To my friend Luc, without whom this story would not have been written.

1

UNHINGED

APRIL 21ST, 1989

A crack of thunder split the air and continued to rumble angrily across the heavens. Its force was finally played out by the distant skies which oversaw the majestic mountain range. Lightning streaked again and thunder boomed in response.

"Looks like it's gonna be quite a storm out there," the man noted in his shaky voice. He drew back a side of the curtain from the window and stared intently into the dark sky. His skin was wrinkled and worn by the many hard years of mountain life, but his hands still held a measure of strength that belied his great age.

The old woman straightened her hand-knitted sweater and, with some difficulty, pulled herself up from the creaking rocking chair to join her husband at the window. She pushed her large-framed glasses up on her nose and squinted into the darkness.

The black clouds ominously floated across the sky, covering many of the peaks in its ghostly darkness. Breaks in the seemingly otherworldly cover allowed for points of light to shine through from the stars and the bright full moon at times, but they quickly retreated behind the dark cover as it continued by.

The rain became more torrential; it bounced against the wooden shingles then rolled in waves to the gutters where it filled the muddy street just outside the aged house. The old man heard the baying and nervousness of the livestock in the basement below as the storm increased in intensity. "We better make sure everything is ready then." He turned to his wife and patted her on the shoulder. He offered her a weak smile, but knew that it was a failed attempt to calm the rush of nerves he knew were exploding within her at that moment.

She stared at him with concern in her eyes. He gave her shoulder a tight comforting squeeze. His wife did seem to deflate a bit and relax from the gentle touch of her husband. "It is time," she stated after taking a deep breath. "I'll get the windows and the doors." She pulled the blinds aside and reached for the wooden shutters that latched over the glass of the large window before them.

The old man looked into her light blue eyes as she turned to face him. "Maybe it will pass by our house again," he said reassuringly with another forced smile. He then nodded and walked on shaky legs over towards the door at the base of the stairs. The large door was set at a forty five degree angle and inset slightly into the wall.

"Don't forget to leave—"

"Yes, I know," the old man interjected dismissively with a wave of his hand before she was able to finish the comment. He had lived this night thousands of times in his life and wasn't about to jeopardize anything by forgetting the smallest detail.

With some effort he swung open the door. The pungent smell of the livestock hit his nose as he descended into the dark. The old stairs creaked and groaned under his weight even though he wasn't more than a hundred and forty pounds. He almost fell more than once on the rotting wood but managed to catch his balance and continued on. When the old man reached the bottom he grabbed the thin cord above him and pulled it, causing the dangling light to come to life. The goats moved about, nervously bleating in their pen, and the chickens danced around their cage showcasing their restlessness—pecking and clucking with abandon. The two cows mooed loudly in distress and stared at the old man with their black eyes—almost as though they were pleading with him. He could see that they sensed something was different about this night. That, in fact, it was *that night*.

"Easy," he said, trying to reassure them as he checked to make certain their stalls were securely closed and locked. "Easy."

He then turned to the barn door that led out to the street. The double door was thick and solid, made of oak and held together with steel strips that lined it vertically and horizontally. Sweat began to drip down the old man's forehead and his heart beat more forcefully in his chest as he knew he was running out of time. He pulled the door and found that it was fastened shut; water streamed through the seams and leaked into the barn creating small rivers on the muddy floor. As swiftly as he could with his trembling hands he turned the handle and opened it a crack. He quickly glanced outside and saw that his neighbor's barn doors across the street were slamming in the wind.

More water raced into the barn. He could feel the wind and smelled the fresh scent of the spring downpour waft through the crack. The moisture in the air felt good on his weathered face and reminded him of the blessings of a fresh downpour, but he knew that the good feeling was merely a facade in the face of this evil night. Despite that realization, he was about to take another long pull of the fresh scent when a flash of lightning and a crack of thunder shook him back to his senses. He knew that time was short and this was the last place in all the world he wanted to be at that moment. He hobbled to the stairs and began to ascend them as quickly as his old legs would carry him; glancing at his livestock, maybe for the last time, as he went up. Their eyes pierced through him and he felt as though they were judging him, condemning him for his actions this night.

He tried to push those dark thoughts away. "Maybe tonight won't be your night," he whispered to them, trying desperately to justify his actions as he hurriedly climbed the last of the stairs back into the house.

"Did you leave it—"

"Yes, yes!" he cut her off again sternly as he fumbled to get the door closed. He would leave nothing to chance. Once shut, he locked it up tight. He spun his head around and glanced at the front door. His wife had fastened the two deadbolts and the heavy chain. With a nod of satisfaction, he turned to her.

"Well, all the windows are done up tight," the old woman stated confidently. "We have done everything we were supposed to."

"Very good then, very good," he replied in that shaky voice—which was a little shakier than before—as he took his wife by the hand and led her upstairs. The two shambled their way up the steep staircase, holding onto each other and the railings for balance.

After locking down all the windows in the upper floor and getting hastily ready for bed the old couple laid down for the night. The only light that was on in the room was that of the small oil lamp which was sitting on the night-stand beside their bed. The small flame of that lighted wick danced in the slight breeze that ushered through the worn seals on the old windows.

The old man huddled close to his wife and held her tightly. He stared out from under the thick woollen blankets, refusing to take his eyes off the bedroom door that was also now locked down. He turned his head slightly and saw that she was also looking intently at that old door. The man's heart continued to race as the storm outside intensified. Flashes of light shot through cracks in the shutters, followed shortly by the boom of thunder. The animals in the cellar continued to knock loudly at their pens in complete agitation, which was easily heard through the sparsely insulated house, even so far as to the second floor.

An hour later the storm seemed to pass over and all that could be heard of the remnant from the tumult was the light patter of rain which continued to fall in a steady stream from the sky. Even the animals seemed to settle from their agitated state. The old man looked to his wife and saw relief in her eyes. He smiled and was about to turn over when he heard a creak from the large barn door in the cellar. The relief in his wife's eyes turned to horror as she too must have detected the sound.

The old man felt his wife begin to tremble, then he too started to shake slightly. They knew it was here. They knew what was coming.

The creak became more pronounced as the barn door opened widely. A low growl resonated up through all the cracks of the weathered house and into the ears of the man and his wife. The livestock became violently loud as if pleading for their very lives. Each terrified sound they made almost took on a human quality in the ears of the old man. Those pleading sounds assaulted and pierced through him.

The growl became a roar that bounded through the house from the cellar and was enough to freeze the couple in place. The man smelled the stench of urine as he and his wife's bodies released their contents. He cupped his hands over his ears when the shrieks of the slaughter rang out and looked to see that his wife was doing the same thing. It felt to him as though it would last forever: the pleading, the pain, the suffering. His lips quivered and moved in prayer.

Then all was quiet.

The old man dared to pull his hands from his ears. He could hear another low growl resonate, as though it was carried through the house by the calm wind of the post storm torrent. The sound made it seem as though the creature was everywhere and yet nowhere. Finally, after a long while, the growl stopped. He perked his head up a little and suddenly heard a loud crack as a stair runner snapped under the weight of something that was much heavier than himself. Creak, creak, crack, creak, the sounds issued forth.

He looked at his wife who was trembling so violently he thought she might be on the verge of a heart attack. Her lips quivered and tears streamed down her cheeks.

The old man then looked back toward the door and heard the loud sound of a creaky stair again, and a slight rattle of the basement door.

"It never comes in ... it never comes in ..." his wife stammered.

He clamped his hand down hard on her mouth. He

heard another rattle and his wife shook her head violently from side to side. He had to hold her tighter and feared he might suffocate her if she didn't calm down. His mind whirled, trying to retrace his steps. Did he forget something?

The seconds seemed like hours but then the man heard another growl—snap!—then something banged through the barn door and slipped out into the night.

2

JEREMY JACKSON

MAY 20TH, 1989

The sweet smell of the forest air put a smile on the young man's ruddy face. He walked the narrow country road taking in the sights and sounds of the mountain pass. He would have taken the train if it weren't for the intermittent railway strikes on the French lines, but perhaps this was better: more scenic. Early spring was beautiful in the French Alps: birds chirped, squirrels hustled from tree to tree, and the ground was moist with the early rain. Life had come again after hiding away from the winter's snow and chill, and it was wonderful to behold. Yes, Jeremy Jackson was glad he made this trip.

Jeremy reached around and pulled a small canteen from his pack and took a long drink of the refreshing water. He wiped his mouth as he stood transfixed, staring at the majestic peaks before him. After a long moment he replaced the canteen and continued on down the road.

Almost an hour later he rounded the bend of the narrow road and saw before him the small town of Le Lieu. The tiny houses of the village spread along throughout the valley surrounding a main market area. The quaint chimney stacks of the homesteads issued streams of smoke into the mountain skyline. He made out the sight of a distant train pulling away from the small hamlet and going off into the mountain passes.

"That would have been handy to have a couple days ago," he said in a sarcastic tone as his eyes followed the disappearing train. He chuckled and shook his head.

As Jeremy drank in the scene before him, he was glad the rail-strike forced him to take the more scenic route through the Alps. Off the beaten path. The train would have been picturesque he knew, but not near as nice and refreshing as the hike. He was always trying to find the positive aspect in the midst of his setbacks. He brushed his hand through his curly brown hair and began to hum a tune to himself as he descended into the valley.

The main square and market was abuzz with activity. Le Lieu seemed much larger than it had appeared while looking at it from above. At that distance it appeared as merely a small forgotten mountain town nestled into a low valley—hidden from the world. The town actually sprawled its way throughout the valley floor and reached up the sides of the mountains encompassing it. He could see a tram rising to the peak of one close mountain where a large chateau overlooked the town like an imposing sentry.

He made his way through the market and into the nearest pub: La Pomme D'Eve. The young man sat down at a table in the corner, unloading his large pack and placing it to the side.

"What can I get for you?" the waitress asked in French. The old wood floor creaked beneath her feet as she shifted her weight from one foot to the other. Even though it was a cool, May day, a bead of sweat marked its path down her round face.

"I'll have ... um ... a beer ... please," Jeremy stuttered through broken French, hoping he had said the right thing, or at least enough of the right thing to be understood.

"Are you American?" she asked in English with her thick French accent.

"Oui, madame."

"I am Jannette," she replied. "It was beer you wanted then?"

Jeremy smiled and nodded.

"And where are you heading? We do not get many visitors around here. Our town is not as well known as the others that are in the Alps, and we rarely get visitors up this way," she replied.

Jeremy held up his finger for a moment while he rummaged through one of the inside pockets of his jacket and produced a map. He unfolded it, laid it on the table, and scanned across it for a moment. Placing his finger on a certain spot he said, "The town of L'accord." He looked up and shrugged.

A dark shadow suddenly fell over the woman's face when he mentioned the name of the town. "You do not want to go there," she said in all seriousness. "There is a curse that lay upon that town."

"Cursed, huh?" Jeremy couldn't quite keep the smirk off his face. He tried to school his features back to seriousness when he saw Jannette scowl at him.

"Believe it or not, but I would not go there."

"So, is this town abandoned, then?"

"No," Jannette said, drawing the word out longer than needed.

"Is there something wrong with the people? Are they normal?"

Jannette glared at him, her lips pressed into a thin line. "I suppose they are."

"Then why do you say it's cursed?" Jeremy's initial excitement about exploring a "cursed" town waned.

"Because of the stories ..." The woman eyed him for a moment, as though she was contemplating whether or not to tell him what she was thinking. After taking a deep breath she said, "There is something not right about the place and everyone who is not from there avoids it like the plague."

"Well that just heightens my desire to go and see it," the young man replied as he folded the map up again. "When I come back, Jannette, I'll tell you all about it then maybe you'll come to realize that they were just stories."

Jannette looked at him with that same dark expression. "*If* you come back," she said cryptically as she turned and padded away.

Jeremy was struck by the seriousness of Jannette's response, but quickly shrugged it off with a chuckle. No. This was going to be the best vacation he had ever had. Ghost stories weren't going to deter him; not since he knew that once he went back to San Francisco he would be hard pressed to make his way to Europe with the pressures of school and work looming over him. He knew his MBA was going to take at least two years to complete, then he would have to find a job and settle in to normal life. There wouldn't be much time until later in life—if he was lucky or made it a priority—for him to see the world which was unacceptable to him. He was going to enjoy every sight, every place, and every experience during his time here.

A few hours later, after taking in the sights of the sprawling mountain town, he found himself standing on the small platform waiting for the next train to pull into the station. The air had turned cool as a northern breeze blew over the mountains and into the valley; the sun having retreated well over the western peaks. He cinched up his light jacket and waited patiently with his hands in his pockets. The clouds began to roll in and a darkness descended upon the town.

"Great," he whispered to himself knowing that a rainstorm was on its way. It wasn't unexpected given the time of year, but he had hoped to make it to L'accord before there was any significant change in the weather. He shook his head and forced a smile onto his face. No. The rain wasn't going to dampen his spirit.

A few minutes later he heard the clatter of the train roll down the track toward the village. The diesel engine rolled by him—breaks screeching—to finally stop before the platform. There were two passenger cars and six cargo cars attached together which struck the man as strange but he merely shrugged, thinking the small communities were probably best served by the joint service.

He glanced around and saw only three other passengers boarding: an old man, a middle-aged woman, and her daughter. As the door opened he was greeted by the conductor. "Tickets please," he said in French.

Jeremy flashed him the train pass he had purchased.

"Merci," the conductor, an older man dressed in a blue uniform, sporting large glasses and a gray moustache, said as he stepped aside for the young man to board.

Jeremy stepped onto the train and was hit by a pungent odour that smelled like a combination of wet dog and an old piece of wood that had begun to rot. He stepped lightly down the aisle, eyes scanning between the seats, searching for one where the leather hadn't cracked straight through. He kept a wary eye on the overhead rack, wondering if the wood was strong enough to carry his backpack. With a shrug, he swung into a seat, wincing when his thumb came away with a sliver.

It was all part of the experience, he thought to himself.

He noted that there were four more people seated throughout the carriage. They all appeared to be plain-looking folk; probably just heading up the line to other towns along the route. He unslung his large pack and placed it beside him on the seat. He watched the workman outside, busy shifting supplies on and off the cargo cars. After a forty minute wait the train began to roll on.

An hour into the ride the clouds thickened and darkened even more. The rain fell in large drops splashing off the carriage and rolling in rivers down the windows. He moved away from the window as water started to seep in through the broken seals.

Shortly after the deluge started the train began to slow as it approached its first destination.

"Excuse me sir," Jeremy said in French, trying to flag the conductor down.

The man came over. "Pardon?" he asked.

Jeremy was a little flustered, not knowing exactly how he would phrase his next question. Instead he decided on another tactic. "Do you speak English?" he asked hopefully.

"Yes," the conductor replied. "What do you need sir?" His accent was thicker than Jannette's.

"What town are we approaching?"

Jeremy saw a flash of fear in the man's eyes. "This town?" he said. "This is L'accord."

Jeremy glanced out the window briefly. He couldn't see any buildings at the platform which made it look like the town wasn't close to the train station and the rain was coming down pretty hard. He wasn't even sure how far of a walk it would be, but he quickly shoved those thoughts aside, smiled widely, and started to stand.

The conductor put a hand on his shoulder. "You do not want to get out here monsieur. It is not ... good. No one goes to L'accord."

"So I hear," Jeremy replied as he removed the man's hand. "I'll be fine." He grabbed his pack and moved past the man.

"Please sir, I must protest. I can not let you out," the conductor pleaded.

"So am I a prisoner on this train then?" Jeremy asked indignantly and raising his voice so that the others on the car could hear.

"No. Of course not. I just wish you would reconsider."

"Can you or anyone tell me why then?" he asked flourishing his hand around the cabin and looking at everyone else. "Or is it just because of some silly tale you heard when you were a kid?" He looked the conductor in the eyes. "Unless you can tell me anything specific as to what is rumoured to be going on here, then I'm going to L'accord."

The conductor returned Jeremy's intense stare for a long moment, then stepped aside. The train screeched to a final halt. "Thank you," the young man said curtly as he moved to the exit and stepped off the train.

The rain was coming down in sheets again and Jeremy

ducked into the open platform hoping that the roof structure would provide some protection from the torrent. He looked back at the door to the train as it closed and seriously considered getting back on. He glanced over and noticed again that workmen were busy at work unloading supplies onto the deck. This particular train deck seemed to be in the middle of nowhere with a single road departing from it.

He was about to turn and get back on when he noticed a truck off to the side that was being loaded with supplies by the workmen from the train.

I'll catch a ride with whoever owns that truck! he reasoned to himself as he turned away from the door.

He walked down the platform and noted that the three workmen had slipped back onto the train, and the truck was now loaded.

"Hello!" he called in French.

No response.

"Hello!" he called again as he quickened his pace.

Again, there was no response as the two men quickly battened down their load and jumped into the vehicle.

"Wait!" Jeremy yelled as he broke into a run. "Wait! I need a ride!"

The truck fired to life then sped off down the road just as he ran to the edge of the platform. "Great!" he exclaimed aloud.

The sudden sound of the couplings banging together on the train as it departed startled the young man and made him flinch. He turned to see that the passengers and conductor were all staring at him as they pulled away. He smiled sarcastically at them and offered a wave.

"Well, I guess there's only one thing to do," he said

aloud, throwing his backpack to the deck and pulling out his flashlight.

He shined the light onto the road and scanned around. To call it a road was an overstatement as it seemed more of a track carved through the forest. Large trees and thick brush rose from either side of the narrow path up the mountain. To Jeremy's surprise the truck had disappeared quickly up that muddy trail leaving him on the platform in the dark.

With a sigh he jumped from the deck; water and mud splashed as he landed on the soft ground. He found it difficult at that point to maintain his normally positive disposition in the midst of the mess he found himself in. He took a deep breath, shook his head disapprovingly, and started walking up the road. He felt the pull of the mud on his boots and knew that it was only a matter of time before water began to seep in.

The young man made it about twenty feet. Twenty miserable feet of mud and rain and slipping, only to arrive at the steep incline up the mountainside. He flicked his flashlight up the slope and froze, his heart leaping in his chest.

There, staring back at him through the darkness, were two yellow, unblinking eyes.

3

L'ACCORD

MAY 20TH, 1989

Jeremy backed up a step. His hand shook as he moved the light around so he could get a better look at the creature in front of him. He breathed a sigh of relief as the silhouette in front of him of a large deer came into focus. It blinked then walked off into the nearby forest. Jeremy chuckled at his paranoia, then continued on.

He trudged up the path through the forest, his feet slipping in the thick mud as they searched for purchase. The world at the edge of the light of his flashlight fell away into blackness, as if disappearing into the maw of some giant monster.

Jeremy shook his head. "Letting silly stories get to you," he muttered. "There isn't a monster. It's just nighttime."

He had hiked through many mountain ranges in his life: the Rocky Mountains of western Canada, the White Mountains of New Hampshire, and the Sierra Nevada range in his native California, but never before had he felt the deep darkness he now felt. It reached into his soul and conjured the nightmares of his childhood. It dimmed the light of hope and dampened his spirit. He shook his head again and dismissed the ridiculous thoughts. He was just frustrated that those men hadn't given him a ride, forcing him to walk in the rain.

The muck from the gravel road was thick about his boots now as he trudged on through the darkness. A branch snapped over the sound of the pounding rain. He jolted his head to the side and moved the flashlight, trying to peer into the gloom of the tightly packed trees. His heart raced. Nothing. A crash in the forest. He swung to the other side. Nothing.

It's probably just more deer, he reasoned to himself.

The young man's nerves were strung taught, bringing him to the edge of himself, as his eyes moved back and forth. Despite his insistence that there was nothing to be afraid of—which he repeated over and over again in his head—he quickened his pace into a jog. His light bounced off the trees and road in front as he scrambled up that incline. He even shined it back a few times as if he was expecting some great creature to leap upon him from the darkness.

Relief flooded through him a few minutes later when the road started to flatten out slightly and he noticed a faint glow coming out of the gloom—lights from houses! His pace grew more urgent and desperate, wanting with all his heart to be out of the darkness and into the light of the town. As Jeremy crested the top of the road he saw, laying before him down in a low valley, a small town. He slowed up momentarily so he could take in the view, then began sprinting once more, down the narrow winding road. The rain still pounded down on him, but he hardly cared as he knew he was getting close to shelter.

Jeremy nearly slipped and fell a few times on the muddy road as he navigated his way down into the town onto what appeared to be the main road of this rustic village: an uneven cobblestone surface. Houses and shops lined the rocky street but were spaced far enough apart, and at different distances back from the road, to make the town feel less populated than it probably was. Street-lights—sparsely spaced—throughout the town provided that same soft glow he saw from above which illuminated enough of the street for Jeremy to negotiate his way.

The town was positioned in a tight valley between two peaks. He heard the sound of flowing water and was able to make out, through the haze and rain, a small river to his right and down an embankment which flowed through the middle of the valley. Jeremy squinted his eyes and could see the outline of a bridge in the distance that crossed over the river. He looked around and noted that there were houses on both sides of the river, and many that stretched up on either side of the mountains. The town was significantly smaller than Le Lieu at first glance, but it was hard to tell in the dark with the limited lighting as to the actual size of the place.

Jeremy walked down the main road looking for a hotel or hostel. There was nothing. The rain slammed down harder than it had before. He knew he needed to find a place to stay. He needed to find a place fast!

With more urgency Jeremy went to the nearest house and began to bang on the door. "Hello! Is anyone there?" he asked, trying to articulate the French words as correctly as he could.

The lights inside were on, but no one answered. After a moment at that house, he moved to the next one.

"Hello! Please! I need a place to stay for the night," he pleaded. "Even if you just direct me to the hotel." In his urgency he abandoned trying to speak in French and reverted back to English.

No response.

He banged again and again, but no one answered.

Jeremy walked through the town, soaked and haggard. *Why isn't anyone answering?* he asked himself. His normally positive nature and outlook dampened with each ensuing drop of rain that fell on his thoroughly soaked body.

He even banged on some of the shops—doors and windows—even though there were no lights on inside. Not surprisingly there was no answer. Jeremy considered the possibility of breaking into one of those apparently empty places but pushed the thought away. He wasn't to that level of desperation ... yet. No. He knew there had to be someone in the town who would open up to him. The young man moved onto more houses pleading for them to have some compassion.

Nothing.

He had to believe that someone in the town would help him; someone *had* to help him. He moved through the narrow, uneven, streets continuing his knocking and pleas. It wasn't until he was about halfway through the village that he noticed that most houses had large doors attached to the front that were just off to the side from the main doorsteps. At first he thought these were garages, but then he heard what sounded like sheep and chickens coming from one. He also noticed that the door to that particular house was open slightly, rocking gently in the cold breeze. Jeremy took a step back, under one of the street-lamps, and looked up and down the road to see that the three houses which were beside each other all had these same doors, and that they were all unlocked and swaying in the breeze, rocking open and closed.

"That's weird," he whispered to himself. "Why would they lock their houses tight but leave these open?"

He approached the one right in front of him and pushed on it. The door swung open. He slowly entered as he shined his light inside. There were pens and coops and dozens of animals locked inside. He further stepped in and looked around. There were stairs leading up to a door that he could only assume led into the house. The thought struck him then that, in a worst case scenario, he could shelter in the barn if no one let him in. Then, in the morning, he could talk to someone and find out more about this strange little place.

He sighed. "You guys won't mind if I stay with you for the night will you?" he asked the sheep with a chuckle. "It wouldn't be the first time I spent a night in a barn." The sheep looked at him and bleated. He noticed that it sounded almost nervous, like it was scared or pleading with him in some way. It was weird.

Suddenly the animals became agitated. Jeremy flinched. "Whoa," he said to them. "Whoa. Talk about the whole place being inhospitable. Even the animals don't want me to bunk with—" He didn't finish the sentence as the hairs on the back of his neck stood up. He glanced all around as his heart leaped in his chest. Jeremy spun, searching for the unknown fear in the darkness like he had done back on the road when all he could feel coming from the gloom was some cryptic terror.

The flashlight's small beam whirled with him but there was nothing. Fear struck the young man like never before and a foul rotting smell adrift on the breeze assaulted his nose. He knew he had to get out of there, but he didn't know why. He had to get out of there now, but he couldn't move as the fear chained him to the floor.

There was a long scraping sound at the side of the barn, like someone dragging a rake across the old stone. He heard, over the tumult of the animals, what sounded like footsteps slopping in the mud outside; big, heavy footsteps. His eyes stared at the place on the wall where it was coming from. He knew, whatever it was, it was outside between the buildings and heading toward the street. His eyes moved with the sound. Whatever it was, it moved slowly and methodically like it had all the time in the world as it scraped against the wall. It had all the time in the world to ... Jeremy's eyes popped open wide and his heart raced even faster when the realization hit him ... stalk its prey.

I have to move! he shouted to himself. *I have to move now!*

His legs shook so badly he feared he would fall over, and his breath came in quick short gasps.

The scraping continued in one long horrid note. Then it stopped.

The sheep bleated uncontrollably and knocked their heads into the pen's gate as though they were attempting to smash it open. Chickens fluttered and clucked like mad. It was the closest thing Jeremy had ever heard to a chicken screaming!

"Hello!" he called out. "Who's there? I need a place to stay." He wasn't sure what else to do or say as his heart pounded.

A long moment drifted by then he heard a long scrape

again on the wall. His heart stopped. The animals' noise was leading, whatever it was, straight to him. His gaze darted at the three, secure walls, then landed again on the barn door. If he didn't move, he would be trapped in here with the animals.

The young man forced himself—willed himself—with every fibre of his being to move. He lunged for the door—his only thought was to get out. He thew it open, and ran up the street in the pouring rain. He heard the animals' distress impossibly heighten even more as he sprinted from the barn to the next house.

"Please let me in!" he yelled; pleading, begging. But there was no answer. He continued his forceful hammering on the door until despair mixed with his fear. Then he smelled it again: the smell of death. A low throaty growl entered the young man's ears causing a shiver to course up his spine.

"No. Please," he whined as he turned around slowly to look death in the face. Those eyes! Those horrific, hateful, eyes were the last thing that Jeremy Jackson ever saw. The scream—his own scream—was the last thing Jeremy Jackson ever heard before he felt the sting of his throat being torn open; his voice silenced as his windpipe was ripped out, and his precious blood poured forth from his severed arteries.

4

TRISTAN

MAY 21ST, 1989

Tristan Berger stared at the door for a long while. He had heard the pleas and the banging last night, but was frozen with fear. He didn't want to open the door.

This had never happened before. They had never had anyone outside during *that* night and he didn't know what to do. He had done everything he was supposed to in order to prepare for the night, but he wasn't expecting this. How could he have expected it? He prayed that it was all just a bad dream and that, when he opened the door, everything would be as it should be.

Maybe he made it to another house? Tristan tried to reason it out; tried to find another way that this ended for the stranger.

But what about the screams? He knew he heard screams. Or did he? Maybe his mind was playing tricks on him last night?

Tristan scratched at his medium-length beard as his thoughts and fears spun within him.

What would Charlotte have done? he asked himself. Tears welled up in his eyes at the thought.

His wife Charlotte, who had passed away suddenly two years earlier, was the most caring person he had ever known.

"She would have let him in," Tristan whispered to himself. "She would have let him in." A tear streamed down his cheek.

He could hear the screams in his head. But his mind questioned the reality of that. Were they really screams? Was someone actually out there? Or did he imagine the whole thing?

The screams did go away at that moment from inside his head. But that was the most terrifying realization of all: the pleas for help went away.

No. There weren't any screams, he determined. Whoever was out there went to a neighbors' and sheltered with them.

He took a deep breath, shook his head, and reached for the door with his calloused hand. Slowly—very slowly—he opened it up.

Tristan's heart sank.

His greatest fears were realized as the scene became clear to this gentle giant. The steps were coated with blood and torn pieces of flesh and clothing. His door was splattered, and there was a trail that led out onto the cobblestone roadway. Large black crows circled around, and some even landed near the doorway and were picking pieces of flesh up and flying away with them. The main mass of the man's body was lying in the street, ripped and torn. His entrails laid across the cobblestones; a feast for the hungry birds. Surprisingly, the man's face was still relatively intact and appeared to be disfigured and twisted, transfixed in an expression of absolute horror.

Aside from being the town's electrician, Tristan was also a butcher and had gutted countless animals and wasn't squeamish of blood or the smell of death, but this was a man! A man who had been killed at his door while he cowered in the relative safety of his house.

"Oh Charlotte. What have I done?" He whispered in anguish.

Tristan's stomach lurched and he jolted forward, vomiting violently onto the doorstep. He pulled himself up and wiped his mouth, then he leaned forward again and threw up some more. The puke drizzled onto his beard and tears began to run down his rough face. The bitter taste of the stomach acid burned at his throat.

He stood up once more in time to see Luis Moreau, an older man from down the street, and his small dog, gaping at him and the scene at his front door. The dog began to bark, then tugged violently at the leash which caused Luis to lose his grip. Before he could grab the leash again, the dog ran up to the corpse and tore some flesh from the body.

"Remy!" Luis yelled, running up and grabbing the leash.

Birds scattered at the movement of Remy. Luis tugged on the leash and pulled the dog away. The two sprinted back down the street.

Tristan nearly vomited again at seeing Remy tear a chunk off the dead man.

He knew he had to let Mayor Boucher know what had happened, and he had to be the one to tell him before the whole town found out that someone had been killed. In the history of L'accord this had never happened. They had always been so careful, but now ... now things had changed —someone had been killed.

Tristan darted inside and grabbed the phone, dialling the Mayor's number on the rotary dial with all haste.

"Hello," Mayor Jean Boucher answered in a groggy voice.

"Jean, it's Tristan. Something ... something ... has ..." He wasn't able to get the words out.

"It's okay Tristan, just calm down. What's the matter?" the Mayor replied, seeming much more awake now.

Tristan took a deep breath. "Someone came into town last night."

There was silence. "Jean? Did you hear what I said?" Tristan asked with urgency.

"Yes. I heard you. Are you certain?"

Tristan's thoughts spun. He wasn't sure how to even tell him what he found. "I found the remains on my doorstep and in the street," he said bluntly.

There was silence again.

"Jean, someone was killed last night," Tristan stated. "There's blood everywhere. And Luis and Remy ... I don't know what ... I can't ... The body ..."

"Is there something wrong with Luis? Is he okay?"

"Yes. It's not Luis. It's someone else. A stranger." Tristan's voice broke up as tears welled in his eyes again.

"Okay Tristan. It's okay. I'll be right there," Jean responded. "Just don't do or touch anything. Do you understand?"

Tristan grunted in affirmation then hung up the phone. He rubbed his hands together nervously then brushed them through his thick brown hair. What did he do? How could he have let that person die? He could have helped but he didn't. Charlotte would have helped, but he ... he ... he was a coward.

Within minutes Tristan heard the front door creek open. He turned to see Mayor Jean Boucher carefully stepping into the house, trying to avoid as much of the mess as possible. The Mayor—a short portly man with white thinning hair—adjusted his coke-bottle glasses as he looked around at the scene. Tristan also noticed that a crowd was beginning to form outside: people from all over town gathering and gawking at the scene before his house.

Mayor Boucher walked over to Tristan and put a hand on his shoulder. "It's going to be okay," he reassured him, but Tristan didn't share his optimism. Despite that, he nodded anyway.

"I'll convene a meeting with the council members right away and discuss what actions we need to take and how to handle this ... circumstance."

Again, Tristan felt numb.

"Did it kill any of your livestock?" the Mayor asked.

That question shook Tristan from his stupor. He hadn't actually looked to see if his livestock was killed or not. "I ... I don't know," he stammered as he rose and headed for the cellar. He flung the door open and quickly descended the stairs with Mayor Boucher close at his heels. The barn door swung slightly in the light breeze from outside. Tristan scanned the barn and noted that all his livestock were peacefully grazing within their pens. He looked to the Mayor, puzzled as to why none of his animals were harmed.

The Mayor shrugged. "Maybe it was satisfied with the —" he paused as if looking for the right words to use, "the intruder."

Tristan's eyes went wide at Jean's choice of words. Intruder?

Jean must have noticed his shocked expression. He smiled and led Tristan outside where a number of the town's people had assembled, all gawking at the torn up body. "Tristan has done us a great service by locking out the intruder," he stated loudly. "For centuries we have lived in peace with the Protector and nothing like this has ever happened. Our way of life must be preserved above all else and we can't let intruders disrupt that."

The Mayor turned back to Tristan and put a hand on his large arm. "Don't trouble yourself, my friend, by the incident. This man was nothing but a mere beast, fit for the sacrifice, like any of our animals."

Tristan swallowed hard.

The Mayor turned back around to face the town's people again. "The beast saw fit to take this man instead of any of our livestock this month. It is a blessing!" he said with a flourish of his hand toward the bloody mess.

He turned back to Tristan again. "Do you understand?" he asked in a soft voice.

Tristan nodded. He wasn't sure he really understood, but found himself accepting Mayor Boucher's assessment. He knew that Jean would do that which was best for the town and its people. He had to believe that.

"Come, my friend," Jean said. "I'll find others to help you clean up the mess."

He nodded again slightly and, after closing the barn door, stepped over to stand beside Mayor Boucher.

Tristan noticed that there had to be above thirty people by now, all whispering, talking, and staring at the remains, and more were running up the street from both directions.

A hush came over them as the Mayor stepped forth with his hands upraised.

The crows still circled and perched nearby, their greedy eyes focused on the prize. "Now I know that you are all stupefied by the events that we now witness here within the limits of our fair town," he began, "and I know that you have many questions that, I assure you, will be answered in due course. But first I must convene an immediate emergency council meeting with the honourable members in order to decide how we are to handle this ... intrusion."

He stepped away from Tristan and scanned the crowd with his steely expression. Tristan looked at their faces—some stoic, others shocked.

"It's all his fault!" one man screamed and pointed a finger Tristan's way. Other voices rose in agreement. Tristan visibly shrank back at the accusation.

"Now you know that's not true, Martin!" an older woman cut in. "The poor soul banged on a few doors. I heard him too, but did any of us open up to him?" The crowd quieted. "No," she continued, eyeing many in the crowd one by one and waving a finger menacingly. "We were all huddled in our own beds hoping that our house wasn't the one that was being visited. Weren't we?"

Mayor Boucher walked over to her and put a hand on her shoulder. "Thank you, Aline. I don't think anyone wants to lay the burden for this situation upon our dear friend Tristan do they? Besides, as I said earlier: He did us a service by allowing the protector to deal with the intruder." He looked at Martin threateningly when he spoke.

"No. We have lived here for generations, and if there are to be generations more then we must stick together and support one another *and* the actions of the Protector."

"How are we going to have generations beyond us when many of our young people are leaving?" another middle-aged woman asked in disgust.

"Now you know that the council and I are working to address that question, Bridgette. But now's not the time for that debate. We need to immediately deal with this situation first in order to preserve our ways," the Mayor answered.

Most of the people in the crowd began nodding their heads in agreement with the Mayor's assessment of the situation, but Bridgette waved her hand dismissively at the man and walked away.

"Now, can I please have some volunteers to help Tristan clean up this mess?" the Mayor asked as he waved his arm toward the gore and the remains. Five volunteers stepped forward from the crowd. "Good. Thank you, my friends. You will have news as to what our plan is shortly. Now, the rest of you, please go back to your daily duties and work. This will pass in time."

Tristan looked out at the crowd, amazed at Mayor Boucher's handling of the situation. The man was so eloquent and always knew what it was they were to do. He was more than a little disturbed, however, at the seemingly relative ease of mind that the Mayor was displaying. Tristan didn't know how this was going to turn out even though the Mayor was confident that life would get back to normal. The one thing he did know was that this event had shaken him to the core. How was he going to reconcile this event in his mind? He could have helped, but he didn't. And the Mayor telling him that it was good for the intruder to die didn't sit well with him at all.

He knew the screams he heard were going to resonate in his mind for a while and follow him to his bed at night.

Tristan and the five volunteers scooped up the body and large parts into a plastic bag. They then sprayed down the steps and street, scrubbing them thoroughly with soap and disinfectants. He was starting to feel more relieved about the situation now that the body was bagged and his steps were cleaned up. Not having the visual reminder of what happened seemed to work in calming down his nerves.

By the time they were finished, Tristan noticed Mayor Boucher walking back up the road toward them.

The Mayor nodded at each of the men as he approached. "Good work. It looks like nothing ever happened here."

Again, the nonchalant nature Mayor Boucher displayed was shocking to Tristan, but he wisely kept that to himself.

"So we have discussed the situation and have decided that we will bury the remains outside of town, and we will never discuss this event again.

"Mathieu, can I have you and Nicolas take care of that for us?" Mayor Boucher asked one of the men that helped clean up the remains.

Tristan saw Mathieu nod and sensed that there was some secret communication between him and the Mayor when he saw the look the two exchanged, but just shrugged off the feeling. He had been traumatized by the incident and his emotions were raw at that moment and probably not to be trusted.

He was also unsettled about Jean's assessment that the man who was banging on his door last night was some sort of intruder. "How can I forget that this happened, Jean?" he whispered, walking closer to the Mayor.

The Mayor offered a slight smile. "Because you have to," came his simple reply. "We have to if we want to preserve our way of life. We need to walk a fine line if we are to preserve the town and, as I said, our way of life, or rather, our very lives. I will not put any of that in jeopardy —I can not allow it." He raised his voice at that last statement.

The other five men were nodding their heads in agreement, but Tristan was too shocked to do anything but stare in disbelief. This man that was killed was someone's son, maybe even a brother, or worse: a husband. But that didn't matter to the town of L'accord.

Tristan wanted to scream out in protest but he knew he couldn't. He knew Jean was right. He knew that, in order to survive, the whole town would have to play along. Maybe it was for the best that the Protector was here last night, defending their way of life; eliminating the intruder.

Preservation was everything. To preserve meant life. To put that at risk meant ... Tristan didn't know what it meant, but how could he continue to live with himself?

Two weeks later Tristan stood in his butcher's shop staring at the hunk of meat in front of him. The cutting table was stained with blood as were his big hands. But it wasn't the blood of the cow he was butchering that he saw, it was the blood of the man. The sights of the incident assaulted him. He hadn't slept well since that fateful day as he was visited by the sights, smells, and sound—the sound of the screams! —in his dreams.

He placed the knife down and walked to the cabinet on the other side of his small shop. Tristan opened the door and pulled out a .12 gauge shotgun. He put a slug round into the chamber and cocked the gun. Tears formed in his eyes as he placed the barrel in his mouth.

The screams of the man who was slaughtered at his house sounded in his mind as his finger glided over the trigger.

5

NO ONE LEAVES L'ACCORD

JUNE 4TH, 1989

Tristan scrunched up his face and closed his eyes. Great drops of sweat rolled down his forehead. The taste of the steel was bitter, but not as bitter as the thoughts of death that now permeated his mind. The tormented man wanted it all to end. He wanted the emotional pain to be over. He wanted the screams to stop. He wanted the sight of the man's broken and torn body to be gone from his memory.

He tried to reconcile the sights in his mind with the Mayor's comments about defending the town against this "intruder," but he wasn't sure he could. If he was a hero then why did he feel like a coward?

He began to pull down on the trigger and felt the movement keenly on his thumb. Just another quarter inch and it would all be over. Just another quarter inch and his pain and confusion would be over.

Tristan growled. His face screwed up even more; his teeth bit down on the barrel of the gun. His growl came to a crescendo, then ... he released the trigger and placed the gun to the side. He cupped his face in his hands and sobbed. He didn't even have the courage to kill himself! What a wretch! A tormented wretch who would live out the rest of his life knowing the truth of who he was: a coward.

June 12th, 1989

Julien threw the last of his bags in the back of the old car. Despite the fact that L'accord was closed off, for the most part, from the rest of the world, people from the town still went to Le Lieu once in a while—albeit rarely—in order to pick up supplies: food, fuel for their vehicles and farm equipment, clothes, and such. The train wasn't always reliable so they made a habit of keeping some of the cars in town serviceable. Julien's Dad had passed this one down to him and had shown him how to keep it in working condition.

There were also a number of trucks in the community that helped with hauling wood, animals, and building supplies when needed. It was a balance between being detached and surviving using the means of modern technology.

Julien's Mom stood by watching the display with concern etched on her face. He could feel her eyes boring into him, as if she was looking for an answer that he could not give to her. But there was no secret answer. He had already told her his reasons for leaving but she just couldn't accept that. L'accord was not the place where he was going to live the rest of his life.

Julien finally turned and looked at his Mother. Her graying hair hung down across her shoulders. She still retained much of her youthful appearance despite the hard mountain life. And, in truth, she wasn't really that old yet: merely forty six. Her eyes normally sparkled with energy and life. Now, he saw only sadness in them.

Without saying a word he walked over and wrapped her in a tight hug. She held onto him as though it was the last time she would ever see him again.

Julien pulled away and held her at arms length, offering her a warm smile. "It's okay Mama. I'll call as soon as I get to the next town to let you know I'm okay."

"Will you?" his Mother asked in an accusatory tone.

"Yes. Of course."

"None of the other young people who have left have ever called or written home," she said harshly. "How am I supposed to believe that you will?"

Julien wrapped her in another hug, but she pushed him away this time.

"I will Mama. You'll see," he replied.

"You should listen to your mother, Julien," came the familiar voice of Mayor Boucher.

Julien spun around to see the Mayor walking up to the house. "Oh ... Hi Mayor Boucher," he stuttered. He felt instant guilt which he couldn't explain. He knew that the Mayor disapproved of anyone leaving the town, but he always figured that it was due to his desire to care for all the citizens of L'accord. He was a nice man and didn't want to see anyone leave.

The Mayor smiled and put a hand on Julien's shoulder. "We just care about you son. Our town will not be the same without you."

Julien appreciated the Mayor's concern, but he had made up his mind. "Thanks Mayor, but I have to do this."

"But why?" his Mom blurted as more tears formed in her eyes.

Julien smiled sympathetically at her. "I love you Mom, and I *will* be in touch."

She wiped the tears from her cheek. "Just go then," she said angrily as she turned away and went back into the small house.

Julien watched her go and stood staring at the closed door for a long while. He didn't want to hurt his Mom, but he also couldn't stay here any longer, not now that someone had been killed during one of *those* nights.

"Please, son. Don't do this," Mayor Boucher pleaded. "If there is anything I can do to convince you to stay, please let me know. I will do anything."

Julien was struck by the Mayor's evident emotion, but he had made up his mind. He couldn't live here any longer. "Thank you, Mayor, but I have to do this."

Mayor Boucher backed up and nodded at him, a grim expression spread across his face. "So be it," he said coldly.

Julien was struck by the Mayor's sudden change in demeanor but shook the negative thought away. It's not like he was the first one to ever leave L'accord, this town he had grown up in. A few others in recent times had left, and it was true that they were never heard of since, but Julien knew it was just because the outside world was so much better than the life they had known. They must have found a freedom they never knew existed. A freedom to choose where to live, what to do for a job, more prospects for marriage, freedom from *those* nights ...

Julien had tried to convince his Mother to leave with him after the incident of a few weeks ago, but she would not. She would not abandon her home, friends, and family.

Despite the loss of Julien's Father years earlier, she still would not leave her brothers, sister, and nieces and nephews. They were so dear to her, and even the mention of possibly leaving seemed to break her heart.

Now that he was leaving, Julien knew for sure he had indeed broken her heart, but he just couldn't stay any longer.

With those thoughts swirling around in his mind, Julien nodded good-bye to the Mayor and climbed into the car. The engine fired to life and sped away down the only road out of town. A road he had never traveled before.

Mayor Boucher watched the car speed away. He shook his head in dismay. It was getting harder and harder to convince these younger people who wanted to leave to stay. He would have success once in a while, but, more often than not, they would not heed his pleas.

Their fate was sealed.

He knew Mathieu and Nicolas would do what they needed to.

The road wound through the mountains, trees whipping by. Julien rolled down the window and took a deep breath of the pine-scented air. The wind whipped his hair around. He turned on the radio and fiddled with the stations, only keeping one eye on the road. No one ever traveled this road.

A moment later, music blared through the radio, songs Julien had never heard before. New songs. He leaned back and grinned, drumming the beat onto the steering wheel. This. This was freedom, something he'd never truly felt in L'accord.

He looked left and right, taking in all the new sights he could. He couldn't believe it had taken him this long to make the decision to leave. It felt as though a huge burden was removed from his back. Now, he knew he could be free of L'accord.

He dipped down into a lower section of road, then it went up and right. As the car came around the corner his eyes widened and his heart leaped within his chest as he saw a man standing in the middle of the road.

Julien pulled the wheel to the left and slammed on the breaks. The wheels locked up and the car went into a skid. He slammed into a large tree with the rear of the vehicle, the impact jarring him violently and causing the car to spin the other way which bounced off another tree and soared into the ditch.

The car hit tree after tree, and Julien smashed his head on the steering wheel and then the side window which exploded, shattering glass all over him. Eventually it came to a stop.

Julien's head throbbed, and he was pretty sure he had broken his right arm. His vision blurred and he could feel the warmth of his blood pouring from the many cuts on his head. He grabbed for the door handle and tried to open it. Miraculously, it swung free. He waited a moment for his vision to clear a bit, then stumbled out of the car and fell on the soft ground. As he hit the ground, pain shot through his injured arm causing him to yell out.

He laid there on the cold ground for, what seemed to

him, a long while when suddenly he heard footsteps coming down the hill towards him.

He looked over to see two older men coming into view. He recognized them from L'accord though he couldn't remember their names.

"Help!" he managed to say. "Help me!"

The first man reached him and looked down with his piercing dark eyes. "Look at that. Right on time," he said as he readjusted his baseball cap then stroked his dark beard. "Well. What do you think Nicolas?" he hollered back to the other man.

Julien's mind spun. *Right on time for what?*

"I think it's going to be hell trying to get his car back up that hill when we're done."

"Ya," the first man replied as he looked around, seemingly oblivious that Julien was injured and bleeding at his feet. "But we could always leave it here. It's not like anyone is going to see it from the road anyway."

"I know that, Mathieu. But it's going to be that much harder to strip the parts unless we put it with the others," Nicolas replied as he approached.

Mathieu appeared to be deep in thought.

Julien groaned as another wave of pain shot through his arm. That sound seemed to shake Mathieu from his contemplations as he turned and looked down at the broken man.

Julien looked up at him wondering why he seemed so distant from his plight. He was injured, bleeding, and needed help and these two were just standing there!

"Well. I guess we'd better take care of this first," Mathieu said as he pulled something from behind him.

Julien's eyes widened in horror as he saw Mathieu pull out a gun and cock the lever.

"No! Wait!" Julien screamed in protest. "What are you doing?"

"We can't have anyone leaving L'accord," Mathieu replied with a grin. "It's not our way."

Everything seemed to go into slow motion at that moment for Julien. He saw the gun levelled at his head. Mathieu's finger slowly pulled the trigger. There was a flash, smoke, intense pain, then ... darkness.

6

HAZELY SILVERSTON

JUNE 14TH, 1989

Hazely leaned back in her chair, watching her client digest the information she had just given him. She glanced over at the window beside her desk absently, and watched a large black fly bounce mercilessly off the glass trying to escape. The mid morning sun shone through in straight lines disclosing thousands of previously hidden dust particles that floated about her office.

She tried not to appear too bored while she waited for her client to work out in his own mind what he figured must have happened in his relationship with his wife to drive her away.

He stared at the picture, his face showing signs of disbelief. He straightened his silver-framed glasses—as if that would change what was on the picture—and held the damning evidence closer to his face. "I can't ... I just ... it's that ..." he stammered.

Hazely rolled her eyes. She had become accustomed to this kind of shock once she uncovered what was actually happening with the client's spouse. In truth she would have preferred that at least some of her cases had a happy ending, but she was so jaded and cynical that, if that were ever the case the shock would be enough to knock her on her ass.

In her line of work she came to realize that spouses who began to draw suspicion from their partner meant they were hiding some dark secret: almost always adulterous dirty secrets. But these cheating partners were always smart enough to evade the other's prying investigations, which is where Hazely fit in. None of them could keep their secrets for long from her. She always found the truth as to what was going on, and exposed them for what they were: adulterers and adulteresses with carnal appetites and dark passions.

Hazely brushed her thick wavy blonde hair from her face and leaned forward, placing her elbows on her solid dark-oak desk. She felt she needed to say something constructive so she struck a pensive pose. "Listen Dwayne, it's not the first time I've caught a man's wife cheating on him with another woman." As soon as the words were out of her mouth she realized that it was the wrong thing to say.

Dwayne's eyes widened as he looked at her in horror! She could tell that he was broken up inside and, unfortunately, she had never been good on the consoling side of things. He started to weep.

Great! Hazely thought to herself. She got up and moved to stand beside the broken man who had now slumped his shoulders and was sobbing uncontrollably. "There, there," she said in a flat tone as she stroked his back while rolling her eyes. She tried to sound sympathetic but knew she was failing miserably. "At least it's going to be way easier having the judge decide in your favor with these babies in your possession," she reassured. "Look here at this one." She pulled one of the pictures from his hand. "There's no mistaking what these women are up to here and we can clearly see your wife's face." Hazely brought the photo closer, "Hmmmm." She then held it up at a different angle and cocked her head to the side, looking at it closer. "It's actually amazing that she was able to get into that position. She's quite athletic."

Dwayne looked up at her—horrified—as he wiped the tears from his cheeks.

"She actually looks like she's quite enjoying herself," Hazely said aloud, but then realized her error immediately as Dwayne broke down again.

"You know what you need?" she asked as she stood back and looked at the broken man. He looked at her again. "You need a stiff drink and maybe some female companionship. I'm off at 5:00 if you're interested."

The man's jaw dropped open so wide that Hazely thought it would fall right off his face, and the look in his eyes were of abject horror! Hazely took a step back, placing her hands on her hips and stared at the man coldly. "What? You don't think I'm beautiful?" she asked sarcastically as she moved her hands up and down her shapely body in order to accentuate her curves. The man shook his head then seemed to gain strength as he clenched his jaw and stared at her.

Hazely sighed—actually finding herself a little disappointed—and handed the picture back. "Perhaps not," she said absently.

"The other PI's were right. Letting a woman investigate another woman ... You probably got that photo because you were all in there together. Damn slut."

Hazely eyed him coldly. "You have thirty days to make

payment, Mr. McDermott. If you don't, rest assured that I will find you."

The man—his face a mask of anger—stood up and stormed from her office.

Hazely slumped down in her chair, her eyes landing immediately on the pile of bills that were stacked up on her desk. The anger that had welled up in her at the comments began to subside. She shook her head and sighed again.

A few moments after Dwayne McDermott ran from her presence the phone on the desk buzzed. "Yes, what is it Melinda?" she asked as she answered it.

"There is a couple here to see you," Melinda answered in her high pitched voice. "Their names are Mr. and Mrs. Jackson. They said they called earlier but you never returned their messages."

Hazely rolled her eyes. She remembered the messages: something about their missing son. She was not at all interested in a missing persons case. She would rather focus her private investigator's practice on potential adulterers and the like. With domestic situations at least she knew roughly—through the help of the spouse—where her targets would be and then just trail them until relevant evidence manifested itself. It was easy money, and the time commitment was far less than a missing persons case. If she got caught up in a lengthy investigation she knew she would miss out on a fair amount of other work which she couldn't afford.

Her eyes glanced to the stack of bills again.

Missing people weren't easy to find, and not something she had the stomach for.

If she took a case like this, and was tied up for a while, then she knew her competition—mostly ignorant men who were always trying to prove they had bigger dicks than everyone else—would devastate her business by taking potential work away from her. Most of her competitors were ex-San Francisco Police officers like herself. They were pigheaded, chauvinistic jerks, who were always trying to scoop business from her. Would her business survive the time away?

Hazely sat back and thought about it for a moment. Her gut was telling her not to do it, but she actually didn't have any more jobs lined up immediately. Her eyes went to the stack of bills again and she sighed. Maybe it would be in her best interest to hear them out?

"Ms. Silverston?" Melinda asked when Hazely didn't immediately answer.

The woman sighed. "Okay, let them in."

A moment later a man and a woman tentatively entered the office. Hazely put on a fake smile and walked over with her hand extended. "I'm Hazely Silverston," she said, trying to seem as concerned and sensitive as she could while shaking their hands.

"I'm Jonah Jackson, and this is my wife Maria," the man replied.

Jonah was tall—at least six foot three—with a solid frame underneath his neatly pressed business suit. His hair was mostly gray and he had lines at the side of his eyes. Maria was short with long black hair and she was dressed in a smart looking business skirt and top.

"Please, won't you come and sit down," Hazely said to the two as she motioned to the chairs in front of her desk.

"Thank you," Jonah replied and moved over to hold the seat for his wife before he sat down.

A perfect gentleman, Hazely mused to herself as she noted how Jonah held the chair for his wife. *And he's kind of cute even though he's older. I wonder if his marriage is happy?* Hazely smiled inwardly then shook the thoughts away as she shuffled to the other side of the desk and quickly sat. "Listen—"

"Before you say no," Jonah cut her off. "I want you to hear our story and what we're willing to pay for you to find out what happened to our son."

Hazely's anger welled up inside her as she was cutoff. She narrowed her eyes at Jonah and clenched her jaw. All she saw at that moment was a wall of red. She was about to shut down the conversation and escort them from her office when she glanced at the stack of bills on her desk. That quick reminder was enough to help calm her down and refocus her thoughts. She took a deep breath and tried to relax.

"Okay," she replied. "Tell me your story." She sat back in her chair and folded her arms.

Jonah and Maria glanced over at each other, probably for strength, then turned back toward Hazely. "About three weeks ago our son Jeremy was backpacking through France," Jonah began. "The reason we knew where he was, even though he was in Europe for more than a month before that, is because he always checked in with us once a week—every Sunday—finding some way to make a collect call. We were expecting such a call on May 7th but it never came."

"It was part of the agreement we made with him," Maria quickly added.

Jonah looked at her and patted her on the knee. He then turned back to Hazely. "Well, he called us just before heading into the French Alps. He told us the route he was planning on taking—a more scenic, less traveled area—but that was the last time we heard from him.

"We contacted the French police when he failed to call again the second time and they said they would search for him. A week after that they contacted us and said they found nothing. They added that many people go missing in the Alps every year; it's a vast sprawling wilderness they said."

"And why do you have trouble believing them?" Hazely asked, sensing their skepticism.

"Because our Jeremy wouldn't be foolish enough to head through raw wilderness. He would stay to the roads and towns of the area," Maria blurted.

Hazely sat back, digesting the information. She really did not want to take this case. The time away from her business in San Francisco would be more than she wanted. "I don't know if I can help you," she stated bluntly.

"We know that you don't normally take on missing persons cases," Jonah quickly interjected. "Your secretary told us as much, but we ask you to consider taking this on. We will pay for all expenses incurred and pay you three times your regular fee." He cleared his throat. "We'll pay anything to find him, or at least, find out what happened to him, or ..." he shifted uneasily. "Even if you don't find him, or what happened to him, we have to know that we tried everything we could."

That last statement perked Hazely up. "Even if I don't find your son?" she asked with a raised eyebrow. Most cases had motivational aspects where a positive conclusion to the work reaped a greater value for services rendered.

Maybe an all-expenses paid trip to France on the Jacksons dime would be a worth it, she reasoned to herself.

Maria leaned forward. “Yes. We will pay three times your full fees even if you don’t find our son. But if you do find him—or what happened to him—then we will pay five times your fee,” she replied with tears rimming her eyes. “We just want to know what happened to Jeremy. Whether he is alive or dead.”

Jonah put an arm around his emotional wife. “Will you help us?” he asked.

Hazely sat back again. She placed her fingers together and held them up to her chin. “Why me?” she asked bluntly. She knew there were a number of PI’s in San Francisco, and she had to wonder why they had actively pursued her for this.

Jonah shifted uneasily. “It’s because—”

“It’s because what Jonah?” she cut him off, fixing him with her intense blue eyes. She knew it was because no one else would take the case, and that they had probably heard that Hazely’s case load was a lot less than the other P.I.’s in the field. She was a last resort.

Jonah shifted uncomfortably again. “We heard that you were one of the best,” he finally declared.

Hazely stared at him for another uncomfortable moment. She could see through the lie. She knew that, oftentimes, she ended up with the leftovers in this male-dominated field. She also knew that the sexism, harassment, alpha-dog crap that predominated the career wouldn’t go away anytime soon. It was the same at the SFPD.

“Okay, we’ll go with that.” Her icy stare bore into them.

Jonah and Maria looked at each other, seemingly uneasy at that moment.

Hazely leaned forward then and placed her hands on the desk. “I’ll take your case,” she said with intensity.

Maria smiled at her husband. Jonah pulled a picture from his inside jacket pocket and slid it across the desk. Hazely picked it up. "He's quite handsome," she commented. "How old is he?"

"He's twenty-three," Jonah replied.

"And why was he in Europe?"

"Just backpacking before he started his MBA program at the Golden Gate University," Maria replied. "He wanted to see the world." She looked over at Jonah and offered him a smile. "He's got an adventurous spirit just like his dad," she said, then turned back to look at Hazely once more. "He's a good kid."

Hazely nodded. "Do you have any more information that would help me establish a starting point? You said he contacted you before going into the Alps?"

"That's right," replied Jonah. "We mapped out where we believe he was." He pulled out a folded map and laid it on Hazely's desk. "You see this?" He pointed at an X that was penned near a town called Le Lieu. "This is the last place we knew he was going to. He called us the day before heading there and mentioned it on the phone. He said he might have to walk because of the current rail strike but wasn't concerned about it. Apparently, the town wasn't far from where he was, maybe ten miles up the road."

Hazely grabbed the map and looked it over. "That is really remote, isn't it? He really did want to be off the beaten path."

The couple nodded.

"And do you have the contact number of the police officer you spoke with?"

"Yes. It's all here." Jonah produced a few more pieces of paper with numbers and names scribbled down on them.

"Okay," Hazely said as she looked at them both intensely. "You have acquired my services. You can leave a cheque for half the payment with my secretary."

Jonah and Maria smiled brightly as they looked at each other. She smiled back weakly, not entertaining any illusions about her results, but willing to give it her best shot, if only to prove something to those block-headed chauvinistic jackasses who demeaned her over the years.

After Mr. and Mrs. Jackson left the office Hazely found herself staring at the picture of Jeremy for a long while. "What happened to you?" she whispered to herself. "What indeed?"

A moment later Melinda walked to the open door and looked at Hazely with a somewhat apprehensive posture.

"What is it now?" an exasperated Hazely asked.

Melinda adjusted her tight skirt and strode in the rest of the way to stand before her desk. "Your sister called again."

Hazely rolled her eyes and sighed as she leaned back in the chair.

"Actually, she called three more times. I think you should—"

"Should what? Pretend like nothing happened?" Hazely asked angrily as she stood up.

The movement must have startled Melinda as she slid back a step.

"I don't think you understand the dynamics of the situation Melinda. You don't understand the knife that bitch stuck in my back when she sided with our parents over me! The abusive—" her voice trailed off as she choked back the tears. Tears she swore she would never shed again.

Melinda seemed shocked and a little frightened by the outburst at first, then composed herself. "You're right. I don't understand," she answered evenly. "But it seems to me that she is trying to reach out, and maybe even make amends for what happened to you. Don't you think you should at least hear her out? She's the only sister you have."

Hazely tightened her lips. "I don't need anyone, especially not her," she declared coldly, then sat back down at her desk and picked up the picture of Jeremy again.

After an awkward moment she looked up at Melinda. "You'll have to manage the office without me for a while," she said, trying to change the subject. "It appears as though I'm going to France." She held up the picture of Jeremy Jackson for Melinda to see.

"Take some of the payment that the Jacksons left and use it for advertising," Hazely instructed. "I'm really hoping that, by the time I get back, I have a number of cases waiting for me. With the amount this client is paying, we just might be able to get out of the hole we're in."

Melinda stared at her for a few heartbeats then nodded and turned away. When she reached the doorway she turned around and looked at Hazely. "Everyone needs someone," she said softly before disappearing from the office.

Hazely sat back in her chair and shook her head in defiance.

Not me, she thought to herself. *Not me.*

7

THE LEAD

JUNE 17TH, 1989

Hazely walked from the terminal. Her hair whipped in the cool breeze, and the smell of exhaust from the many cars cruising to and from the airport wafted through the air. The low buzz of people talking and walking throughout the busy center filled her ears.

She looked down at the pad of paper she held in her hand looking at the notes she had made from her conversation with the Jacksons. While reviewing the pages on the plane she had circled Inspector Renaud's name, number, and the address of the station. She knew he would have to be the first point of contact in order for her to start the investigation. She really hoped he would have a little more information than the Jacksons were able to provide, but she wasn't confident that this was going to be the case.

Hazely glanced at her watch, noting that it was 1:30 pm already. Melinda had booked her an appointment with the inspector at 2:30 pm. She looked up quickly and raised her hand as a yellow cab rolled up. The cab stopped and she scrambled inside.

"Please take me to the police station," she said. "This one here," she clarified as she held up the paper with the station the Inspector was assigned to.

The cabby nodded. "Oui, Madame."

Hazely sat back in the seat as the car sped away. She looked out the window. Her thoughts drifted into silent contemplation about the case. She really hoped the French police would be of a different breed to the ones she had interacted with at SFPD. She had fought so long and hard to just get to where she was, and she really needed a break—she needed some cooperation.

She quickly pushed those thoughts aside and silently berated herself. No. She was tougher than that. She didn't need anyone else. All she needed was information and if that was all she received from the Inspector then she would be glad with that.

Even her family—the ones who were supposed to be there for her—abandoned her, so why should she expect anything different from anyone else?

Hazely's teeth ground in her mouth. Only then did she realize how wound up she had made herself. The frustration welled up in her and she felt like she might explode at any moment. She took a deep breath and consciously tried to relax. It took a few heartbeats, but eventually Hazely felt herself calming down.

Either way, she knew this meeting with Inspector Renaud would be interesting. She just hoped for a productive end.

~

"Madame, as I already told you, people go missing in the Alps all the time," the portly Inspector Renaud explained to Hazely. "Sometimes we find them and sometimes we do not." He reached over to a drawer in his desk and pulled out a package of cigarettes, then motioned toward Hazely, offering her one. She held up her hand and shook her head. The inspector merely shrugged and placed one in his mouth. "I really do wish I could help you, but we cannot expend that many resources looking for one man."

"Can you at least tell me where your investigation led?" the young woman asked, leaning forward in her chair. "Maybe I can pick up the trail from there?"

The inspector lit the cigarette and took a long pull on it; the end sparked to life. "All we had, Miss Silverston, was the same information you do from his parents," he stated matter-of-factly. He took another pull on the cigarette then exhaled. He leaned over and tapped it on the ashtray. "We even have a group of Chasseurs Alpin doing maneuvers in the area and they haven't reported anything unusual."

"Chasseurs Alpins?"

"Yes. Alpine Hunters. A ... French special forces outfit. I'm sure if they saw anything suspicious they would have reported it."

"And did you question their commander about our missing person?" Hazely asked skeptically.

The Inspector shifted uncomfortably. "Well ... no."

"The French Alps are pretty vast. What do you think the chances are of them stumbling on something without them actively looking for it?" Hazely questioned.

The Inspector seemed like he was at a loss for words. "I—"

Hazely waved her hand to cut him off. She wasn't interested in hearing his excuses, but decided instead to move in a different direction. "And where did you start your investigation?" she pried. She saw the inspector shift slightly under her scrutiny. She knew this conversation was getting really uncomfortable for Inspector Renaud.

"Ah ... well ... we searched all the areas the Jacksons told us about," he stated quickly.

Hazely narrowed her eyes at the man. She knew this inspector hadn't taken the case seriously from the beginning. She suspected that he probably put limited resources on it, if any. She even wondered if they actually went to Le Lieu at all! The anger bubbled up in her, removing all restraint. "Well, thank you for your help, you ignorant ass."

The inspector's eyes went wide at the comment.

"I know it's just another stupid American getting lost in the Alps so why would you give a shit about that?" she stated more than asked indignantly as she stood up. "You probably didn't even send an investigator to Le Lieu. No. You're just saying what you can to get me out of your office because I'm an equally dumb woman investigator who should just shut up and go home. Is that right?"

"Now listen here madame," the inspector said—his voice rising—as he came out of his seat. "You have no right—"

"No right to what?" Hazely cut him off with an upraised hand. "No right to actually do my job? If I was part of the French police I'd probably get a promotion for doing a half-ass investigation and telling others that I've done my best."

The inspector's face reddened and he looked to be on the verge of an explosion. *What a pompous fool!* she thought to herself. "I won't trouble you further." She narrowed her eyes at him, then scoffed and stormed out of the man's office before he was able to say another word.

"Miss Silverston!" the inspector yelled after her, catching the attention of all the other officers in the main office.

Hazely turned to regard him. "What?" she snapped.

He was silent for a moment and looked to be composing himself as all eyes were on him. "I ... I ..." he stammered. "Don't be disappointed if you can't find the man," he finally said coolly. "Some people just disappear, even though we do expend incredible effort trying to find them, and many times we never know why. Trust me."

Hazely didn't relent in her penetrating look. The fact was that she *didn't* trust him. She had dealt with many people like the Inspector in her eleven years of law enforcement and investigating. She could tell when people didn't give a damn, and this inspector was evidencing himself as one of those people. She was sure that if Jeremy was a French citizen, they would have put far more effort into finding him.

The fiery woman turned and walked away without another word.

The next day Hazely found herself driving through the scenic Alps. The road turned and weaved as it snaked its way through the beautiful mountains. There was a freshness to the air as life flourished from the green landscape. The peaks remained snow-covered and the air was still cool and crisp at the high altitudes. She had never been to France before and was quite enjoying the majestic scenes. They had mountain ranges in California, but, in her estimation, they paled in comparison to this—at least the ones she had visited. And the fact that the French drove on the right side of the road put her at ease.

Hazely glanced over at the unfolded map laying across the passenger seat and placed her finger on the road she was driving down. She was sure she was almost to Le Lieu.

She focused again on the road and brought her thoughts back to why she was here when she crested a hill and saw, stretched out in the valley before her, a small town. She whipped by the welcome sign for Le Lieu and in a few minutes found herself slowly driving down the main street to the Alpine town.

Her first order of business was to find the police station. Hazely pulled her car into the first gas station she could find and went to talk to the clerk.

"Excuse me?" she said, walking right up to the counter. A young scrawny man looked up and smiled as he saw her approach. "Can you please tell me where the police station is?"

"Are you American?" he asked enthusiastically.

She nodded and smiled. "Yes. Can you please tell me where the police station is?" she asked again.

He smiled back. "But of course! It is just down the road here then take your second right. You will find the place."

"Thank you. You speak pretty good English for being so secluded," she commented.

"Thank you. We learn two or more different languages in school. Most of us choose English," he replied.

"Well, I appreciate your help," she said as she smiled one last time and walked out of the gas station.

A few moments later she was pulling up to the local police station: a one story building that couldn't have been more than a thousand square feet in total. There was a single police cruiser out front.

"What did I expect," she lamented aloud with a chuckle as she put the car in park and turned off the ignition. This whole experience so far had been a major shock for the young woman, coming from a massive sprawling metropolis like San Francisco to this back water town in the French Alps. She had been to small towns back in California and neighboring states, but this was different. This was really secluded. What a change indeed!

When she walked in the front door she saw a desk off to the side with a few papers strewn about. On top of the pile was a crossword puzzle from a French paper which had scribbles and corrections riddled through it. The smell of burned coffee filled the air. Her eyes glanced around and she saw a small table with a coffee pot on it which looked extremely well used. The liquid within the pot was extremely dark. Cups littered the table. All of them looked used and unwashed.

Hazely heard grumbling coming from the hallway that led to the back of the building and someone was yelling in French. "Hello," she called. The man continued to rant. She cleared her throat. "Hello!" she yelled more insistently. Suddenly the ranting stopped, then she heard a large crash, and some more yelling.

"Are you okay?" she asked, moving toward the hall.

"Oui! Oui!" the voice came back. "Une minute," he said.

After a few more moments a tall gangling man came around the corner at the end of the hall. He brushed his thinning hair to one side and tried to straighten his disheveled uniform. He had what appeared to be grease on one of his hands and a small splotch on his cheek. Hazely noticed that he got some grease on his uniform when he tried to straighten it which caused her to smirk.

"Oh hi," Hazely said with a smile. "I was wondering if you could help me?" she asked innocently.

"Ah ... of course madame," the officer replied as he continued to adjust his shirt. "Sorry for my appearance. I was just trying to fix the air conditioning unit," he explained.

"No worries," she replied. "May I sit down?"

"Yes, yes. By all means," the officer replied, motioning her to the chair opposite his desk. He sat down and leaned forward.

Hazely slipped easily into the chair. "My name is Hazely Silverston and I'm investigating a missing person who was last reported to have been seen in your town."

That statement seemed to perk the officer up. "Really? And who is this missing person?"

Hazely produced the picture of Jeremy and laid in on the desk. "His name is Jeremy Jackson and he disappeared almost two months ago. I spoke with the Inspector who was assigned to the case—Inspector Renaud—and he said there were no leads he could provide for me. In fact, he seemed dismissive of the case stating that many people go missing in the Alps every year. But I have reason to believe that Jeremy did in fact come through your town, and from here, no one seems to know what happened to him."

"Inspector who? This is the first I've heard of this case."

"Really?" Hazely asked. "The Inspector was sure he did his diligence in this case." She could feel the anger rising in her again. This only confirmed the Inspector's incompetence.

The Officer shook his head. “Sorry Madame. I don’t know what to tell you.”

“That’s okay. This just confirms my earlier suspicions about the lack of care involved in attempting to solve this case,” she replied. “Which means I can probably assume that there was no questioning done by anyone here at Le Lieu.”

“Not that I remember,” came the officer’s honest reply. “I would know if someone from another department was investigating in my town. There aren’t many secrets that can stay secret here at Le Lieu.

“I’m sorry that’s not what you wanted to hear,” he said sincerely.

“That’s okay,” Hazely replied. “You’re just confirming what I suspected all along.” She worked hard to keep the frustration and anger out of her voice as she took the picture from the desk and stood. “Sorry to have bothered you. If you don’t mind I would like to start my search for any evidence of Jeremy passing through your town by questioning your citizens about any possible sightings they may have had of him.”

“By all means,” the officer stated as he rose. “You might want to start with asking Albert Lefevre. He seems to know most of what’s going on around here.” He grabbed a pen and scribbled something down on the pad that was on his desk. Tearing the paper from the pad he handed it to Hazely. “Here’s his address.”

Hazely took the paper. “Thank you. This is very helpful.” She worked hard trying to keep the surprise out of her voice.

The officer smiled. “The street he lives on is a few miles down the main road here. Just follow that and you’ll see it on the left. And before you go why don't you take my card and call me if you need anything." He handed her a business card. "My name is Maxime, Maxime Vaux."

Hazely smiled and took the card. "Thanks, Maxime."

After stepping back outside she looked down at the address. *Is this guy really going to be able to help?* Hazely shook her head. *It was worth a try.*

After leaving the police station she drove down the main road and in no time found the street she was looking for. Albert's house was the fifth one in on the right. Hazely pulled the car up in front of the small house. The house looked really old, like most of the buildings in this part of the country. It was made mostly of brick with a steep roof that had a chimney shooting out the top on the right side. Light smoke billowed from the chimney. There was an old truck parked on the grass to the side of the house. The yard appeared unkept with grass growing at uneven lengths mingled with weeds.

"Great," Hazely remarked aloud. "This looks promising," she said sarcastically as she got out of the car.

She carefully walked up the broken sidewalk and came to the front door. It was made of wood and had large patches of paint missing from various areas on it. Hazely looked for a doorbell but didn't see anything. She shrugged then knocked loudly.

A moment drifted by but there was no answer.

She knocked again. "Hello! Mr. Lefevre!" Hazely shouted.

Another moment passed then she heard someone shuffling to the door. The lock clicked and it opened. Standing there was a short old man with thinning gray hair and piercing brown eyes. He wore tattered overalls and a dirty t-shirt. His nose was large and bulbous with long white hairs protruding from it that curled up slightly.

"Mr. Lefevre?" Hazely asked.

"Yes?" the man replied in a thick French accent.

"I'm Hazely Silverston. I'm an investigator from the US and I'm looking for a young man who went missing around here about two months ago." She pulled out the picture of Jeremy and showed it to him. "Have you seen him?"

Albert glanced at the picture for a moment then looked back at Hazely. "No," he replied.

"Well do you know if anyone else had mentioned him coming through town?"

"No," he said again.

Hazely sighed as she put the picture away. "Do you have any suggestions as to where I can begin looking in order to get information on this man?"

Albert shook his head. "No."

Hazely rolled her eyes. "Okay. I'm sorry to have bothered you."

Albert closed the door and Hazely heard the distinctive click of the lock. She stood there for a moment staring at the aged door wondering how she got herself into this. She took out Maxime's card and looked at it. "Thanks for nothing," she said aloud as she crumpled up the card and threw it to the ground.

Hazely spun around and stormed back to the car, muttering curses to herself.

She climbed in and sat there for a long time, trying to collect her thoughts. She hated doing cold contacts. It was not the most efficient way to get information, but she knew now that she didn't have much of a choice. Hazely really thought that Maxime's lead would have turned into something substantial. How could she have been such a fool for getting her hopes up!

With a growl she turned the key in the ignition and drove away.

Hazely drove back to the main road, parked her car, and sat in silence thinking it through. "Okay, he was in this town, but stated to his parents that he walked to Le Lieu because of the rail strike. That means he entered town here. If I'd just hiked ten miles or more then I'd probably be thirsty, hungry, and tired. So, where's the nearest place a guy could sit down and have something to eat?"

She looked out the window and glanced over to see a sign hanging from an overhead banner: La Pomme D'Eve. It wasn't the only pub she had seen in town on her short drive through, but figured she had to start somewhere.

Hazely walked in and noticed immediately that the place was bustling with patrons. She did manage to find a seat in the corner and made herself comfortable. A moment later a middle aged portly waitress padded over to her. "Quelque chose a bore, madame?" she asked.

"Do you speak English?"

"Yes, madame. I asked if you would like something to drink?"

Hazely sighed in relief. "I'll have whatever your house beer is." She thought about questioning the waitress regarding Jeremy, but decided that she could use a drink and something to eat first.

"And would you like a menu?"

"Yes. That would be great," Hazely replied as she pulled her thick blonde hair back and tied it in a ponytail.

After the waitress left she pulled out the picture of Jeremy, the map of the surrounding area she had, and a notepad. She opened the notepad and began to document her progress, or lack thereof, thus far:

"Day 2 of the investigation. No sign of Jeremy. This is just as bad as working for the SFPD. No one wants to do more work than they have to. Missing—or dead?—men lie, I guess"

She was jarred from her thoughts as the waitress returned and placed the drink in front of her and gave her a menu. She was about to leave when she suddenly stopped and stared at the picture that was laying on the table. Hazely noticed the sudden shift in the woman's posture.

"You've seen this man? Haven't you?" she asked. Hazely leaned forward, pushing the picture closer to the waitress. Could this be her first lead?

The woman seemed hesitant to respond, looking to Hazely then back to the picture.

"If you know where this man has gone I ask you now that you share the information with me," Hazely pressed.

"Why are you looking for him?"

"I'm looking for him because he went missing a month or more ago, and his parents have hired me to find out where he is."

The waitress's face seemed to blanch at that moment. "You've seen him," Hazely pressed again. "Where did he go? And when?"

"I ... I don't know for sure. It was, I think, about a month ago. I don't know where he went but I know where he was planning on going."

"And where is that?"

The waitress leaned forward and got very close to Hazely. "He said he was going to L'accord, a small town a few hours up the road. I told him not to go but he must have ignored my warning," she whispered.

"Okay ... and why is that a problem?" Hazely asked, not understanding why the woman got quiet all of a sudden.

"No one goes to L'accord. It is not safe," she replied cryptically.

Hazely cocked her head to the side and looked at her curiously. "And why is that?"

"It's cursed."

"Cursed? What kind of curse?" Hazely asked skeptically, a little louder than she intended.

The waitress looked around as if trying to collect her thoughts, then turned back to Hazely. "No one who is not from the town goes to the town ... ever. We were warned as children not to go there if we value our lives and so we don't."

Hazely scoffed. "And I suppose everyone in the area believes that?" she asked skeptically.

"I am not the one looking for a missing person, am I?"

That comment caught Hazely off guard, but then she quickly dismissed the woman's paranoia.

The waitress turned to walk away but Hazely grabbed her arm. She turned and looked Hazely in the eyes. "If Jeremy went to this town do you happen to know how he was planning on getting there?" she asked.

The waitress was silent for a moment. "I do not know exactly," she replied. "He could have walked or maybe taken the train, depending if there was a strike at the time or not."

Hazely let go of her arm. "You don't think he could have hitched a ride?"

The waitress laughed. "No, madame. I already told you that no one goes to L'accord." With that she turned and walked away.

Hazely didn't know what to think. This was one of the

weirdest conversations she had ever had and wasn't really sure she knew what she should do next.

Sure, working the streets of San Fran brought her into contact with strange people and crazy circumstances, but those were, for the most part, drug and alcohol induced. This seemed to be on a totally different level. This woman completely believed what she was telling her.

Hazely suddenly felt like she was out of her depth. This was the last thing she expected to hear, but she knew that the unexpected often came with the job.

After a few more moments of thought she turned back to her notepad and wrote:

"Cursed town? Or foul play? Who's hiding what? At least I know a definite last sighting of Jeremy and an intended next location."

8

MAYOR BOUCHER

JUNE 18TH, 1989

Hazely was up early the next morning and, after a quick bite to eat, she headed to the train station. The platform was small and well maintained. There was a large brick building beside it with signage she could only assume had the name of the station on it, and probably information as to where tickets could be purchased.

She pulled open the thick door and walked up to the nearest ticket booth.

"Excuse me, but do you speak English?" Hazely asked the older man with light brown hair flecked with grey, and a somewhat crooked nose who stood behind the glass at the ticket booth.

"Oui, madame," he responded. "What can I help you with?" His accent wasn't as thick as the other people she had met since landing in France which brought some relief to the woman.

"I'm looking for this man," she replied as she placed Jeremy's picture under the glass.

He picked it up and looked at it for a few moments before putting it back down. "Sorry madame, but he does not look familiar. Why are you looking for him?"

Hazely placed the picture back in her pocket. "He went missing about four weeks ago while traveling around here, and I have information that he might have boarded a train from this platform."

The man shook his head. "Sorry."

Hazely thought for a moment then held up a finger as an idea came to her. She reached in her purse and produced her PI ID. She slid it under the glass. "I don't suppose I could look at your surveillance recordings? I just need the ones from between May 1st to the 25th."

The older man looked at the ID for a moment then nodded. "It might take a while for you to look through the footage."

"That's okay. I have the time."

The man came out of the booth and walked her back to the security room. They were met by another man who, after hearing Hazely's request, took her back to the room where the tapes were kept.

"Thanks for your help," Hazely said with a smile as she sat down with a small TV and video player.

The security guard grabbed a box of old tapes which were date stamped on the outside of their cases. Hazely wasted no time in finding the ones she needed and began to go through them one by one, fast forwarding through the footage looking for anyone that matched Jeremy. An hour and a half later she made it to May 20th. Her eyes were getting heavy and the hope that she would find what she was looking for began to drift from her until something flashed across the screen that caught her eye. She bolted up in the chair, immediately awake, and stopped the playback. The woman rewound the tape until she saw it again then began to play it at normal speed. When the man she saw entered the screen again she paused it. The quality on the camera wasn't very good, but she recognized that it was definitely Jeremy Jackson!

She looked at the time on the screen: 20:21. She pulled out her pad of paper and scribbled down the date and time on her notes.

"Excuse me?" Hazely tried to get the security guards attention when she came out of the room. "Do you have records of what trains were leaving the station on May 20th around 8:30 pm?"

"I can probably find out for you," he replied as he walked over to the phone and picked it up. After a quick conversation in French he hung it up and turned to the woman. "It was the Alpine Express which was traveling South East."

Hazely ruffled around in her bag and produced her map. She unfolded it and came to stand beside the guard. "Does it go through this town?" she asked pointing to L'accord.

The guard nodded.

Hazely smiled. Thanks!" she said as she bounded out of the security room. She now had two confirmations of a possible location and, in her books, that was good enough.

After staying the night at Le Lieu, Hazely packed up the car early and left for L'accord which was, according to the map, at least a three hour drive if the roads were good. She felt confident that she had found a significant lead and was going to chase it down with all the determination and skill she could muster. She still didn't know what she would face or what she would find, but that was the excitement of chasing the mystery. To her, Jeremy was not just a case anymore, he was a story, or rather, had a story—a hidden story—that she needed to uncover. Her hope that he was still alive was minuscule, but there was a good chance—at least in her mind—of finding out what happened to him. It was that thought that now spurred her on.

A couple hours into the drive the young woman quickly realized that the trip was going to probably take a little longer than she had first estimated. The narrow high mountain roads were pitted and rough. She had to wonder if people didn't come out here because of the state of the roads and not because of the talk of this silly curse! She also missed a couple turns that weren't marked at all and had to backtrack. The roads were so narrow and, in the thick forest, hard to navigate.

The going was slow, but eventually, just over four hours from when she left Le Lieu, she pulled into the small mountain town of L'accord. Most of the last few miles of the road were a significant uphill climb with a sheer cliff on the right side leading down into a deep valley. The view from this height was breathtaking with the forested mountains spiraling into the air, their iced caps poking into the clouds. The road twisted and turned as it climbed higher and higher. The thing that most unnerved the woman was the fact that she had seen zero traffic either going towards or away from this place. It was a desolate wilderness until she finally crested the hill and saw the mountain town laid out before her.

Many houses were sprinkled on the mountain side and

throughout this small valley. She noticed, to the North of the town, there appeared to be a large industrial building on the side of the mountain across the river that flowed through the bottom of the valley. There were houses on either side of the river with one aged-looking bridge spanning the gap. The bridge was framed on its sides with thick planks that extended about ten feet above the decking, and large solid-looking trusses ran the length of it forming an open roof structure. The town itself was smaller than Le Lieu but was spread out more throughout the valley which made it seem expansive.

As she wound down into the valley, she saw a large radio tower spiring into the sky on the South part of the town up on the mountain side. *Well, at least there's some semblance of civilization*, she thought to herself. As that notion took shape in her mind she also noticed power lines running through the length of the valley and across the river, connecting to every building within the town. That sight, along with the tower, gave her a little hope that this place wasn't quite as secluded or cutoff as the others she had spoken to implied that it was. She also noticed a small building with an electrical service truck parked out front. The building was down by the bank of the river. There were what looked like small power transformers around the building and it actually stretched out over the water for twenty feet or so. It resembled a small electrical grid where the main power from it went out into the small village, giving the houses and town the power they needed.

She drove slowly down the main road and many heads turned to take note of her; many of them huddled and whispered to one another as she passed by.

The woman felt uneasy as she rolled on. There was definitely something odd about the reaction of the people, but she shrugged it off to the comments of the waitress the previous night where she said that no one visits L'accord. She figured that the town's folk probably weren't used to seeing strangers come strolling through.

Hazely observed that, like any small town she had been through in the area, they had a market which bustled with people as they traded and sold their wares, a small library which was attached to the school building, and town hall. The one noticeable absence—outside of any hotels which was to be expected from this place—was that of any emergency response buildings: no police, fire, or ambulance.

The main road was made of cobblestones, and all the town's houses were mainly stone with wooden roofs. The stonework was some sort of worked masonry that was smoothed out to appear as one solid piece for the walls. Most of the houses were small two story designs. The library, town hall, school, and many of the downtown shops were exceptions in that they were made of brick and sturdier looking materials. The library and school were small compared to the towering town hall.

She glanced at her watch and noted that it was only 11:20 am. In the absence of any law enforcement she figured that the best place for her to start was probably at the town hall. She actually wondered if anyone would even be there given the size of this place, but what other choice did she have?

Hazely parked her car across the street and eyed the building for a moment before getting out. She walked up the large stone steps of the town hall, noticing a big statue over the main entranceway. It was of a man holding out a rolled parchment to the sky. To the left and right of the doors were statues of large wolves.

Hazely was transfixed for a moment at the imposing pieces of artwork. It was truly magnificent and not really befitting the nature of this small village. She walked over to one of the wolves and ran her hand down the carved stone. It was smooth and well worked. She stared into the thing's eyes which were painted but looked so real. They were blue and almost appeared to be the eyes of a human. She moved slightly to the side and it looked as though they were tracking her. She stepped back and shook her head, then came closer again. No. They were just really well painted. She chuckled to herself then moved to the large wooden doors and pushed on them. They opened easily and led to a main hall with vaulted ceilings and various pieces of ancient looking artwork adorning the walls. Again, this seemed out of place to the small town, but she didn't let that bother her and instead strolled up to the reception desk at the end of the room.

An older woman sat behind the large desk filing pieces of paper into a large drawer. She glanced up when Hazely approached. Her eyes went wide when she saw the stranger.

"Puis-je nous aider?" she asked.

Hazely shook her head. "Do you speak English?"

The lady rose and came over. "Yes. Is there something I can do for you?"

"Is there a place to stay in town and maybe a pub where someone can get a bite to eat?" She didn't see anything at first glance when she entered L'accord, but she figured it couldn't hurt to ask.

"No. I'm afraid not Madame."

"You don't get many visitors?" Hazely stated more than asked.

"We do not get any visitors," came the half-expected reply. "Are you lost?"

"No," Hazely responded. "I'm here to see the Mayor or someone who is in charge. I'm here looking for a young man that probably came through here about six weeks ago. His name is Jeremy Jackson." She pulled out the picture and placed it on the desk.

The woman adjusted her glasses and looked at the picture. "I do not recognize him. And, as I said, we do not get visitors to our small town. The only ones who ever come here are servicemen from the government whenever they need to fix our power lines which doesn't happen often."

Hazely fixed her with an intense stare as she picked up the picture. "And why is that I wonder?"

Her blunt question must have taken the woman aback as she retreated a step. "I will get the Mayor," she replied as she turned to go.

"Ya, why don't you do that," Hazely said sarcastically. She knew she shouldn't have been as harsh as she was, but Hazely could feel the anger rise in her and wasn't exactly sure why. Others had remarked before that she was an angry woman but she always brushed the comments off to justifying her attitude with the abuse she had suffered most of her life. The anger now was a part of her and often rose to the surface when she least expected it to.

In truth, despite the lack of help in this case so far, she knew she should actually be pleased with her progress, but she couldn't bring herself to take pleasure in even the little victories, and she didn't know why. One question always haunted her and she either didn't know the answer, or didn't want to dig deep into herself to find the answer: Was she broken beyond repair?

Moments later a shorter man with a large belly and coke-bottle glasses came through the door the lady had disappeared through earlier. His appearance pulled Hazely from her thoughts. "Theresa tells me that you are looking for a missing person miss ..."

"Hazely. Hazely Silverston," she responded, extending her hand to the Mayor.

"Well, miss Silverston—"

"Please call me Hazely."

"Hazely," I would love to help you but we do not normally get—"

"Visitors," Hazely finished for him. "I heard. As a matter of fact, I get the sense that people say that a lot when inquiring about your little town. The problem is," she pressed, "is that the trail I have followed of Jeremy Jackson seems to lead here. A town that I have been told not to come to.

"In fact I was told that Mr. Jackson was warned not to come here as well before he disappeared. Do you find that odd Mayor ...?" she let her voice trail off, fishing for his name.

"Mayor Boucher," the Mayor replied, obviously taking the hint. "And no, I do not find that odd," he stated. "What are you implying? Maybe Mr. Jackson never made it here. Have you thought about that?"

"Well ... the problem is that I know he boarded a train on May 20th heading in this direction with the intent of getting off at your small town. I find that, in itself, intriguing. Don't you?"

The Mayor's stone-cold facial expression didn't give the slightest hint of being shaken or of knowing anything of what Hazely was talking about. He was completely cool. "It could be a coincidence. Maybe Jeremy decided to get off somewhere else?"

"You know, I did think about that but, according to the map this is the next place that has a stop and, the fact that the train ride was later at night, I find it hard to believe he would change his mind."

The Mayor shrugged. "Who knows what some people do these days. The postulations you are making are a little stretched don't you think?

"The answer to your next question which you will be asking is no. I have not seen anyone come to our town in some time."

Hazely thought about what the Mayor was saying for a moment. It's true that Jeremy could have just kept going to the next stop passed L'accord and had gone missing somewhere else, but, being here anyway, she decided that she needed to do justice to this lead she received and shake it down as far as she could. The woman knew now that there were two ways of handling this: the professional way of using tact, which she wasn't very good at or, her way.

"I think you're hiding something," Hazely stated boldly —accusingly—as she looked to see what reaction she would get from her comment. "And I intend to find out what that is as I suspect it has something to do with Jeremy's disappearance."

The Mayor's eyes went wide for a moment then he quickly composed himself. "I assure you, Hazely, we have nothing to hide.

"Why would you come in here and start making wild accusations? You don't even know who we are yet," he replied indignantly.

"Excellent," the woman said without missing a beat.

"Then you won't mind if I stay in town and look around will you?"

"Ah ... no, of course not," Mayor Boucher stammered. "But our little town does not have any hotels for you to stay in," he argued.

"Oh I'm sure you'll be able to set me up with a room in a house somewhere in your respectable town as ... an honored guest?"

The Mayor stared at her for a moment as if he was thinking carefully of a reply. "Of course," he finally said. "But you will have to give me some time to set that up.

"How about you come back at 3:00 this afternoon. I will have something arranged for you by then."

Hazely stared at him intently, trying to see if his mannerisms would give her a clue as to whether or not he was hiding something. She couldn't be sure but felt that something wasn't right, and she suspected that the Mayor knew more than he let on. Either that, or he was just caught off guard by her blunt behavior. "That sounds agreeable, and appreciated," she responded with a slight nod. "I'll see you at 3:00 then."

She turned to leave then looked back at the man. "I do have one more question: What's with this curse I've heard about?" she asked jokingly with a chuckle.

A shadow fell over the Mayor's face. "It was nice talking to you Miss Silverston," he replied coolly as he turned and disappeared back down the hall.

That wasn't the response Hazely was expecting. She stood there staring down the hall for a few long moments before turning and exiting the town hall.

She had a few hours to burn while waiting to find out what the Mayor could do in finding a place for her to stay so she decided she would poke around town a bit. She left the car parked in front of the town hall and took off on foot, asking anyone she came across about Jeremy and showing them the picture if they stopped to talk to her. Unfortunately, most people avoided her when they saw her coming, and the ones she talked to claimed they couldn't speak English and hurried on. She felt incredibly frustrated!

The walk through the town itself was pleasant, however. There was a slight breeze drifting through the valley which carried the fresh scent of the surrounding forests with it. She inhaled deeply, enjoying the fragrance. Birds also perched around or flew overhead chirping wildly as they chased each other across the sky. Small squirrels scampered about searching for food.

After an hour, she decided to walk across the bridge and check out the North side of town. The river was high and rapid, being mere feet from the bottom of the bridge. The old planks creaked and groaned as she walked along but on a whole the bridge appeared strong and sturdy. She made it across in a few minutes and began strolling along the broken roads. Hazely noticed that there were a number of abandoned houses on that side, just as there were on the South side. Some of the townspeople were out working their small plots of land or feeding their cattle.

People eyed her suspiciously as she walked by. She tried to smile and wave at them for no other reason than to see what reaction she would receive; they always just turned away from her and went back to their work. She knew she wasn't the friendliest person, even when she was faking it, but the response from the townspeople unnerved her. Small towns in the US were always full of friendly people who were willing to bend over backwards to help others out, even strangers. Her experience at L'accord so far was completely different than anything she had experienced that was similar to this in the past.

Despite the many people out and working there seemed to be an eerie quiet about the place and she couldn't quite put her finger on why that was.

Hazely got a better look at the large building on the mountain side and discovered that it was actually an old foundry. The other peculiar building on this side of the river was an old church. It was constructed of mostly stone, like the rest of the buildings in this strange town. She walked up to the front of the large open stairs that led to the huge wooden doors of the building. As she scanned around the entranceway, she noticed a big circular stone off to the right of the stairs which was covered in grass and moss. She bent down and began to brush the debris away from it. The only thing written on it were Roman Numerals MDCLXVI.

"One thousand six hundred and sixty six," she mouthed. "What does that mean? Is that the street address?" It was hard for her to tell as none of the buildings seemed to have address numbers which didn't really surprise her at all.

She pulled her camera from her pocket, wound the film, and snapped a picture. Then she took a picture of the entranceway. She walked around the perimeter and noted that the large stained glass windows, which were at the back, seemed to be intact, although the rest of the building showed significant wear. It didn't even look as though the building was in use anymore.

While at the back of the church, she noticed a large cemetery that stretched out on the hillside. The headstones weren't in any logical order, almost as though the bodies were just thrown in the ground. Many of the markers were damaged and weathered and a few were even toppled over. She walked into the graveyard and began roaming through the site. She brushed the dirt and dust away from a few of the stones and read the names and dates on them. One was dated as far back as 1497 which amazed her. This small town was old; older than any in North America. Hazely was shocked that it had survived for so long being as secluded, and seemingly locked away from the world, as it was.

"Hello miss!"

Hazely jumped and turned around at the sudden sound of the man's voice. Her heart jumped and she had to settle herself in order to catch her breath. She looked up to see a large man standing on the road near the church.

"Sorry, I didn't mean to startle you," the man apologized. "But the Mayor wanted me to come and fetch you as he sorted out a place for you to stay."

Hazely nodded. "It's okay," she replied as she walked toward the man. "I'm Hazely," she said, extending her hand.

"I know. I'm Tristan," the man said stoically, staring at her but not offering his hand to shake in response. "You shouldn't be here at the Church."

Hazely pulled her hand away when he refused to shake it and cocked her head to the side. "Why is that?"

"Because it's not safe." He turned and walked back toward the road.

Hazely stood there staring at him for a moment as he walked away. "How is it not safe?" she called out as she hurried to catch up.

Tristan didn't answer as he made it to his truck, which was parked in front of the Church, and climbed in.

"Okay ..." Hazely said to herself as she opened the passenger door and got in.

Tristan fired up the old truck and they drove across the bridge. Hazely was shocked that the old structure was able to hold the weight, but it did.

"I noticed that there's not many vehicles in town," the woman said, trying to start up a conversation.

The man grunted.

"Is that because you don't need them? Or are they too expensive?"

The man grunted.

Hazely felt her frustration rising with the total lack of civility she was experiencing. "Maybe it's because everyone else in town is too stupid to drive," she blurted as she looked at the man.

Tristan did turn his head and glared at her when she made that comment.

The cheeky woman smiled back innocently and shrugged.

The big man looked back at the road and in no time they found themselves at the town hall.

"Bye, Tristan. It was nice talking to you," Hazely said sarcastically as she left the truck.

Tristan drove away without saying a word.

The Mayor was standing on the front steps. "It's not much, but it will keep you warm and dry for your stay here," he said to her as she approached. He handed her a key.

"As you might have noticed, we have a number of abandoned buildings. Here's the key to the best one we could find. You can stay there rent free." He handed her a piece of paper and the key.

Hazely took the key and paper. "Thank you." She looked at the paper and saw a rough drawing of the town. The house they had assigned to her was circled. *This town doesn't even have addresses or street names?*

"And how long are you planning on staying?" the Mayor asked, pulling Hazely from her thoughts. The way he asked it seemed a little too intent for Hazely's liking.

"Until I either find out what happened to Jeremy Jackson, or the trail runs cold," she stated matter-of-factly.

"Of course, of course. I hope it will not take that long for you to find out that we have never seen the man," he stated confidently.

He then nodded and walked by her. "Well, feel free Miss Silverston to come and see me anytime you wish and ask any questions you have," the Mayor said to her as he headed down the street.

Hazely watched him go then looked down at the key and then back to the other side of the river. "Cursed or not, this place is just plain creepy," she said to herself. "There is something going on here and I'm going to find out what it is."

9

THE FOUNDRY AND THE CHURCH

JUNE 18TH, 1989

Hazely turned the handle after unlocking the door and pushed, but the door didn't budge. She pushed harder—shouldering into the solid wood—and the door gave way, swinging open and causing dust to explode into the air. She coughed and waved her hand before her, trying to curtail the dust cloud. A musty smell was thick in the air, but Hazely figured that was normal for a house that had sat for so long.

The main entranceway opened into a small living area with a kitchen backing onto it. There was a large front window which was covered with sheets. Two chairs sat before the aged-looking hearth. The chairs were covered with thick plastic and layer upon layer of dust encompassed those.

Hazely reached over to the switch on the wall to her right and, a second later, the lights came to life. "Well, at least there's electricity," she commented as she strolled the rest of the way into the house carrying her small suitcase with her.

The kitchen area was bare, but still had the old gas stove in one corner. There was a door at the other end of the kitchen that led to the backyard. This door was also hard for her to open, but with a little extra effort, she managed to pry it loose. The fresh smell of the greenery from the forest, that lay about five hundred feet to the back of the house, was a refreshing scent to the musty smell that consumed the house. After taking a few minutes of reprieve in the yard, Hazely went back into the house. As she walked through the kitchen, she noticed a phone on the counter. She picked it up and, to her surprise, heard a dial tone.

"Well at least I have some sort of access to the outside world," she commented to herself.

Hazely checked her watch and did a quick calculation of the time change between here and San Fransisco. She knew that Melinda wound't be at the office yet, but decided to call anyway and leave a message.

The line rang five times before the answering machine picked up. "Hi. You've reached Silverston PI services. Unfortunately, we are unable to take your call at this time. If you leave us a detailed message with the reason for your call, and a number we can reach you at, we'll get back to you as soon as possible. Thank you." *She is way too chipper*, Hazely thought to herself. *But I guess that's why I hired her*.

The line beeped. "Hi Melinda. This is Hazely. I just wanted you to know that I'm in a small town in the French Alps called L'accord. I traced Jeremy's trail here but haven't been able to get any concrete evidence yet as to his whereabouts." She paused for a moment as she glanced out the window. "There's something strange about this place, but I'm not sure what that is. It's probably nothing. Anyway, I'll let you know when I have something solid. Bye."

After hanging up, Hazely went upstairs. It was more of the same and she did her best to pull the sheets off the furniture without disturbing too much of the dust. She also opened all the windows in an effort to air the place out. There were two modest bedrooms and a washroom upstairs. She checked the water and, after a few seconds, brown liquid began to flow. She was actually shocked to see that the water was still connected even though this was an abandoned house, but just shrugged the thought away. They obviously did things differently in L'accord. Hazely let the water run for a couple minutes and eventually, to her relief, it turned clear.

After spending some time wiping everything down, and making sure the places she was going to be using primarily in the house were free of mice and other rodents, she left, went to the small market in town, and picked up a few items that would make her stay in the old house more comfortable. She purchased sheets and blankets for the bed, a few cooking supplies, fire wood, and some food. By now the townsfolk must have gotten wind about the stranger that had come to town as the odd looks she received weren't as pronounced as they were when she first arrived.

By the time she had purchased the goods and brought them to the house, the sun was just going down beyond the mountainous horizon. The darkness that suddenly dropped over the valley due to the retreating sun was incredible. With that darkness came a deepening coldness that seemed to sink through Hazely's clothes and into her very skin even though the first day of Summer was merely two days away. She shivered as it pierced into her, but shrugged it off because she knew she had work to do.

After making herself a quick sandwich Hazely walked

out into the chill air and spent a moment looking around. The sparse street lights had flared to life by this time and the stars had come out to evidence their glory in the night sky. She was in awe of the magnificent sight of the nighttime canopy. Rarely had she seen such beauty, especially in San Francisco where the light pollution was so great you could barely see any stars, let alone the explosion of brilliance that was now before her.

Only a couple times in her life was she privileged enough to escape the city with her parents and sister to experience half of what she now was witnessing. Those were the happy moments—few though they were—from her childhood before her mother had died. That event manifested her father's true character, who became abusive to her, almost as though singling her out as some conspirator in her mother's death. Just the thought of that time caused the blood to boil in her veins! And her sister ... that wench who always made excuses for him and covered up his abuse, even to the point of siding with him over her during a domestic disturbance call she had made to the police. After that incident, the abuse got worse, even sexual. It was shortly after that when she ran away and lived on the street for a few years, selling herself as a prostitute in order to survive, before joining the SFPD. And the men she met in the SFPD weren't much different than the ones who had abused and used her for their own pleasures on the street. Sure, they were white collared cops, but their attitudes were the same: abusive, arrogant, calloused, and manipulative.

Hazely shook those dark thoughts away and pushed them far down inside of her where she locked them up. From there she would release them from their cell once in a while when she needed extra strength and motivation to make it through another day.

She cleared her mind and inhaled deeply the fresh scent of the forest. The sweet smell seemed to melt away the darkness.

Most of the townsfolk had retreated for the night with the exception of a few who were still trying to stable the rest of their animals.

"Where to start?" she asked herself. She had a long day, and was starting to feel the effects of it, but pushed the fatigue aside. The sandwich had helped in giving her the energy she needed to continue. No. She had a few hours before it got too late and wanted to make the most of her time. Besides, poking around at night was preferable to having the townsfolks' eyes on her as she was investigating.

The house the Mayor had loaned her was across the bridge on the other side of the river from where she had entered the town. She looked up on the hillside and noted a number of houses, the old church was here on this side, and the foundry which was up on the hill at the edge of the forest. The foundry looked abandoned.

With a shrug the woman zipped her jacket up tight, made sure her flashlight worked, and double-checked that she had her hand gun tucked away in its holster at her back. She walked down the street, veered up another road where she passed a number of houses, then came to the wide main road that led up the hill to the foundry. The road was in disrepair and overgrown. She made it up to the parking area and noted that the lot was riddled with cracks where weeds and other grasses sprouted up through.

Hazely made her way to the main entrance: a large steel

door with a chain wrapped around the handles and held together with a massive padlock. She examined the lock and gave a couple tugs on it seeing if it had lost any of its integrity over time. It was solid. She thought about shooting the lock off, but quickly decided against that as she didn't want to attract any attention to herself—at least any more attention than she already had. She decided instead to check the perimeter and see if there was any other way in the building.

Just around the corner she noticed a shattered window at ground level. Hazely shined her light in and saw broken tables, chairs, and other debris strewn throughout the place. She brushed some of the broken glass away from the frame with the sleeve of her jacket, then placed her hand on the sill and was about to jump in when she heard a shuffling sound to her left, back toward the way she had come. Her heart suddenly ramped up as she spun and shined the light over there.

"Hello!" she called. "Who's there?" Hazely walked back towards the corner of the building and pulled her gun. "I don't want any trouble," she said as she spun around the corner. Nothing. She listened for a moment and all she heard were owls hooting, some other critters chattering, and a far off howl of a wolf.

She shook her head, went back to the window, and quickly hopped inside. After taking a quick look around this small room she moved to the door. Before heading into the hallway, she flicked the light switch but nothing happened. This didn't really surprise her at all as this place looked like it was abandoned years ago. She walked into the hallway and shined the light down each direction. Hazely figured it probably didn't matter which way she went so she turned right. Every room she came to she opened the door and took a quick look. Most of the rooms looked like they used to be offices with dusty desks, broken chairs, and other furniture.

She went around the corner and saw that the hallway continued straight, but there was another hall that turned right. As she came to the junction, she shined her light down and saw a door at the end. Hazely walked down and attempted to open it, but it was locked. She aimed her gun at the lock and put a round into it. The old metal blew apart and she had no trouble kicking the door in. She hoped that no one had heard the gunfire as she knew that sound in the mountains traveled a long way. After a moment to contemplate that, she shrugged and walked through the door.

The room opened into a massive area that had, what appeared to be, boilers and electrical boxes positioned throughout. Cobwebs and dust hung like uneven tapestries over all the equipment and from the ceiling. Hazely had to swipe them away as she entered the mechanical room.

At the end of the room was an area with a chain-linked wall with a locked gate that went from floor to ceiling. Inside were a number of desks, filing cabinets, and chairs. She saw, hanging on one wall, a blueprint of the foundry. Hazely continued to scan her light around the room, but there didn't appear to be anything of significance. She thought to break the lock and get a better look inside the maintenance crib but shook that idea away. After a few more moments she backed away from the maintenance office and searched around the rest of the vast mechanical room. Other than the electrical panels, boilers, and furnaces, she found table saws, punch presses, table-top drill presses, and other pieces of old equipment.

Hazely thought it was strange that this place had obviously been out of operation for a long while and yet the company who owned it didn't collect their equipment when they folded it up.

After searching the room thoroughly, she backtracked and continued down the hall. As Hazely walked she glanced back and noted that her footprints were evident in the thick dust that coated everything in this place. The fact that there was so much dust told her that no one really came in here anyway so she didn't feel at all concerned that the Mayor would be upset with her snooping around. Hazely merely shrugged and continued on.

She found more offices, a locker room, and a set of stairs that led up. Hazely went to the next floor, which housed more offices and a long wide balcony that overlooked the main floor of the foundry. From this height she was able to view the factory floor. There were large pieces of equipment at different work stations and a few rail cars in different stages of production.

"I wonder when it went out of business?" she said aloud. The sound of her voice in the midst of the dead silence startled her.

This place was more massive than she first realized and she felt the scope of what she was doing baring down heavily on her. She had to remind herself that she wasn't going to leave any stone unturned. Abandoned buildings were perfect places to stash bodies, especially ones that are this secluded. With that thought in mind, she continued through the rest of the foundry until she was totally satisfied that the search wasn't turning up any clues. She literally found nothing. There were no traces that this place had been disturbed for years, except the one smashed window she had come through.

Three hours later, as the night darkened, Hazely walked down the wide road back into the town, content that she had thoroughly searched the foundry. She glanced at her watch and noted that it was only 10:32 pm. It looked much later than that due to the darkness which prevailed in the valley. As she continued down the uneven roads, she came around the corner that led to the house she was borrowing. She was struck again by the sight of the old church, only a few houses away from where she was staying. There was a flickering old streetlight cascading the front of the aged building with its incandescent glow.

Hazley's pace slowed as she approached. She knew this building was abandoned like the foundry and figured that she would be searching it sooner or later. She glanced at her watch again. In truth, she wasn't really tired yet—which could have been a result of the fresh mountain air. She wanted to use every moment to turn up every stone and eliminate all the possibilities in this case. That included searching the church, and every other building in town if she had to.

She was sure that Jeremy was dropped off in L'accord—even though she couldn't prove it yet—right around the time he had disappeared, which made this entire place open to investigation. With a determined stride she walked up to the large front door of the building. Hazely shined her light on the door and tried to open it. To her surprise it swung inward easily. She examined the latching mechanism and noted that it had been broken; how long ago that happened she couldn't be sure. The large doors creaked on their ancient hinges as she pushed them all the way open. She shined her light in and noted that the church was really just one large room with pews lining the left and right of a main aisle which led down to a raised dais. She found a light switch just off to the side and flicked it. Nothing happened. That surprised her a little as the house she was borrowing had electricity, but then again, maybe the Mayor had someone turn it on for her before she occupied it? This church looked like it hadn't been used in a long, long time. Maybe they were conscious about which buildings to power and which ones to not? The foundry didn't have power either.

She noted that there was nothing on the dais when she pointed her light down there again, but behind it she saw the glint of something but wasn't close enough to make it out. Slowly, she made it down the aisle shining her light all around, but particularly at the spot on the far wall. As she neared, she saw that the glint the light was refracting off was a large crucifix that hung on that wall with its base about three feet off the ground. The edges were lined with what looked like copper or brass.

She moved in closer and examined it. The main parts for the cross, and the body of Jesus that hung from it, were made out of some sort of hardened clay which gave it a really life-looking quality. She thought that it was strange that this hadn't been taken by the Catholic clergy who must have abandoned this place a while ago. It was a wonder that no mischievous kids had thrown rocks through the windows. She shrugged at the thought. This town was so different; she wouldn't be surprised if the punishment for breaking windows was public stoning!

After glancing around a little more, nothing further stood out as unusual. She turned to leave, but before taking a step she noticed a staircase to her left that led down. "This place has a basement?" she said aloud—almost shocked.

Hazely moved through some pews, navigating toward the staircase, when she heard a sudden "crack!" from above. The woman flinched and shot her head up to see something drop from out of the darkness.

10

ST. AIBHE

JUNE 18TH, 1989

Hazely jumped to the side in between two pews. The pews smashed apart and pain exploded up her left arm as something struck her. She landed hard on the floor, hard enough she lost her breath. Her hand banged against one of the pews on her way down and she lost her grip on the flashlight. It bounced a few feet away, the light dancing and spinning until it came to a stop.

It took a moment for the dust to settle. Her hand brushed against something that was under the pew, knocking it away. She had no idea what it was and was too disoriented to sort it out. She coughed and sputtered and tried to get up, but was pinned. She attempted to squirm out but was unable to move. Panic struck as her heart began to race. "Help!" she yelled, but knew no one would be able to hear her. "Help!" she screamed again.

She was about to yell out a third time when she heard some of the debris being shifted. A moment later the wood that was piled on her was moved aside, she saw a light, and a strong hand grabbed her. As she was pulled out over one of the broken pews she looked up and saw Tristan hoisting her out.

"Wha ... what are you doing here?" the shocked woman asked.

"I was coming to see if you needed anything when I saw you go into the church," Tristan replied. "Come. We need to get out. You shouldn't be in here."

"I know," she said, thinking that the fallen beam was evidence enough as to why she shouldn't be in this dilapidated old building.

"No. I don't think you do know," Tristan replied cryptically as he helped her out of the church. "This is no place for you."

Hazely stared at him, not quite understanding. "Are you saying that I shouldn't be in the church or in the town?" she asked pointedly. "I mean ... you didn't exactly make me feel welcomed after our last conversation."

Tristan didn't respond as he helped her to the house. "It would be better for you if you just left," he said sombrely. "There's nothing for you here."

"Not even information as to what happened to Jeremy Jackson?" the woman asked slyly.

Tristan shook his head and turned to leave.

"You know something don't you?" Hazely called after him, seeing if she could get a response from him.

The big man paused for a moment then shook his head and continued walking into the night. If Tristan was hoping that Hazely would be leaving town any time soon because of his veiled warning, then he was going to be sorely mistaken. His attitude and cryptic exhortations to leave only solidified the fact in Hazely's mind that there was something going on here. No. She wouldn't be leaving. She knew the answer as to what happened to Jeremy was somewhere in L'accord.

June 19th, 1989

"You want me to let you do what?" Mayor Boucher asked indignantly.

Hazely smiled disarmingly. "Why is that an issue if you are certain the town has nothing to hide?" she asked pointedly. "Besides, you already said that you would allow me to question the people of your town. If, as you have stated previously, no one has ever seen Jeremy Jackson, then there should be no issue in letting me go door to door with your sanction, in order to question the citizens of L'accord."

The Mayor was silent and Hazely knew he was working out any possible ramifications for him and his small town. He probably had no issues of her walking around and asking her questions, but to systematically work through the town like she was proposing might put him in an awkward spot if someone said something that he didn't want them to. If it was true that Jeremy had never come here, then they should have nothing to worry about with the scrutiny. She sensed, however, that the Mayor was concerned about something that was happening within the town, and was troubled that her systemization would find it.

"Fine," he eventually agreed grudgingly. "But you have to promise not to invade more of their privacy than you are already asking to do."

Hazely smiled again. "I'm not asking to invade anyone's privacy," she replied innocently. "I would just like to get to know your people a little bit and ask them about Jeremy. How harmful can that be?"

The Mayor scoffed: she sensed that it was at her display of innocence. "There is one more caveat," he said to her as he walked over and lifted his jacket from the nearby coat rack. "I'm coming with you."

Hazely wasn't really shocked that the Mayor would make such a request. She couldn't think of any reasons as to why she wouldn't let him, other than the fact that he might try to manipulate some of the conversations away from her investigation. She figured if that happened then she would just steer it back on course. Not to mention that, in his attempted manipulation, he would be implying knowledge of something that he was hiding which, she was sure, she could maneuver to her advantage. "That's fine with me," she agreed, "but it could take a while. Do you have the time?"

"I will make the time," Mayor Boucher replied curtly. "This is obviously important to you and to Jeremy's parents —which I completely understand being a father myself—so then it is important to me as well. Besides, not everyone in L'accord speaks English. You're going to need a translator."

Hazely nodded and motioned for the Mayor to lead the way out.

"The first house I would like you to take me to is Tristan's," Hazely stated as she and the Mayor walked down the stairs of the Town Hall.

Mayor Boucher stopped and eyed her for a moment.

"Is there a problem with that?" she asked.

"No. Not at all," the Mayor answered without hesitation. "It's right this way." He veered down the street and led her through the Southern portion of town. Within minutes they were standing before a small stone house. The narrow stairs led up to a thick wooden door.

Mayor Boucher knocked on the door, then waited. A moment later, Hazely could hear someone coming. The door swung open and Tristan stood there staring down at the two. He looked like he was confused as to why they were standing in his doorway.

"Sorry to bother you, Tristan, but Miss Silverston here would like to ask you some questions about her missing person? Is it okay if we come in?"

Tristan looked from the Mayor to Hazely then back to the Mayor. "Yes. Of course. Please come in," he stated, then led them into the house.

Hazely walked in behind the Mayor. She saw a comfortable living room with a cozy-looking fireplace in the corner. To the left of the fireplace was a small book shelf, sparsely populated with a variety of different sized books. There were a few photographs in old frames placed in various spots on the shelf. The smell of bacon hung in the air.

"Would you like some coffee or tea?" Tristan asked.

"Tea would be fine," Mayor Boucher replied. "Anything for you Miss Silverston?"

"Coffee," Hazely replied. She walked over to the bookshelf. Her eyes were transfixed on the pictures there. "Is this your wife?" she asked, picking up one of the frames. A middle-aged woman with short brown hair smiled at the camera. She wore a blue flowered dress that had smatterings of mud down one side, and was holding the end of a rope that was tied to a goat. Her face was also smeared with mud and so was the goat.

"Yes," Tristan answered. "Her name was Charlotte. She passed away a few years ago."

"I'm sorry to hear that," Hazely replied.

She then turned to the Mayor. "How are you able to get pictures developed being such a small community cut-off from the rest of the world?"

The Mayor chuckled. "We are not completely cut-off," he stated. "We do go into Le Lieu when needed to trade some of our goods and get supplies—especially when the trains aren't working—and, yes, we get some of these little niceties as well.

"It must be extremely foreign to you, living this simply."

Hazely nodded and put the frame down. "I must admit, your little town is not like anything I have ever seen before."

Tristan brought the Mayor his tea and Hazely a cup of coffee. "Please, sit."

Hazely sat in an old wooden chair. She sipped her coffee then put the cup down on the small table that was beside her. "As you have probably heard already, Tristan, I am looking for the whereabouts of this man," she said as she pulled out Jeremy's picture. "Have you seen him?"

Tristan took the picture and looked at it for a moment. "No," he replied, handing it back to her.

"And you don't know of anyone else who might have seen him come through here on May 20th?"

Tristan looked to Mayor Boucher, then back to Hazely. "No," he replied again.

"Did you hear of any rumors of a stranger coming through L'accord about that time? It is a small town after all and people talk."

Again, Tristan looked to the Mayor then back to Hazely. "No. I heard nothing."

Hazely was beginning to feel the frustration rise in her again but quickly calmed herself down. Maybe it was time for a different approach. "Okay, so if you haven't seen Jeremy, or heard rumors that someone came through here, then why did you tell me last night that there is nothing for me here and that I should just leave?"

She glanced at the Mayor and noticed that he seemed uneasy for a moment, but then recovered his composure.

Tristan also looked to the Mayor for a moment then back to Hazely. "It's because you are disturbing the peace of our town."

"The peace of your town!" Hazely blurted. "I'm looking for a young man who went missing around here."

"Yes, and you're accusing us of some wrongdoing that we didn't commit."

"I'm just trying to get to the bottom of this in order to bring some peace to his family and, if there is some criminal activity, to bring those responsible to justice."

"Well, I'm afraid you're going to be disappointed then, Miss Silverston," the Mayor interjected. "As Tristan has said, we are a peaceful town. You are accusing us of doing something we didn't do."

"I'm not accusing you of anything yet," Hazely replied. "I've just followed the trail and it has led here. I think someone in your town knows something and I'm going to find out what."

Hazely stood up. "Thank you for the coffee. Come on Mayor. We have a lot more houses to visit."

Mayor Boucher smiled and stood. "Yes of course." He turned to Tristan. "Thank you for your hospitality, my friend. Have a good day. Don't worry. You have done nothing wrong."

Tristan nodded, but remained stone-faced.

Hazely stared at the big man for a moment, then wheeled around and left the house.

The rest of the morning passed quickly with visitations to numerous other households. Not everyone was available at each house, but Hazely made notes of those places and people who were absent so she could come back later. With the Mayor right beside her, she questioned everyone she could and Hazely quickly grew frustrated with the lack of progress to her case. She was sure that Jeremy had come through here but no one would admit to ever seeing him.

After the tenth meeting as Hazely and the Mayor were walking to the next house she turned and stated, "I find it hard to believe that a stranger came into your town and no one seems to have any recollection of that."

"Then maybe your conclusion that the man came here is wrong?" the Mayor stated calmly. He turned his body so that he was standing fully before her. "Being an investigator, you must know that if you start with a wrong premise then you, in no way, can come to the correct conclusion. You assume that Jeremy came here without any actual physical evidence to the case."

Hazely thought about the Mayor's logic for a moment. It was true that she didn't have physical evidence that Jeremy had made it to L'accord, but the circumstantial evidence was really compelling. She couldn't shake the fact that Jeremy had actually boarded a train with the specific intent of coming here.

Hazely steeled her expression and decided to press the point, just to see if she could shake anything from Mayor Boucher. "You're wrong about that," she stated coolly. "I do have a record that Jeremy was indeed dropped off by the train that travels through here delivering supplies," she lied, as she really didn't have definitive proof of his dropped location.

"Well, maybe your information is in error," Mayor Boucher deflected.

"I find that very hard to believe," the woman replied, trying to match the Mayor's calmness.

"If he was dropped off then maybe he was attacked by a wild animal before reaching the town? It is a bit of a walk from the train dock to the outskirts of L'accord, and if he came in at night, it's not an entirely preposterous assumption. This is a practically untouched piece of wilderness you are standing in, with the exception of our little town of course."

"Maybe," she conceded, and made a mental note to go and search the road from the dock to town tomorrow. "But there's something you're not telling me," she stated evenly.

The Mayor's eyes went wide at the blunt accusation. "Why would you say that?" he complained, his voice rising. "I have been as accommodating and helpful as possible for you, and you claim that we are hiding something," he scoffed.

"I don't know what it is, but something isn't right and I'm going to find out what that is," Hazely responded without missing a beat. She put a finger to her lips. "Maybe I should talk to Tristan again," she said. "He was very helpful last night at that old church." She wanted to see what the Mayor's reaction would be to that information.

Boucher stepped back, his face full of disbelief. "Tristan has told you everything he knows," he shot back. "And you should not have gone into that building, or any of our buildings" he said sternly.

"I didn't think it was an issue," she replied. "The church

is abandoned, and I assumed you were being cooperative with me in my investigation." She tried to sound innocent but knew she wasn't pulling it off. "I guess I should have asked before barging in but—"

"You have no right!" Mayor Boucher screamed at her as his face reddened. Hazely glanced around and noticed that a few of the townspeople must have heard the outburst and were staring in their direction.

Hazely didn't expect such an explosive response. "I'm sorry. I—"

"No! Madame! You are forbidden to go into any of our abandoned buildings, do you hear me? Especially the church!" He then stormed away.

Hazely stood there watching the portly man depart. The fact that Mayor Boucher had gotten so upset with her snooping around only strengthened her resolve to do more of it. She saw the hushed whispers of a few people as they scurried away.

This whole situation was surreal to her: she was in the middle of the French Alps, trying to solve this mystery, in a town that seemed so backwards in many ways, with people that acted very suspicious about something that she couldn't nail down. It was like being in an Alfred Hitchcock film!

Hazely knew now that she needed more information, and she was certain she wouldn't be getting it from any of the town's members anytime soon. She thought hard about what her next move should be. Should she go back to the church right now? The mention of her being in that building seemed to set the Mayor off. Maybe there was something there she could find? As she thought about it, her eyes suddenly settled on a young woman walking up the path by the town hall. She walked passed the hall and up the stairs that led into the library that was connected to the school.

"Yes!" she exclaimed aloud as she ran across the square to the small building. She knew that most communities had some sort of preserved record in their libraries about their town. She figured it was worth a shot to see if L'accord had something like that; and besides, at minimum, she would be able to question that woman and anyone else who was in the library about Jeremy. She wasn't holding her breath on it, but it was better than nothing.

Hazely stepped up to the door, grasped the handle, and opened it.

The building itself was fairly small, made of stone like all the other structures in town, but the inside walls were lined from floor to ceiling with books. It made sense that the town would accumulate such a supply of literature since L'accord was far removed from anywhere else in civilization. The only medium they had which allowed them to stay in contact with the outside world was the telephone, radio, and their limited trips to the market at Le Lieu. Books, therefore, must be a coveted item in the secluded mountain town.

At the far end of the building to the left was a door that most-likely allowed entrance from the school.

The woman she had seen enter just moments earlier was taking her jacket off at a desk in the center of the room and hanging it on the chair. She appeared to be in her mid twenties with long brown hair that bounced on her shoulders when she moved. She wore a green dress that came down to just below her knees that had a black belt around the waist which was fastened by a small gold buckle.

When Hazely entered, the woman looked over at her but

didn't seem shocked to see a stranger standing there. Obviously, the woman had heard that she was in town.

"Hello ... Uh ... I mean Bonjour," Hazely greeted as she walked up.

"Can I help you?" the woman asked back in her French accent.

"Yes. I think so. I'm Hazely Silverston," she said extending her hand.

The woman turned and, after a long look at her, grasped Hazely's hand tentatively. "I'm Isabella."

"Well it's nice to meet you Isabella. I have a couple questions I'd like to ask. First, as you probably already know—or not—I'm a private investigator from San Francisco, and I'm looking for this man here." She pulled out the picture of Jeremy and showed it to her. "His name is Jeremy Jackson and his last reported sighting was here at L'accord. Have you seen him?"

Isabella shook her head. "I haven't seen him. We don't get—"

"Visitors here," Hazely finished for her as she rolled her eyes. "Ya, I've heard that. The other question I have for you is if you have any books on the history of L'accord and ..." she paused for a moment, trying to collect her thoughts, "that old church on the other side of town?"

"Why do you want to know about that old building?" Isabella asked with a tone of suspicion as she brushed her long brown hair from the right side of her head and back over her ear. "It's just a run down piece of crap."

"Oh it's nothing; just that I love history and architecture and being in your antique town is bringing that love out in me again," Hazely lied.

Hazely noticed the look Isabella was giving her. It was as

though she wanted to ask a question but was afraid to do so. "What's on your mind Isabella?"

The young woman chewed on her lower lip.

"It's okay," Hazely reassured her. "It will be just between you and me."

Isabella looked to the side for a moment as though she was thinking of how to put her question into words.

"It's okay. Really." Hazely put her hand on the woman's arm.

Isabella looked at her. Hazely noticed tears coming to her eyes. "It's just that ... my boyfriend, Julien, left a week ago and hasn't called yet. He promised to call me as soon as he got settled, then I was going to go with him. We were going to travel the world! I know he would not forget me."

Hazely felt sorry for the poor girl. It's not the first time she had heard of men jamming out on their woman.

Isabella must have sensed her skepticism. "It's not normal. You don't understand. There have been others who have left and have never been heard of again."

"Disappearances like Jeremey?"

Isabella shook her head. "No. These are people who have grown up here and have left. They aren't strangers. You are a private investigator. Maybe you can find out what has happened to them?"

Hazely didn't know what to think. She had enough of a case trying to find out what happened to Jeremey. Was there a connection? She had no idea, but she knew that, if there was a connection, she would find out what it is. "I can't promise anything, but I'll do what I can," she replied.

The woman wiped the tears from her eyes, then came out from behind the desk. "I will do what I can to help you, Miss Silverston."

"Thank you. Please, call me Hazely."

Isabella nodded. "We have some history books in this section over here," she said as she led Hazely over to a shelf by the wall, "and there is one that talks about the founding of this town. Unfortunately, it is in French. Do you read French?"

Hazely shook her head. "Maybe you can help me?"

Isabella smiled. "I can do that."

The door at the far end of the building opened and three small kids about seven to ten years old came bursting through. Hazely and Isabella looked over at them. The kids froze in their tracks, then wheeled about and ran from the room.

"We don't get many—"

"Visitors," Hazely finished for her again. "Ya, I get that," she said dryly.

Isabella smiled sweetly then sifted through a number of books on the shelf until she came upon a large hardbound tome with a black cover that was falling apart at the seams. "We have to be careful. This book is very old," she commented.

Hazely looked at her amused and bit back her sarcastic reply about that being quite obvious from the style and condition of the book.

"I've actually never read this book so it should be interesting for both of us," Isabella stated as she carefully took the ancient-looking book over to the desk and gently opened it up. A few pages almost fell out, but she caught them and put them back in place.

"Wait a second," Hazely said. "You're telling me that you don't know the history of your town either?"

Isabella eyed here curiously. "Why is that so surprising

to you? A lot of people do not know the histories of their own towns or cities."

Hazely conceded the point. She was beginning to like Isabella. The woman seemed to have a spunkiness to her that Hazely admired. It was at that moment that Hazely decided to turn the conversation to more pointed questions as she felt that she had nothing to lose. Maybe Isabella was a kindred spirit to herself in attitude. "So you don't know the history of your town you say, but I have a feeling that there is something strange going on here and I want to know what it is. Do you know?"

Isabella looked away from her and nervously brushed her hair back over her ear again. "All I know is that we never get visitors here, and we rarely venture out." She then cocked her head to the side. "Are you referring to the practice we have of leaving the doors to the barns that are in our houses open once a month?"

"What? I didn't know that was a thing."

"Yes. It's the tradition we have. It's said to bring good luck and protect us from misfortune."

That comment caught Hazely off guard. It was probably one of the last things she thought she would hear. "Okay ... that's not something I expected you to say."

Isabella smiled. "If you don't have any animals in the house you are staying at, you should buy some. Tonight is the night of the tradition. If you don't follow the tradition, then you should leave and come back in the morning. I would hate for something bad to happen to you."

Hazely snickered inwardly at the comment. She was never a superstitious person, and this tradition sounded ridiculous to her. She was about to say something sarcastic to Isabella, but decided against it as she still needed her help with the research. "Thanks for the warning," she replied instead.

Isabella nodded then turned her attention to the book. She flipped through a few pages then pointed to a drawing made of the town.

Hazely glanced down and saw many similarities in that drawing to what the town looked like today. "When does it say this town was founded?"

Isabella moved her finger across the ornate text. "It says here that the original settlers to this area were in 945 AD, and that the townsfolk were practitioners of magic and witchcraft."

Hazely glanced at Isabella for a moment then looked back down as the young woman flipped through a few more pages, skimming over the text. "What else does it say?"

"It is just detailing some of the early members of the town and the prominent witches and warlocks who practiced here." She flipped over the page again and both women looked down at it intently as they saw a drawing of the church.

"Okay what does it say about that?" Hazely questioned.

Isabella scrolled her finger back and forth for a moment. "This church was known as St. Aibhe after the Patron Saint of Wolves and was founded in 1666 by a priest named Vincent of Wales."

"1666?" Hazely asked. "That was the number I saw on the stone outside the church." She glanced at the librarian who looked over at her.

"It must be a founding marking," she replied. The young woman turned to the book again and continued to scroll down the page. "Vincent apparently was able to convince the townspeople to abandon their dark ways and accept the

Roman Catholic faith. They burned all their books and items of witchcraft and sorcery." She pointed to a drawing of the flaming pile that showed Vincent tossing in books and other items of sorcery.

Isabella turned the page and continued to read. Suddenly her finger stopped and she stood staring at the page as if in shock.

"What is it?" Hazely asked urgently.

"Shortly after Vincent burned the books he disappeared, never to be seen or heard of again." She flipped the page and a look of confusion splayed across her face.

"What is it?"

Isabella flipped a few more pages. "It says that, shortly after his disappearance, the townsfolk reverted back to their witchcraft and sorcery."

"How is that possible with all of the books burned?"

"I ... I don't know. Maybe they imported more from neighboring communities? In any case, the Catholic mission of evangelization never really took hold in this part of the mountains after Vincent disappeared," Isabella replied.

"Does anyone you know of in the town still practice witchcraft today?" Hazely asked.

Isabella shook her head.

"What else does it say about the town after these events?"

Isabella scrolled her finger across a few more pages. "It just moves on to other aspects of the history about other towns in the Alps and France in general—nothing interesting."

Hazely stood up and placed a finger on her lips as she pondered her next move. This seemed like a sidetrack to her purpose of finding out what happened to Jeremy, but could this story be somehow connected to Jeremy's disappearance? How could it? Hazely was torn. She didn't believe in witchcraft, and the events this book described happened centuries ago. How could they have something to do with the disappearance of Jeremy Jackson?

Maybe Jeremy stumbled upon something he wasn't supposed to and one of the town's people—perhaps even Mayor Boucher—did something to him? But what could the town possibly be hiding that would be important enough to kill over?

All her doubts assaulted her at that moment. Maybe Jeremy didn't make it to L'accord after all? She quickly reviewed in her mind all the information she knew about his travels and was convinced that he made it here. It seemed like the most logical conclusion with the data she had.

No. She wasn't about to turn away from L'accord just yet. She didn't know why, but something deep down inside her —like an intuition—told her that something else was happening here, and that Jeremy had somehow gotten caught up in it.

"Miss? Are you okay?" Isabella asked when Hazely, who was engrossed in her thoughts, didn't say anything for a long while.

"What? Oh ... ya. I'm fine. I was just thinking," she replied.

"About what?"

"Why doesn't the mayor want anyone to go in the church?" Hazely said absently to herself.

"What?" Isabella asked.

"Oh nothing," replied Hazely. "You've been very helpful.

Thank you." She flashed Isabella a disarming smile and headed for the door.

"Where are you going now?" she heard the librarian ask as she opened the door.

She didn't bother to answer the question as she walked into the fresh mountain air once more. She knew what she had to do next. She had to go back to the church of St. Aibhe, this time in full daylight and with purpose. Her instincts were telling her that something was there; something that would help her explain what was going on here in little old L'accord.

11

THE CHURCH

JUNE 19TH, 1989

Tristan sat motionless in the large cushioned chair as he stared out the window, a stoic expression upon his face. Images of the gruesome scene played through his tortured mind.

And the screams!

Tristan heard the plea for help in his dreams every night since the incident occurred. He would wake up in a cold sweat gasping for air that seemed difficult in coming. Jeremy Jackson would appear over the large man at night with half a face—brain matter and blood oozing from the fractured skull—limbs hanging grotesquely off his torn up frame.

"Why?" the raspy voice asked accusingly.

But then, beside Jeremy, would appear the Mayor. He would smile and push the man away. "You did well, Tristan. Because of you our town is now safe from the intruder. He would have ruined our whole way of life. You know that."

Tristan was confused. He despised himself and yet knew that somehow he had acted correctly. The Mayor reassured him that he had acted correctly with the best interest of the town in mind.

But now *she* was here. What if this investigator dug something up that they had missed? What if she did find out that he was the one who let Jeremy die? It was too late, in his mind, to do what his wife Charlotte would have done. He failed.

Or, did he?

If Jeremy would have survived that night, then he would have found out about their secret. If he found out about their secret, then he would have exposed the town to the world. If that happened, then their very existence would have ended. Yes. He did do right in letting the man die. The Protector knew that the stranger had to die and so he assisted in doing just that.

Tristan spun the events around in his mind and slowly —ever so slowly—began to realize and understand that he was a hero, and that his actions were necessary. Jeremy had to die, and he helped in doing that.

A smile spread across his face as he thought more about it.

The smile then transformed into a frown when he saw, through the large window, Hazely walking down the road toward the bridge. Tristan sat up and observed the woman move with a sense of urgency; a sense of purpose. She was relentless in her search for Jeremy Jackson and Tristan knew that eventually she would find out the truth. A truth that the town, he knew now, could not afford. A truth that he could not afford.

Why didn't I let you die in the church? he asked himself.

That was a mistake—a mistake he had to remedy.

Hazely tied back her thick mop of blonde curly hair with an elastic. She glanced around ensuring that no one was watching her then pushed open the door. She was immediately struck by how much damage the fallen beam had done to the pews and was shocked that she didn't get seriously injured or even killed. The whole place looked different in the daylight. She gingerly stepped inside, looking up to see if there were any more timbers on the verge of collapse. Hazely noted spots of sunlight streaming through cracks in the ceiling and walls at various places. There was quite a bit of water damage on the wooden structures within the building which explained how such a large piece of roof truss could have rotted away so thoroughly.

Tristan's warning to her about being in the church echoed in her mind, but when she replayed that conversation she felt that he was hinting at something deeper. Did he not want her to be in here because of the danger of the dilapidated building? or was it something else? It had to be something else. The Mayor's display of outrage when she mentioned the church threw up a red flag in her mind. There was something else here, and she had to find out what that was.

Carefully, she stepped through the entranceway and into the pew area. Hazely went left of the fallen beam glancing up as she plodded her course just in case another support structure gave way. Dust and cobwebs coated the walls and corners of the stone frame seemingly in every section. And why shouldn't they? This building was more than three hundred years old! It was amazing that it still stood at all, but here it was.

Hazely finally made it to the platform at the front of the building and stepped up on it with ease. She was still amazed that the stained glass windows of saints and angels were fully intact. The light shone through those painted panes to refract in a multi-colored display throughout the church. Despite the age of the building, the varying colors mingling together made a beautiful display as they splashed around the room.

In between those dazzling windows hung the large crucifix she had seen the night before. In the daylight she saw clearly now that it was lined with some sort of tarnished metal—probably copper. She put her hand on it and wiped some of the dust away. It looked like any other large crucifix she had seen in the Catholic churches at home except she knew this was much older than probably all of those. Again, the thought struck her as to why they would have left this piece of artwork here in the church instead of sending it to a museum or selling it?

She moved her hand across the artwork as she inspected it. She noted in a few spots what looked like red flecks of paint which she thought was curious, but nothing too out of the ordinary, especially if they ever painted inside the building over the years without taking it down. The crucifix felt a little warm which, she figured, was due to the light from the windows hitting the copper.

Hazely shrugged then moved to the other side of the church—heading toward the stairs she had seen the previous night. She slipped around the broken benches and pieces of wood that laid strewn throughout.

She gasped and jumped back as a number of rats scurried in all directions as she flicked over a piece of rotted board. Many of them ran under the pews.

"Great," she sighed. "I hate rats."

She watched as one of the large rodents scurried under the fallen beam. A flash came back to her as she remember brushing against something when she was pinned.

Hazely took a step and crouched down.

"You shouldn't be in here," a deep voice echoed.

Her heart jumped. She snapped her head up and saw Tristan standing there, staring at her. His demeanor was different than it had been before. Before he seemed soft-spoken and gentle—albeit in a strange way—but now he wore a somber expression, and his eyes narrowed at her threateningly.

He seemed even more intimidating standing before the open door with the light silhouetting his large form. Hazely steeled herself as she stood up. "I'm sorry Tristan, but I have to complete my investigation and find out what happened to—"

"You're not supposed to be here," he cut her off through gritted teeth. He advanced a couple steps then closed the door, grabbed a large piece of wood from the side of the door, and dropped that old locking beam across the metal brackets. As he faced toward her again Hazely took a step back as she saw what looked like a large butcher knife in his hand.

Hazely felt her heart race. "Listen, I don't want any trouble," she said as she slowly reached her hand behind her back. She winced a little when she realized that she had forgotten to bring her gun with her this time.

"It's too late for that now," Tristan replied cryptically. "We can't have you disturbing things. You'll ruin us."

"What are you talking about?" Hazely tried to reason with him.

The large man walked toward her methodically, picking his way through the debris; advancing on her like a man possessed. "It was me," he said in a low voice. "I killed the man. And now, I have to kill you, too."

Hazely's eyes went wide at the confession. "You killed Jeremy? But why?"

Tristan didn't answer, he just continued to advance with singular purpose.

Hazely looked around to see if there was any other way out. She saw a door at the back of the church but it was too far away for her to make a run for. She didn't even know if it was locked or not. No. Instead, she scooped down and picked up a large piece of wood. "Come on then," she said, waving the stick menacingly at him. He was only ten feet away.

Hazely lunged left then ran right, jumping up on one of the pews and running down its length. Tristan lunged, swinging the knife at her, but fell short. The woman went to leap from the pew but tripped as the wood from the bench cracked and fell apart. She landed on her side with a thud and groaned from the impact. The sound of her attacker rang out in her ears as he threw debris aside, advancing on her.

Hazely glanced over her shoulder and saw the cleaver descending. At the last moment she twisted to the side. The large blade sank into the wood right beside her. She swung the stick up as Tristan retracted the blade. The wood hit the man in the wrist causing him to grimace from the blow, but he stubbornly held on to the weapon. Hazely fully turned herself and held the stick up. Tristan pulled back his arm readying for another strike when Hazely swung the stick again, this time hitting him in the face. There was a loud crack and the big man reeled back. Blood flowed freely from his smashed nose.

Hazely took the opportunity to jump to her feet. She swung again and hit him on the wrist which dislodged the knife from his hand. Tristan came forward but Hazely smashed the board across his face again. The blow rocked him back, but he came on more furiously than before. The behemoth grabbed her with both hands and threw her toward the wall. Hazely crashed into the unforgiving stone and slumped to the floor—the board fell from her grasp. She felt blood trickle down her forehead and darkness threatened to overcome her. Hazely shook her head, trying to shrug off the dizziness.

Tristan growled as he approached. Hazely glanced over to where she dropped the board. It was only a few feet from her. She reached for it, battling her dizziness. Her fingertips brushed the edges of the board when pain erupted in her side. Tristan landed a second kick. The force of the blow threw her up against the wall.

Spots and light danced in front of her gaze. She saw Tristan lean down. She felt him close his massive hands around her throat. With frightening strength, he hoisted Hazely into the air and slammed her against the wall.

Hazely grabbed futilely at his iron grip. The air was being crushed from her. With as much energy as she could muster, she swung her leg into the man's groin. Tristan flinched from the blow and his grip lessened, but he refused to let go. Tears streamed down her cheeks, but she knew she couldn't give up. He was crushing the life from her! She hit him again, and again, and again in rapid succession. He finally let go and hunched over.

Hazely dropped to the ground gasping for air. She

reached over and grabbed the board with both hands and swung it as hard as she could, clubbing the man over the head. He rocked to the side but didn't fall over. She pulled back in order to hit him again but when the board came in he caught it and snarled at her, ripping it from her grasp and sending it flying across the room.

Hazely scrambled back from him, trying to gain as much distance from her attacker as possible. Tristan was moving for her again.

Unfortunately, in her mad scramble to distance herself she found that she was heading back to the platform instead of toward the door. Hazely knew she was in trouble; her heart pumped so fast she feared it would pound out of her chest at any moment.

She leaped onto the platform and turned just in time to see Tristan lunge for her. He tackled her with the force of a train.

Hazely heard the shattering of glass. Stinging pain erupted through her body as she and Tristan hurtled through the window.

12

FEAR

JUNE 19TH, 1989

The window shattered and Hazely found herself flying through the air and onto the ground just outside the church. Tristan landed on top of her and she felt the wind being blown from her lungs.

She grunted and groaned, and tried to suck in the precious air she so craved. Her eyes watered and the world seemed to spin as she laid there, trying to make sense of what had just happened. A few heartbeats later her mind cleared from the disorientation and she felt something warm on her chest and heard Tristan gurgling. The man rolled off her and seemed panicked as he grabbed at his throat. Hazely squirmed up onto her elbows and looked over at her attacker as a spray of blood splattered her face. She scrambled away from Tristan and looked at him as he writhed on the ground, eyes wide: the bright red flow continued to pulse out of his body where a large piece of stained glass had cut his throat.

Hazely looked away from the gruesome sight knowing there was nothing she could do for him. Within seconds the large man lay very still—dead—in a pool of his own blood, his body growing ghostly pale as the light left his eyes.

She sat there looking around at the strangely quiet surroundings. The back of the church was positioned in such a way so as not to be easily seen from any of the residents living on this side of the river. Two or three houses were up the hill beyond the cemetery, but they were far enough away that it would be difficult for people up there to see what was happening down here. There was a small stretch of grass that led immediately into the vast sprawling cemetery. The dead man in front of her struck her as symbolically representative of this quiet solitude before the cemetery: life was very absent. That thought hit even harder—and a shiver went down her spine—when she realized she was mere feet from that place which housed the dead generations which had lived and died here at L'accord. Tristan would be buried here now too.

After a few more heartbeats, she managed to collect herself enough to stand and shake off the dust and dirt. She tried to wipe the blood from her face with the sleeve of her jacket and noted that a bunch of it was matted in her tangled hair. She took a couple deep breaths and tried to compose herself. She had no idea what she was going to do now. The nearest law enforcement was hours up the road. If Tristan was willing to take her life, then would there be others who would do the same?

She stood there in a daze; more of the same types of questions rifled through her mind. Why was Jeremy murdered? Did Tristan act by himself, or was someone else involved? Was the Mayor in on it—whatever *it* was?

She looked out over the open cemetery, deep in thought. How was she ever going to explain this to the Mayor without condemning herself? Tristan confessed to the crime, but now he was dead. Hazely was absolutely sure that Mayor Boucher would never believe her. She had no idea if the Mayor was involved as well. If Tristan killed Jeremy as he claimed to have done, then how come no one else in town even knew he was here? Unless ... the Mayor was actually involved and that was why he insisted on tagging along with her in her investigation. Why else would he want to keep a rein on her?

Yes. He was involved somehow. She could feel it, but she lacked the physical evidence. If only she could find Jeremy's body.

Hazely looked back at Tristan's body, then her gaze drifted to the back door of the building. She knew she couldn't leave him out here. She needed to cover this up until she could find out more information.

It was reassuring to her—in some twisted way—to know now that she was dealing with a homicide. But how deep did this go? Why would Tristan want Jeremy dead? What motive was there? What was the Mayor hiding?

With those thoughts whirling around in her head she went to the door and, after a couple good shoves, managed to open it. "I guess it wasn't locked after all," she muttered to herself.

She then went back to Tristan and pulled her belt off. Hazely slid the belt under Tristan's arms and around his chest then buckled it together. She then pulled off her jacket and wrapped it around the man's neck as tightly as she could so his blood—whatever blood he had left—wouldn't drip everywhere as she moved him. With her makeshift harness she began pulling the large man toward the open door. Minutes drifted by, but the woman managed to pull Tristan into the building and to the top of the stairs.

After taking a short rest she pulled the man's body down the old dusty planks. The bottom landing led to the right. Hazely pulled out her small flashlight and clicked it on.

"Sure," she said to herself sarcastically, "I leave my gun at the house, but remember the flashlight."

Hazely shook her head as she left Tristan's body where it was and walked down the small hallway. It went for about five feet then led to two doors: one on the right and the other on the left. She opened the one on the right. The old hinges creaked as the door swung slowly open. Dust and cobwebs coated the small room, and the only thing in there was some broken wood that she presumed used to be furniture of some sort.

"Good enough then," Hazely said to herself as she went back and collected the body. She dragged Tristan into the empty room. Before leaving him there she searched his pockets. She found his wallet, a lighter, a set of wire cutters, and a screw driver. Hazely thought that was strange, but shook the thought away as this whole circumstance was strange—this whole town was strange!

She unwrapped her bloodied jacket from Tristan's neck and stood up, took one last look at the dead man, then closed the door behind her. Hazely turned and grabbed the handle of the other door when she suddenly heard rustling from upstairs. Her heart leaped in her chest and she froze, straining to hear more. Was this one of Tristan's accomplices?

She pulled her hand from the door and crept as silently as she could back up the old stairs. They creaked and groaned as she went, but she figured she had little choice.

Hazely made it to the top of the stairs and peeked around the corner. A slight breeze blew through the church from the open door and shattered window, but she didn't see anyone. She kept quiet and waited, but when nothing stirred she breathed easier. She was about to head back down the stairs when something under one of the pews caught her eye.

There, under some broken fragments of wood, she saw what looked like a torn up old shoe. It was red and white with the distinctive Nike checkmark on it. She moved towards it and quickly unearthed it, noting immediately that it was stained with blood and torn in half. She pulled her small camera out from her pocket and snapped a picture. She wound the film and snapped another at a different angle.

Hazely grabbed the shoe, turned it around in her hands, and looked over every inch of it. She wondered how it got torn up so badly? Why it was even in here? And who it belonged to? Then it struck her! She fumbled around for a moment in her bloodied jacket and produced the picture of Jeremy. As she looked at him standing there with his backpack on, smiling and proud that he would soon be heading to Europe, she saw them: the white and red Nikes that he wore just before coming to France.

"This is Jeremy's shoe," she said aloud. "But what the hell did Tristan do to him?"

The breeze that blew in through the church caused Hazely's thick hair to move about her shoulders gently. She cupped her head in her hands as she thought about this whole situation. Hazely was incredibly troubled by the turn of events. By Tristan's own admission, he had killed Jeremy. Then he had tried to kill her and had ended up dead himself. And now she found physical evidence, but still had no body.

Hazely glanced back at the stairs where she had unceremoniously dumped Tristan's body, and a shiver went down her spine. She had seen dead bodies before with her work at SFPD, but she had never been involved in the altercation that brought about the death. The thought of it made her stomach churn.

She looked down at the shoe. No. She determined then and there that the Mayor would have to explain these events to her. If Tristan did kill Jeremy the odds of no one else in this small town knowing about it were minuscule. And where was the body?

Her gaze turned back to the stairs. She looked at the shoe again, and then back at the stairs. Without another thought Hazely slipped down the narrow passage which led to the basement. She stepped around the corner and came to the other door.

"Was there a reason the Mayor was so upset that I was here?" she asked herself.

With a shrug she turned the handle and opened the door. Dust exploded into the air as the creaking door cracked open.

The room was dark and cool, almost damp. Hazely shined her light, pushing away the darkness. It was a small room. Right across from the door sat a wooden table. An old chair with four wooden spokes came up from the seat to form the back rest. Each spoke was made of a dark twisted wood that attached to a support on the top of the back rest. The chair was pushed up to the table as though whoever was in here last had finished whatever work they had to do and neatly put the chair back into its proper place. On the table was a large book; it was covered in dust and, from the immediate look of it, appeared to be old and weathered. Behind the book was a candle stand. A pale-looking candle stood out of the holder. It had small waves of wax formed down the sides of it from the burning action of the wick. But from the look of this whole place Hazely knew that it had been years, maybe even decades, or centuries, since that candle had seen any warmth.

She brushed away the cobwebs that hung from the ceiling as she entered and went right to the book that was on the table. Hazely bent down and blew the dust off the cover. She noticed immediately that it was a deep red color—the color of blood. Etched into that cover was a large yellow circle. She pulled her camera out again and took a few pictures.

There was writing that wrapped around the outside of the sphere that was engraved into the cover. Hazely moved her hand across the etched-in characters. As she brushed the dust away she could make out the lettering. "Lupus Est Scriptor Noctem," she read aloud.

Hazely opened it and took a cursory look through the book. It appeared to be written in some sort of French with Latin interspersed. The French writing looked different, like it was old or something. There were depictions throughout, but she couldn't really make sense of their meaning with her quick scan. She closed the tome and wrapped her hands around it and was about to pick it up when she became transfixed with the yellow sphere on its cover.

A shiver coursed down her back. An unintelligible whisper from the darkness came to her ears. Her heart leaped. She spun around, but no one was there. Hazely turned back to look at the aged book. She reached for it again, but fear racked through her. Hazely jerked her hand away. Something wasn't right, but she didn't know what that was. There was something about the ... but how could that be? It was just a book.

Hazely reached for it again. A coldness ripped through her, the whisper in the darkness assaulted her, and the door slammed shut. She jumped and ran for the door. To her surprise, it flew open when she pulled on it. Without looking back she ran from the room and back up the stairs.

Hazely turned around and looked at the stairs, irrationally waiting for someone to come charging up them and attack her. Her breathing came in great heaves. She wasn't sure what had just happened. She wasn't even sure if it was real or if she imagined the whole thing. Either way, she was just glad to be out of that room.

After collecting her thoughts again, Hazely crept through the back door and to the house—ensuring that no one had seen her leave the building. She washed as much of the blood off as she could. By the time she was showered, the sun had dipped well below the mountainous horizon dropping the valley into shadow once more.

This case was now more dangerous than she ever thought it would be. Hazely reached for the phone and paused for a moment. She silently berated herself for throwing away Officer Vaux's business card. She wasn't really sure what she was going to say, but she knew she had to call in some backup. After a moment of thought, she held up the receiver, determined to call the operator and see if they could patch her through anyway.

There was no dial tone.

She pushed a few buttons and hung up the phone, picked it up again, then listened—nothing. "What the—"

Hazely shook her head and hung up the receiver—confused. Then the thought struck her. The tools Tristan had on him! "He must have cut the lines," she gasped. "But when?"

She began to pace. "It had to have been just before he tried to kill me," Hazely muttered to herself. "He must have done it just in case I escaped. He really didn't want me to get away."

Her stomach suddenly grumbled and only then did she realize that she hadn't eaten since this morning. Even though that was the case, she wasn't sure her stomach was churning because of the lack of food; it could, more likely have been, because of Tristan's murder of Jeremy and attempted murder of her.

The day's events rocketed by. It was all too surreal and her mind fought to make sense of it all. She had to crack this case and find out why Jeremy had been murdered, and what happened to his body? In order to do that, she knew she had to break the Mayor and his secrets open and make him tell her the truth.

Hazely grabbed her gun and holster and strapped it through her belt at the back of her pants underneath her sweater, then snatched the torn shoe off the table, and slipped out of the house and ran back to the other side of town. She noted that the folks of L'accord had all but disappeared from the streets—retreating into their homes. With all haste Hazely went to the town hall but found that it was locked up tight. She berated herself for not getting the Mayor's address and knew that her discussion with him would now have to wait until the morning.

~

Agnès Boucher placed a hand on her husband's shoulder. He turned and looked at her. She smiled back with that crooked smile he had fallen in love with those many years ago, then her expression turned grim. "Don't you think you should warn that young woman of the danger she is in by being here?" she asked her husband.

Jean smiled at her, cloaking his real feelings. In truth, if the beast he called 'Protector' took care of her tonight then their problems would go away, so he believed, and so he hoped for that outcome. The only issue would be if someone else came snooping around upon her disappearance. He shook those thoughts away and knew he would deal with that situation if it arose. "She'll be alright," he answered.

Jean had lived in this town his entire life and, with the exception of going to Le Lieu once in a while in order to get supplies and work out deals with the power and rail companies, it was the only place in all the world he had seen. He wasn't upset about any of that. He knew this town was his prison—a prison he had come to love—and that his life would end here one day. His concern now was for the rest of the citizens of L'accord. This incident seemed to have set them on an unprecedented course; one he knew he had to correct.

Agnès looked at him with all seriousness. "Even though the night is upon us once again and she is in our town and doesn't understand our ways?"

That question snapped Jean from his thoughts.

Jean patted his wife's hand with his, then turned to fully stand before her. "The Protector is only interested in satisfying its hunger," Jean stated with confidence. "Its hunger will be satiated with our animals, as it always is."

"Yes, but what about the boy?" she asked. "He wasn't livestock."

"No," Jean conceded. "He was in the wrong place at the wrong time is all. He intruded into our town and the Protector did what it had to do to keep its secret."

"You speak as though that thing is intelligent," Agnès replied skeptically. She took a step back and looked into Jean's eyes.

Jean smiled again. He knew the truth of the creature. He knew more than any other town member. The secret was his to bear. This knowledge gave him the power to manage the situation and turn it in the direction he wanted it to go. "It is," he replied.

Agnès looked shocked at his blunt statement.

Jean chuckled. "It is a reasoning creature. How else would we be able to safely sleep at each full moon?"

Agnès studied Jean's face for a moment. "What if Miss Silverston is in the wrong place at the wrong time? Our ah ... *Protector* ... didn't show any mercy to that poor Jackson boy."

Jean smiled at her use of the title he had given to the creature. He had worked so hard making the people of L'accord accept and appreciate the beast. "No, it didn't," Jean stated matter-of-factly. "It was protecting its secret and us, as those who know of its existence."

"It doesn't seem like much of a Protector to me," Agnès scoffed. "More like a prison guard."

Jean scowled at his wife. Apparently not everyone appreciated the creature the way he did, even his own wife. They hadn't had this much discussion about their situation in years. He didn't like all the questions, especially when those questions came from Agnès. Everyone should just listen and live. He knew best.

He had always done everything he had for the best interest of L'accord, and he was so careful. Even when he took a chance years earlier by making the contract with the rail company in order to bring work and economic development to the valley. When they built the foundry, the contract was specific about days of operation and construction so that no outsiders working on the construction of the building would accidentally be in town during the full moons. Jean had planned everything out meticulously. The town had survived and flourished, and their obligations to the Protector had never wavered.

The foundry had operated for thirty years under the shadow of their secret, but Jean's meticulous ordering of that operation, and the contract's specificity, ensured success. It wasn't until the rail company no longer needed the products they were producing that the foundry shut down. By then, the town had gained enough resources to bring some modern comforts into L'accord.

Jean was actually relieved when they ceased production as he always had the secret of L'accord to protect lingering over him. He always felt like they were on the precipice of disaster.

"Shouldn't you at least warn her of the possible danger?" Agnès pressed again.

Jean's face went very serious at that point. "No!" he snapped. "You know we can't do that," he stated emphatically. "If we do ..." his voice trailed off. "Well," he said with a slight smile trying to calm his wife's fears and defuse the tension, "we just don't know what would happen, do we?" he lied.

The old woman smiled back and nodded. "Well then, I guess all we can do is hope for the best." She turned away from her husband and headed toward the kitchen.

Jean walked up behind her and wrapped his arms around her in a great hug. "We just need to trust that Hazely will survive this night. One wayward traveller being killed is far too many," he lied again, as he secretly hoped that Hazely wouldn't survive the night.

He could feel his wife shiver at the thought.

"This is the curse that is L'accord I guess," Agnès said resignedly as she nuzzled her cheek into his arm. "This is the curse our town has inherited."

Her words pierced through Jean. He could well remember the time when he was just a young man and was told fully by his own father why the town had the tradition it had; why it acted the way it did, and why no one ever left L'accord. That secret had been passed down through certain family lines to only a handful of people who knew the entire scope of what their town had inherited, and Jean's family was one of those custodians. Even now, only a handful of citizens in L'accord knew the entire truth. This was a secret they would carefully pass on selectively to the next generation.

"Did you prepare the house?" Agnès suddenly asked, breaking the silence.

"I just have to make sure the door is open," Jean stated as he let go of his wife and headed to the cellar.

Hazely stepped off the stairs of the Town Hall. She glanced back at the wolf statues and a shiver went down her spine.

The eyes seemed so real, as if they were tracking her movement. She shook the ridiculous thoughts away, whipped her head back around, and picked up her pace, heading back to her house.

Her experience in the room in the basement of the church must have rattled her. She thought of every possible rational explanation as to what she experienced down there. Her mind kept coming back to the fact that she was nearly murdered only minutes before that, and, therefore, her mind must have been playing tricks on her. That had to be it.

She walked back to the bridge as a strong breeze began to soar through the valley. The woman pulled the hood up on her sweater and placed her hands in her pockets trying to fight off the sudden chill. Just before she got to the bridge a loud creak and then a bang rang out in the air causing her to flinch. She glanced over and saw that the house across from the bridge had left their barn door open. She heard livestock rustling about in the barn.

She sighed and walked up to the door of the house, thinking that she had better notify them that their door was open.

She knocked and waited. No answer. "Hello!" she said as she knocked again. No answer. She glanced to the side and saw that the window's were shuttered closed. After a few more moments she shrugged and stepped off the door step. As she did so she noticed that the neighbor's house also had the barn door open. She cocked her head to the side and took a step back. "That's odd," she said to herself.

Hazely walked over and grabbed the door. There was no latch on the outside. She pulled her flashlight out and looked in the barn. Animals were penned inside, milling about.

Weird. But I guess they're not going anywhere.

Again, she stepped back and looked further down the street. Every house on the block seemed to have their barn doors opened and swinging slightly in the breeze. She knew now that this wasn't a coincidence. These people had purposely left all their stables opened. This must have been what Isabella told her about.

Hazely walked up to the next barn door down the street, pulled it open, and went inside. Again, all the cattle and livestock were in here. She examined the doors and noted that there were indeed closing and locking mechanisms on them.

"That's a strange superstition," she remarked aloud.

Was it more than just a superstition though? The fact that all the houses on this street had open barns, for some irrational reason unknown to her, triggered a red flag in her mind and sent a shiver down her spine. Something wasn't right.

She backed out of the barn.

A loud bang rang out. Hazely flinched, pulled her gun, and spun her head to the left, down the darkened street. It sounded like one of the doors slamming hard on its jam, maybe from a gust of wind. She walked slowly in that direction. The cobblestone road wound to the right, and as she started to round the corner she heard some rattling and more banging coming from further down the street. This banging didn't sound like a door slamming, but rather, like a struggle. She stopped as her heart raced. The lights from the lanterns on the poles lining the street seemed to flicker a little as she waited there, in silence. Hazely listened and made out what she thought sounded like animals in distress; it was hard to hear over the ruckus, but she was sure there was something else.

The noises seemed to lessen as she stood there, straining to hear. Hazely slowly went the rest of the way around the corner. She could see one of the barn's doors fully open and swaying in the breeze. She took another step then froze as the hairs on the back of her neck stood up. She glanced down at the torn and bloodied shoe she was carrying and something deep inside her told her to run. Hazely couldn't explain the feeling. It came out of nowhere but the warning was so real. She glanced at her gun thinking she could barge in there and deal with whatever it was, but she was frozen with fear and she didn't know why. She was always so tough and brave, or so she thought. But now she was ... stunned? The only feeling she had at that moment was to run!

She needed to run!

Now!

Without another thought Hazely sprinted for the bridge which was down the adjoining road to her left.

Her legs pumped furiously as she darted down the road. She sensed that something wasn't right, she just didn't know what that was. One thing Hazely knew in that moment of panic was that something was chasing her—hunting her.

She came down the small hill that led to the bridge in a full run. Her breathing came in short quick gasps as she hit the wooden planks of the deck structure. Hazely almost lost her footing from the transition of the stone road to the wooden bridge, but managed to keep her balance and run on.

She dared to glance back a couple of times but didn't see anything. As she neared the end of the bridge, she heard a howl echo through the valley. It sounded like a wolf, but bigger and throatier. She had never heard anything like it before! It was then that she knew—or maybe more feared than knew—that it was close. Whatever it was, Hazely knew that she couldn't outrun it, so she leaped off the side of the structure and onto the soft embankment before the river. Her gun skipped out of her hand as she landed. She thought to retrieve it but decided instead to quickly roll under the bridge.

Hazely laid there, in the mud that was on the bank, trying to control her breathing. Her hands tensed and she felt them squeeze the mud through her fingers. She glanced at her gun which laid ten feet from her, but knew she couldn't get to it. She looked up through the cracks in the old planks to see the clouds crawl lazily across the sky. Suddenly the night lit up as the stars and moon—the full moon—was revealed through the passing of the clouds. It almost seemed peaceful and eerie at the same time. Then Hazely sucked in her breath and held her mouth, feeling the mud spread across her lips and face, as something—something large—stepped on the planks just above her, blocking out her view of the moon. At that moment she dared not breathe.

Hazely saw large, curved claws on the foot that was just above her. It looked like some sort of animal, but she couldn't tell exactly what it was. It lifted its head to the sky and smelled the air as if it was looking for someone —for her!

She moved a hand to her pocket and carefully pulled out her camera. With shaky hands she held it up, but fear gripped her so tightly that it refused to allow her to push the button. Tears rimmed her eyes, and a stench hit her at that moment, carried on the breeze; a stench of corruption and decay. She tried with all her will to keep herself from vomiting. The tears fell from her eyes, cutting small rivers through the dirt and grime that was on her cheeks. She brought the camera down and did all she could to remain completely still and quiet. The seconds felt like hours as Hazely shuddered at the presence of the animal. She laid there, hoping —praying—that it wouldn't find her. Then, without warning, it bounded away.

Hazely, shivering—her brain and body trying to process the experience—laid under that bridge for a long while, not daring to come out until she was sure the thing—whatever it was—was gone. Then again, how could she be sure it was gone? That question horrified her. She had never felt a presence like what she had just experienced: a presence of pure ... evil and death. Yes, she decided, that was how she could only describe it. And that smell!

Terror-stricken, Hazely laid under the bridge throughout the night and, when her body could no longer stay awake due to pure exhaustion, she collapsed into unconsciousness.

13

CHASSEURS ALPINS

JUNE 19TH, 1989

The wash of the helicopter blades laid low the long green grass on the hillside and caused the trees at the edge of the tree-line to sway back and forth from their power. The military chopper hovered thirty feet above the ground, its blades humming menacingly as it swayed slightly in the mountain breeze. The side door slid open and Captain Gabriel Roux surveyed the drop zone by the spot light of the helicopter. The sun had drifted below the mountain peaks, causing the valley below to darken as night descended upon the land.

"Alright men. Be quick about it!" he yelled to his soldiers, two of which came right to the open door and tossed out repel lines.

After the ropes were deployed, they quickly harnessed in and exited the craft.

"I don't like this," Kaplan said as he grabbed the rope and attached it to his harness. Private Fay looked at him curiously.

"What was that Private?" Captain Roux asked sternly.

Kaplan looked the Captain in the eyes for a moment then glanced at Fay and shook his head. "Nothing sir."

He and Fay jumped from the helicopter.

As soon as Kaplan and Fay leaped from the chopper two more took their place, and two after that, and two after that, until all fourteen men—including Captain Roux—had deployed. As the men hit the ground they quickly formed up into a defensive position and waited for the helicopter to buzz away.

Once the sound died down as the chopper soared away, Captain Roux turned to his Lieutenant, Chance Matan. "You know what to do Lieutenant."

Lieutenant Matan nodded. "Okay, let's gather in here," he said to the team as he kneeled down and produced a map. He pulled out his flashlight, compass, and felt marker. "Toussaint and Corbin were dropped here six hours earlier and are headed to the safe zone which is sixty kilometers south west of our current position. Right here," he said as he circled the safe zone on the map.

"Our objective is to make sure they do not make it to that safe zone. This is an escape and evasion exercise."

Captain Roux looked around at his men and saw anticipation in their eyes.

"We cannot allow them to make it to the safe zone," the Lieutenant reiterated, "and, to help us, we have ..." he pulled off his large rucksack and unzipped the main compartment and pulled out two large plastic cases, "these babies to assist us." He opened up one of the cases and produced a large Camera-looking device. They were about a foot wide and two feet long with a narrow lens at one end and a viewing port at the top. It looked like a video camera. The men leaned as if to get a better look at what the Lieutenant was holding up.

"A camera?" one man asked.

"No, Private Faucheux. These are Microbolometers."

"Micro what?"

Lieutenant Matan chuckled and handed it to the Private. "We would normally have given you some training on this equipment in our pre-mission briefing, but decided that it would be best to conduct such training in field conditions.

"Now Private, stand back about ten meters and take a look at us through it." He turned off his flashlight and instructed everyone else to do the same. The large full moon and dazzling display of stars issued forth their glorious light, illuminating the sky enough so they weren't in total darkness.

The Private held up the Microbolometer, but before he could walk away with it Lieutenant Matan grabbed his arm. "Be careful. This thing costs more than your yearly salary, soldier."

Captain Roux could almost sense Private Faucheux blanch at the statement while others chuckled.

The Private turned and walked away then turned back and looked through the lens. He almost fell over as soon as he put the Microbolometer to his eyes. "What the—" he stuttered then held it back up.

Captain Roux watched it all with amusement. He knew his team would enjoy this exercise, especially with the new equipment. "Chasseurs," he said loudly, flicking his flashlight back on. "The Microbolometers, or night-vision cameras as we will refer to them since it's easier than saying Microbolometer," that statement caused the men to chuckle, "are going to change and shape modern warfare.

"These are far better than the Starlight Scopes you may have used in the past. These don't just amplify the ambient light, they allow us to see heat signatures in blackout conditions. And we Chasseurs Alpins have been chosen to assess the equipment in simulated real-life engagement. Hence, our escape and evasion exercise. Sergeant Toussaint and Corporal Corbin have a head start on us, but we have our new equipment which will take that advantage from them if we can catch up.

"This is our mission. Everyone will have a chance to use the new equipment. The Lieutenant here will give you the rest of the briefing we purposely neglected to tell you in our pre-mission briefing." The men glanced at each other with questioning looks when he made that statement, but it didn't phase Captain Roux one bit. "He will go over with you the rules of engagement for this operation," he continued, "so please pay attention and be focused." He waved for the Lieutenant to carry on.

"Thanks Cap," Lieutenant Matan replied. "As the Captain said, we need to be focused. We'll keep together as one team. I'll be the scout, moving ahead and mapping our location. At the head of the team will be the soldiers with the night-vision cameras. With the use of these, you should be able to follow me through the forest and keep pace. We'll be moving fast and so the night-vision operators are going to have to be on the ball with where I am and lead the team."

Captain Roux watched as the Lieutenant leaned over the map and laid out the route that he suspected would be the best way in which to track down their two men in this mountainous terrain. He was convinced that the Lieutenant knew that the topography of the area would limit the possible paths the two men could take to get to their destination and so Matan detailed that in his explanation to the men.

Captain Roux smiled at the efficiency of his Lieutenant and the way in which he planned every detail of the exercise. The Lieutenant was extremely experienced. He even spent some time on exercises in Quebec with the French Canadian Infantry troops called the Van Doos. He always accepted passionately every opportunity in order to enhance and develop his abilities, and never refused a challenge.

He knew he had a great group of men and was eager for them to show him how superior they were to other elite units. After all, this small platoon was part of the *Chasseurs Alpins* (Alpine Hunters) or, as others referred to them: The Blue Devils, a name well earned since their establishment in 1888. And with this new equipment he held great hopes that the field test would bear much fruit and be a game changer in nighttime warfare.

As he watched the briefing he couldn't help but notice how agitated Kaplan looked. The man kept peering around and seemed really distracted. He and Fay whispered behind the Lieutenant's back and did not seem engaged at all in what the Lieutenant was saying.

The Captain walked over and tapped Kaplan on the shoulder. Kaplan snapped his head around and his eyes went wide when he saw the Captain there.

"Is there a problem, Private?" he asked sternly.

"Ah ... no, sir."

"You seem really distracted Kaplan. What's keeping you from paying attention? You haven't been yourself since you learned of our mission here."

Kaplan looked to Fay briefly, then back to the Captain.

He shook his head. “Nothing, sir.”

“Come on, Kaplan. Just tell him,” Fay interjected. “Then maybe one of us can have some peace about your rantings.”

Kaplan scowled at him.

Captain Roux grabbed Kaplan by the arm and pulled him aside. Once they were out of earshot of the others, he turned and faced him. “Well? What is it, soldier?”

Kaplan appeared as though he didn’t know where to start. His eyes darted around until they finally fell on the Captain’s. “It’s just that ... It’s that ... I’m not sure how to say this—”

“Then just say it, son.”

“These woods we’re in are cursed and we shouldn’t be here,” he blurted.

Captain Roux raised his eyebrows. “I didn’t take you for a superstitious man, Kaplan.”

“I’m not sir, but I come from a small town around these parts and there are rumors of something that hunts these woods; something that’s not ... natural.”

“Not natural?”

Kaplan nodded.

“Well, I’ve been conducting training exercises in these mountains for almost two decades now and I’ve never seen anything ... *unnatural.*”

Kaplan nodded, but still looked agitated.

“Now, why don’t you rejoin the others, soldier.”

“Yes, sir.” With that, Kaplan spun around and rejoined the briefing.

Captain Roux chuckled to himself and shook his head as he walked back to catch the last of Lieutenant Matan’s briefing.

With coordinated precision, the Alpine Hunters formed

up and slipped into the forest as the night sky continued to transition into a deeper darkness.

Toussaint and Corbin descended into a small gully and back up over the ridge.

"Hold up," Sergeant Toussaint said, pulling out his flashlight, compass, and map. "We have to be careful not to drift too far off course. No doubt the rest of the platoon will be on us before we know it."

"Ya, especially since I bet Fay a hundred Francs they wouldn't catch us," Corbin stated.

"Well, that's definitely going to motivate him, isn't it?"

Corbin chuckled. He rubbed his hand through his short brown hair and looked up into the night sky which was visible through the canopy of the trees. "It sure is a beautiful night," he said. "Albeit a little chilly." He zipped his thick jacket up more and rubbed his hands together for warmth.

Toussaint paused what he was doing and glanced up at the large full moon that hung serenely in the night sky. He remembered many moments like this while on exercises similar to this one with the Alpine Hunters where he could just lose himself in the stillness and beauty of the mountain nights. He had been an Alpine Hunter for all of his ten year career and loved the job. He couldn't imagine doing anything else. Out here, in the mountains, he felt alive.

"How does your wife like it when you're out on exercise?" Corbin asked, shaking Toussaint from his thoughts.

He shook his head and refocused, going back to his work of finding the best path for them to make it to the safe zone. "She doesn't," Toussaint replied, not even looking up from his map work. “But the girls are even worse than Clarise,” he said with a self-deprecating chuckle. “They make enough fuss that it almost makes me want to quit and find work that keeps me at home.”

Corbin laughed at that. “I can’t see you doing anything else, Sarg.”

“Neither can I. What about you Corbin? You going to get married any time soon?”

Now Corbin did laugh even harder at that statement, then he quieted down and looked around as though he was expecting the rest of the platoon to descend on them at any moment. “I would if I could stay in a relationship longer than six months,” he said in quieter tones.

Toussaint looked up from his work and eyed him curiously. “You seriously can’t stay with a girl longer than six months?”

Corbin shook his head.

“Is something wrong with you?”

“Why would you think it’s me?” Corbin asked feigning being hurt by the comment.

Toussaint laughed as he went back to work. “I just figured that there’s one common denominator in those relationships: you.”

“I just like women too much—all types of women. It’s like grazing at a buffet.”

They shared another laugh, then Toussaint looked over at Corbin. “Okay, I think I have it.” He slid over beside his partner with the map spread out. “If we continue on this side of the mountain and descend into that valley over there we should be able to cross the river and head east around that peak.” He pointed at the dark silhouette of the mountain he was speaking of then back to the map.

Corbin nodded. "Well, let's get a move on so I can win that bet."

Toussaint smiled and clapped the man on the shoulder. He really liked Corporal Corbin's lighthearted nature and his free-spirited attitude. That was probably one of the main reasons he selected the man for the exercise. That, and the fact that he was an excellent soldier. After folding the map up, they began making their way across the mountain and down into the valley.

The two ghosted through the dark woods seemingly making good time. It was hard to judge the distance they were traveling within the thick forest, especially in the dark, but Toussaint kept a brisk pace and constantly reoriented his bearings whenever they entered a clearing. He would stop and check the heading on the compass against the markings he had made on the map and make slight directional adjustments.

Eventually they made it into the bottom of the valley, and the river that flowed freely through it. The river was larger than the two had anticipated, and the current was steady and swift.

"This could put a damper on the plan," Corbin commented as he knelt down at the edge of the river and assessed it in the light of the moon.

"Well ... we could go up river a ways. It will take us a little longer, but there's a small town up there with a bridge. We could cross from there."

Corbin sighed. "How much extra time do you think that will take us?" he asked. He then stood and looked up the river and then back at Toussaint.

Toussaint scratched his chin. "I don't know. Maybe six hours."

"Six hours!"

"Ya, but—" his voice trailed off as he cocked his head to the side and looked up the river.

"What is it?" Corbin asked, pointing his rifle in the same direction.

"I ... I don't know," Toussaint replied. He took a few steps up the river. "I thought I heard something."

"Like what?"

"I don't know. It sounded like ... I don't know what it was. Maybe a growl?"

Corbin rolled his eyes. "Sure, you heard something," he said dryly. "You trying to scare me is not going to work."

"I tell you I heard something," Toussaint insisted.

"Okay, fine. You heard something. Well that's why we train in the mountains with live ammo." Corbin lifted his rifle and patted the side of it to emphasize his point.

Toussaint shined his light into the nearby trees. He peered intently into the dark but didn't see anything.

After a few moments Corbin put his hand on Toussaint's shoulder "There's nothing there, Sarg. So, why don't we just keep going and hopefully whatever it is will lose interest."

Toussaint was quiet for a long time. He then turned back to Corbin and nodded. The two walked the bank heading upriver for an hour until they came to a narrower spot.

"It looks like we won't have to go all the way to the village after all," Toussaint said as he shined his light across the dark water.

"That's a relief."

The two soldiers waded through the chilly water which came up to their chests at the deepest point. The current threatened to wash them away at a few spots but they managed to keep their footing and make it across.

Once on the other side Toussaint reoriented himself again and led Corbin back into the forest. The forest wasn't as thick on this side of the river as it had been on the other which, in the light of the clear sky, gave them more ability to see into the darkness. They walked a few steps in when Toussaint suddenly stopped again.

"What is it?" Corbin whispered.

"Something's not right."

"Would you quit doing that! It's not funny anymore," Corbin snapped.

"I'm not doing anything," Toussaint responded sternly. "I just ... have a feeling that something's not right."

Corbin moved up to kneel beside Toussaint. "Do you think it's the rest of the platoon? Did they find us already?" he asked in hushed tones.

Toussaint shook his head, "I don't know. I just have a—"

"What?"

"Do you smell that?" Toussaint asked crinkling up his nose as he turned to face Corbin.

Corbin sniffed into the air and gagged. "What is that?" he blurted.

"It smells like a dead body," Toussaint replied. His heart began to race. He then heard a low growl resonating on the night air. "Tell me you heard that?"

Corbin nodded and pulled the action back on his FAMAS assault rifle and watched the round load. The chamber on the French rifle was built into the stock so he could easily see the round slide into the firing area when he cocked it. The rifle was also shorter than most military weapons which facilitated ease of carry and movement.

He flicked the front sight down, trying to allow whatever ambient light was around to enter the sight area for better vision. Then holding up the rifle he began looking around as if searching for some unseen enemy.

"Come on Corporal. Let's get as far from this place as we can," Toussaint said, loading his FAMAS and holding it up, as he began to walk through the forest again; this time at a more quickened pace.

He scanned all about, training his rifle in every direction. The scope on the weapon took in more of the light and amplified it slightly, causing him to be able to see a little better than he had been able to without looking through it. Then he heard the growl again to the left. Toussaint spun and peered into the woods. He thought he saw something move across his line of sight.

Corbin looked in the same direction. "What is it?" he whispered loudly.

"I don't ... I don't ..." Bang! Bang! Bang! Toussaint fired shots into the brush.

"What is it?" Corbin yelled, fear evident in his voice.

Toussaint spun to the right. Bang! Bang!

"What are you shooting—" the words stuck in the man's throat as he came up beside Toussaint and looked at where the man was firing. "What the hell!" He let four shots go.

Toussaint ducked and rolled to the side just as the thing charged out from behind some trees. He spun with his weapon around when something hit him in the chest which caused him to stumble back. He glanced down, and in the dim light of the moon and stars, saw Corbin's head staring up at him—his mouth open in a silent scream.

14

REMAINS

JUNE 19, 1989

Captain Roux and Lieutenant Matan pushed the men on mercilessly. The night had deepened and the Captain knew that Sergeant Toussaint and Corporal Corbin would be hard to catch, but he trusted in his men. His Chasseur Alpins platoon had been working together for more than five years now under his command with the newest member, Private Chevrolet, joining the elite team about two years earlier. He knew they were up for the challenge and indeed reveled in the chase! To be a Chasseur Alpins was to be a part of a select group that very few, comparatively, could qualify for in training, but these men under Captain Roux's command didn't just qualify, they excelled.

The Captain was impressed with the speed at which Lieutenant Matan mapped out the course. He seemed to know with almost definite certainty the rough route that Toussaint and Corbin would have taken, given the lay of the land and their objective. It was a guessing game, he knew, of trying to get into the head of the ones you were chasing, but his Lieutenant responded with almost a seemingly clairvoyant ability. At least that's the impression the Lieutenant gave to Captain Roux and the rest of his Chasseurs; they listened to his every command without question.

The Hunters moved through the forest like men possessed for three hours without taking a break as the Lieutenant tore ahead. The two Hunters with the night vision cameras kept a lock on the Lieutenant as he moved which was the only way they could know the direction they were to take. These tactics were a little different than the ones they normally would have employed; it was cumbersome and almost reckless. With the use of night vision they were able to send a point scout out—the Lieutenant—and have the rest follow his lead. Captain Roux wasn't concerned about the lack of stealth as this mission was simply a chase exercise which would prove the use of the Microbolometer in a possible wartime scenario of hunting down a fleeing enemy.

Captain Roux knew that the Sergeant and Corporal—being those who were hunted, and not having any knowledge that the rest of their platoon were testing a prototype night vision equipment that would make finding them all the easier—would be trying to move through the forest and mountainous terrain as quietly and efficiently as possible. The cameras were big and bulky but he knew they would do the job. They had already been useful in keeping an eye on the Lieutenant as he led them through the mountainous forest.

"Is everything okay Lieutenant?" the Captain asked as he and the rest of the platoon came in on his location.

The Lieutenant had stopped. He looked over at the

Captain in the dim light of the night and smiled. "Yes sir. I just thought the pansies here needed a break," he replied.

That comment elicited a scoff from a few of the Hunters who were closest to the Lieutenant to hear the comment. Their response caused the Lieutenant to chuckle and the Captain to smile.

"So do you think we are getting close to them?" the Captain asked, growing serious once more.

The Lieutenant nodded, flicked on his small flashlight, and showed the Captain the partially unfolded marked up map he held in his hand. "I'm sure Toussaint and Corbin will be headed into the valley and across this river. It's the best spot for them to make it up onto the adjacent mountain and around in order for them to get to the extraction point."

"Do you think we'll catch them?"

The only response the Captain received was a wicked-looking smile from his Lieutenant and a call for the men to switch camera operators and form up again.

"I still don't like this," the Captain heard Kaplan mutter under his breath. The man stared nervously up at the sky and into the surrounding forests.

"What was that soldier?" he asked pointedly as he turned to Kaplan.

"Nothing sir," Kaplan responded.

Captain Roux stared at him a moment longer then turned away and motioned for Lieutenant Matan to carry on.

Lieutenant Matan led them swiftly down the slope through the trees. The moon and stars cut through the canopy of the forest enough to provide visibility for them to safely move through the trees, relatively speaking. He refused to let anyone use their flashlights as it would potentially be a beacon for Toussaint and Corbin to pick up kilometers away which would defeat the purpose of the exercise.

Captain Roux heard the distinct sound of the flowing river they were approaching.

His heart pounded in his chest and his breathing increased with the pace of the pursuit. The Captain was in his early forties now, but his muscular frame made him appear as if he were fifteen years younger. He loved pushing his body on. He loved the results he received from pushing his body on. It was exhilarating and refreshing to be able to keep pace and, in many circumstances, outpace those who were half his age.

As a leader he kept a tight rein on the discipline of those in his command and they respected him because they knew he wouldn't ask anything of them that he wasn't willing to do himself. Captain Roux saw too often that leadership positions, even in the military, were occupied by tyrants and overlords. But, through his vast experience and knowledge of human nature, he knew what it was to lead and inspire his men. And now, running through the forest at night with these men whom he would lay his life down for and with, and also allowing Lieutenant Matan to lead the exercise, he was demonstrating that he trusted the Lieutenant, and he was showing his men his ability to develop the next leaders.

The platoon ran on, jumping swiftly over fallen trees and ducking branches, until they came to a steeper decline. The area was more open than most they had run through with small trees spotted throughout the hillside.

The Captain stopped at the top of the hillside with his two night vision camera operators. "Do you see him?" he asked.

There was a momentary pause. "He's at the bottom and moving to the south," the operator to the Captain's right answered.

He chuckled. "The Lieutenant isn't messing around," he stated as he began to pick his way down the decline.

About halfway down, the Captain froze as he heard shots ring out in the night air. The rest of the platoon stopped, all of them looking around at each other and out into the forest.

"I don't like it at all," Kaplan stated, loud enough for everyone around him to hear.

Captain Roux shot his head around and glared at the man. Kaplan stared back unflinchingly.

"What do you make of that Captain?" one of the operators asked. The question pulled his gaze from Kaplan.

"I don't know, but we'll find out," he replied sombrely as he began running down the hill again, this time at a quicker pace. Without a word the rest of the men followed.

It didn't take long to find the Lieutenant who was crouched by the bank of the river with his flashlight out. Captain Roux ran up behind him and glanced down to see what he was looking at.

"Did you hear the gun fire?" he asked without looking up.

"Yes. What do you make of it?"

"I don't know, but what I do know is that they came through here," he replied as he pointed down at some fresh boot marks impressed in the soft mud. "And so did something else." He moved his hand over and showed the Captain a massive dog-like print that was depressed into the mud at least twice as deep as the impressions that Toussaint and Corbin made.

The Captain bent down and looked intently at the tracks. "What kind of wolf made that?" he asked. "The thing must stand at least four feet at the shoulders."

Lieutenant Matan shook his head. The Captain knew he was at as much of a loss as he was.

A few heartbeats later the rest of the Chasseurs were standing on the bank behind the Captain and Lieutenant.

Captain Roux turned around. "Alright men. As a precaution I want your weapons loaded. We don't know if Toussaint and Corbin ran into some wildlife, or even what that wildlife was if that was the case. It looks like they might have had an encounter with a wolf but, if the tracks are any indication of its size, this thing is bigger than any wolf I have ever seen." He never sugarcoated the reality of the situation with his men which was another reason why they loved serving with him. The Captain never fed them any bullshit.

"Are you still comfortable going ahead and leading the way?" he asked Lieutenant Matan.

The Lieutenant stood up and nodded grimly. "I might not keep the same pace, but we'll catch up to our men."

The Captain patted his second in command on the shoulder then motioned for him to lead on.

Shortly after they crossed the river, and as they picked their way through the valley toward the other slope, the Captain heard Lieutenant Matan call out. "Over here!" he whispered loudly. The edged tone of his voice spoke volumes to the Captain who broke into a dead run toward him. He leaped over fallen logs and around trees until he came to stand right before the shaken man.

The Lieutenant looked over at him with a horrified expression on his face. "I found our men," he said sombrely.

"Or at least what's left of them." He moved his light down and across the ground revealing the carnage.

Blood was splattered all over the place! One of the men —he wasn't sure which one—laid prone on the ground, his back looked as though it had been torn out, and he was decapitated. The other man was laying about six feet away, slumped up against a tree with his throat sliced out and his face marred so badly that his features were indecipherable.

The Captain looked over that second man with his light and saw, laying to the man's right was a head. It was then that he clearly saw the details of Corporal Corbin. "My God," he whispered.

The others rushed in behind and abruptly stopped when their collective lights shined upon the remains of Toussaint and Corbin. Many jaws hung open as they gaped at the sight.

"It's the curse," Kaplan whispered loudly. "There's something out here that's going to kill us all."

"Shut your damn mouth!" Captain Roux shouted. "That's your last warning Kaplan."

Kaplan stared hard at him for a moment then nodded.

"What could have done this?" Private Chevrolet asked in barely a whisper.

"I don't know, but we're going to find out," Captain Roux replied with determination. "Do you think you can track where this beast went to?" he asked the Lieutenant.

Lieutenant Matan nodded his head, then immediately went to work trying to discern which direction the animal went off in.

"Give him some room men," the Captain said. "And let's make a perimeter just in case whatever it was that did this comes back."

The men nodded and expertly moved into position around the scene.

What really troubled the Captain was the fact that, whatever it was that did this, didn't appear to eat the bodies. Rarely have there ever been cases where animals killed for sport. It didn't make sense to the Captain.

After a few moments Lieutenant Matan walked back over to him. "Okay sir, I think I have a trail. We can leave as soon as we bag up the bodies."

Captain Roux nodded. "Okay men," he said as he turned to address his Alpine Hunters, "I know this isn't the task you wanted tonight, but we need to package up the remains and haul them out for their families."

"Are we going to split up and send a team with the bodies to the extraction point and another to hunt down the animal?" Voland asked.

Captain Roux thought about it for moment then shook his head. "No. I think it's safer if we stay together as we hunt down this thing."

"But why is that our responsibility?" Kaplan asked. "Shouldn't we head to the point and notify someone so they can send another team to hunt it down?"

"Not our responsibility!" Chevrolet blurted, stepping into Kaplan's space. "This thing just killed two of our men; two of our friends."

The other Hunter's began to murmur and argue.

Lieutenant Matan stepped into the middle of it all. "Shut it!"

The men all quieted at the Lieutenant's command, then looked to Captain Roux who tuned and glanced around at them all.

"No," he stated firmly. "We can't have this thing running

around. It killed fully armed soldiers and there are towns in the area; civilians are in danger. We don't have time to waste. We go after it now and kill it."

The Hunters steeled their expressions and began to nod; all of them except Kaplan, who turned and walked a few feet away to stare out into the forest. Lieutenant Matan stepped toward him, but Captain Roux grabbed him by the shoulder. The lieutenant glanced over and Captain Roux shook his head. With a nod, Lieutenant Matan began organizing the troops in order to efficiently bag up their friends and move out.

Without complaint, the rest of the Alpine Hunters nodded as one and went about their grim work.

15

THE PACT

JUNE 20TH, 1989

Hazely groaned as she opened her eyes. Her body ached all over and her clothes were soaked from the morning dew. She felt disoriented; her mind spun, trying to make sense of the events of last night. She desperately groped for reality to reveal itself.

That couldn't have actually happened? could it? she questioned. *How could something like that exist?*

Hazely glanced to her left and saw the torn up bloodied shoe she had found. Was there a connection to Jeremy's murder and that ... thing? Did Tristan know of that creature's existence and Jeremy maybe found out about it? She shook her head. She knew there was something more going on here than anyone was willing to tell her.

A shudder went through her when she considered what facing a creature like the one she saw last night would do to someone—what it could have done to ... Jeremy? "That can't be right," she said aloud. "Tristan confessed to the murder. Why would he do that if it wasn't him? There has to be a rational explanation." Her mind spun in confusion.

She grabbed the shoe, then slid over and picked up her gun. With great difficulty, Hazely propped herself up on her elbows and looked down at the smooth flowing water. The birds had begun their morning rituals and songs; the fresh smell of the newly watered greenery wafted into her nose filling her with a sense of renewed vigor. Still, as she clambered out from under the bridge and climbed to her feet, she felt worn out. Something had chased her last night—something dangerous, maybe even evil—of that she was starting to accept, but how was she to reconcile that with the known world around her? That creature was ... it was ... and that smell ... Words failed to come to her mind which would help describe the horrifying experience.

She climbed up the embankment and looked back down the bridge toward town. Hazely glanced at the bridge deck where the creature was standing last night but didn't see anything out of the ordinary. She didn't know what she was looking for. Tracks? Fur? Anything? There was nothing. It was simply here then gone. She looked down the bridge again. She had a pretty good idea that Mayor Boucher would know what's going on in little L'accord. Hazely shook her head in disbelief when she thought about this town. A small town in the French Alps that almost no one has ever heard of was now a town that she knew she would now never ever forget.

She pushed the disturbing thoughts away as she began to walk down the old bridge toward town. The Mayor was going to have to answer some very pointed questions.

By the time she got to the other side, some of the weariness had shaken from her body and the woman was now able to move at a quicker pace. With a sense of urgency she sped up the small hill that led to the main road. When she crested the hill she immediately noticed a crowd of people hovering around the front of one of the houses down the road where she had gone the previous night in order to investigate the sound she had heard. Her fast walk now turned into a jog down the cobblestone roadway. As she neared, two of the men in the crowd stepped in front of her.

"There is nothing you see here miss," one of them said in broken English as he held up his hands.

She tried to go around, but the other man, shorter and wider than the first, moved to block her path.

"Let me through!" she yelled at them. "What are you hiding?"

"We are hiding nothing," came the smooth reply of Mayor Boucher as he moved to the front of the crowd. "It's okay Mathieu," he said to the first man, grabbing his arms and gently putting them down.

Mathieu looked to the Mayor for a moment then nodded and turned away from Hazely. The shorter man followed suit.

"You're hiding nothing are you?" Hazely shot back accusingly as she lifted the torn shoe for the Mayor to see. Hazely saw a flash of concern in his face for a moment then it quickly dissipated.

"And what is that supposed to be?" he asked smugly.

"It's the shoe of Jeremy Jackson."

"And how do you know that?"

"Because it's the same ones he was wearing in his picture," the woman explained. "And I know who killed him," she stated confidently. She paused in order to let that information sink into Mayor Boucher's mind. Out of the corner of her eye she noticed Mathieu and the other man glance back in her direction.

Mayor Boucher's expression remained cold and still. Hazely couldn't read him at all which helped to deflate her argument and place some doubt in her mind, but she shook that feeling away as she recalled Tristan's confession and attack.

"I think we should go somewhere more quiet in order to discuss this," he said. "Just you and me."

After a long moment Hazely nodded. As she turned to walk away with the Mayor she noticed, out of the corner of her eye, that some of the town's folk were cleaning something up in the barn. She didn't see much due to the crowd, but she did see shovels and bags. They were scooping something up. Normally, she would have thought that they were merely cleaning out the stalls, but there were far too many people helping out with this for it to be normal.

"Shall we?" Mayor Boucher asked as he grabbed her gently by the shoulder and pulled her along. He turned his head slightly and nodded at Mathieu as he led her away.

"What's—"

"It's none of your concern," the Mayor cut her off before she could get the question out.

Hazely was about to press the point, but decided—in this one rare occasion—to hold her tongue ... this time. She figured she would have time to discuss anything she wanted with the Mayor.

On the way to the Town Hall both Hazely and the Mayor were very quiet. Hazely had to know what was going on. She didn't think she could trust anyone, especially the Mayor, and was more than a little concerned that he might try to kill her like Tristan did yesterday. But now that she was prepared for that possibility—having her gun securely tucked under her sweater at the back of her belt—she felt fairly confident that she would be able to defend herself from the likes of the Mayor if it came to that.

When she got to the steps of the town hall she flinched at the sight of the two wolf statues on either side of the doors. The eyes were so real and looked as though they were piercing through her. Her breathing came in quick short gasps and her heart immediately ramped up.

Mayor Boucher stopped his climb up the stairs and turned toward her. "Is everything okay?" he asked smoothly.

Hazely looked from the statues to the Mayor. She had never felt panic like this before. She had prided herself in being tough, and not taking any shit from anyone, but at that moment—in front of those penetrating eyes—she felt unhinged; and the Mayor's cold calculating expression only accelerated and amplified the feeling.

"Are you okay Miss Silverston?" he asked again when she didn't immediately respond.

"Ah ... ya. I'm fine," Hazely managed to stutter. She took a couple deep breaths then walked up the stairs.

As the Mayor turned from her she thought she saw the slight hint of a grin on his cold face.

The wolves' eyes seemed to dull as she neared. Hazely shook her head. Was she going crazy? Did the encounter last night scramble her brain? She quickly centered herself once more and pushed away the ridiculous thoughts. She wasn't going to let anything shake her from finding out what was going on. She had never been more determined to find out the truth as to what was going on than she was now.

After a few moments they were at the Mayor's office. Mayor Boucher took a seat behind his desk and motioned for Hazely to sit in one of the empty chairs on the other side.

She shook her head. "I think I'll stand."

"It is up to you madame," he stated, again wearing the same smug expression he had earlier.

Hazely wanted to leap over and rip the look off his plump face! Instead, she quickly composed herself and threw the shoe on his desk. "As I mentioned, this is Jeremy's shoe." She leaned over and put both hands on the desk looking down at the man. "And Tristan confessed to killing him."

"That's impossible!" he blurted.

"Impossible that he killed Jeremy, or impossible that he confessed to it?"

"Tristan was a troubled man," the Mayor stated coolly. "He took too much responsibility upon himself."

"He took too much responsibility upon himself!" Hazely repeated angrily. "What the hell is that supposed to mean?"

"It means that I don't believe that Tristan killed Jeremy, Miss Silverston."

"So you admit that Jeremy was murdered?" Hazely shot back.

The Mayor lifted his eyebrows at that statement. "Oh, I did not say that he was murdered."

"But your statement implied that you knew Jeremy was killed."

"That's right. He was killed, but it's not what you think."

"Then why don't you enlighten me as to what happened to my client's son," she stated firmly.

Mayor Boucher stood up, walked to the side of his desk, and looked at her with a steely expression for what seemed a long time.

Hazely could feel her blood boil with rage. She felt the Mayor's evasiveness; his purposeful deviation from the truth as to what was going on here. He knew what happened to Jeremy Jackson and refused to tell her.

"What's ... going ... on ... here?" she asked through gritted teeth, carefully enunciating each word as she tried to contain her anger.

Mayor Boucher chuckled, as if he were mocking her.

Hazely's heart ramped up and she felt her blood pressure skyrocket; her hands tremble with rage.

"I know it's your job to ask questions and get answers, but, trust me, you don't want to know what is happening in L'accord," the Mayor stated cryptically with a cold look. "The more you find out, the closer you are to getting hurt."

"Are you threatening me?" Hazely responded, coming to within inches of his face.

The Mayor grinned. "I am merely stating a fact. People who poke around where they should not tend to regret it. At least, for a few moments they regret it."

Hazely was taken aback by his cryptic comment. What did he mean by that? She composed herself quickly. "Is that what happened to Jeremy? Did he discover something he wasn't supposed to? Is that why Tristan killed him? Is that why Tristan tried to kill me?"

Hazely noted a slight look of confusion when she mentioned that Tristan tried to kill her. He stepped back, then his face was a mask once more. "Tristan tried to kill you?"

Hazely nodded.

"So where is he then? I presume that you have him locked away somewhere?"

"He's dead," she replied in barely a whisper.

The Mayor didn't seem shocked by the revelation. Instead, he moved back around his desk and sat down once more. "Please, Hazely, have a seat and we will talk plainly." He motioned to the chair opposite his.

Hazely was unnerved by the calmness of the man. She had just told him that one of his town's members was dead —presumably a good friend of his—and yet he seemed so sedate by the news.

"Please, sit," he said again.

She moved to the chair and sat down, staring at him.

"So, tell me how he died."

Hazely was silent. She wasn't sure exactly what to say, or where to start. She didn't know if she should be cooperative to the Mayor's request, or guarded. How much should she tell him? His responses weren't at all what she would expect from a man in his position with the disclosure she just laid bare. Maybe she should just get up, find a working phone, and bring in the authorities?

"Come Hazely," the Mayor said softly. "Tristan was a friend of mine and, as I said, he was troubled. I would like to know what happened. If you tell me, then I will cooperate fully with your investigation."

"Will you?" Hazely asked, a little more sharply than she intended.

Mayor Boucher smiled back and nodded. "Yes. I will."

"Well, I was in the church—" she stopped in order to see if she could detect any anger in the Mayor as he told her specifically not to go into that building. He remained calm and collected.

"And I was conducting my investigation," she continued, "when he came in, locked the door, confessed to the murder of Jeremy, and attacked me. We fought. I tried to get away but he tackled me through one of the windows which sliced his throat open. There was nothing I could do for him."

The Mayor was silent for a moment. "And where is the body?"

"I ... I didn't know what to do, so I dragged him into the church, and put him in one of the rooms in the basement."

Mayor Boucher leaned forward. "And did you find anything else in the basement?" he asked smoothly.

Hazely hesitated for a moment. Something wasn't right with the way he asked the question. "No." she lied. "I was pretty shaken up after the ordeal so I hurried out of the building as fast as I could."

"I see." Mayor Boucher leaned back in his chair. "Is there anything else?"

She looked down at her hands. Dried mud still coated parts of her skin between her fingers and under her nails. The smell of the creature flashed in her memory, and the sight of its long sharp claws pervaded her thoughts. "There is one thing," she said as she looked back up to meet the Mayor's gaze. "There was something else last night. Some ... creature. I ... I ... don't know what it was. It looked like a wolf, but it wasn't. I barely escaped." She felt a shiver course down her spine.

Mayor Boucher didn't look surprised. He rubbed his chubby fingers through his thinning gray hair. After a few heartbeats he stood up and walked back around the desk to stand before Hazely. "This is the burden our town has had to endure for centuries."

Hazely was confused. "What are you talking about? Do you know what that thing was I saw?"

"I do. But I don't know if you will understand. For someone like you who lives in your safe and secure world, never really worrying about if you will live or die from month to month, our story will sound ridiculous."

"You'd be surprised what I would believe right now," Hazely replied as she still held the image of that creature—or what little she saw of it—in her mind.

The Mayor sighed. "This is dangerous."

"What's dangerous?"

"Me telling you the truth. You think now that you actually want to know what is happening, but when you find out, inevitable consequences will unfold that can't be stopped. You will regret your decision. I guarantee it."

Hazely stood up. "This is ridiculous," she blurted.

"Is it? You claim to have seen something last night that you cannot explain. I can tell you what that is, but know that there are ... consequences to having that knowledge."

Hazely took a step back. "What kind of consequences?"

"I cannot tell you unless you press the issue that you need to know what is happening here in L'accord."

"Well, maybe the French police would be interested in the story of how Jeremy died?" Hazely retorted.

"And what will you tell them? You already revealed that Tristan confessed to the crime and now he is dead. It seems like they would consider the case closed, and I would be happy if you did just that and left L'accord. But I have a feeling that your inquisitive mind will not stop there. You need to know what you saw last night."

Hazely narrowed her eyes at the man. He was right. Her mind wouldn't stop until that question was answered.

The Mayor chuckled and walked around his desk again to sit down. He motioned for Hazely to do the same. She sensed that he enjoyed toying with her. She clenched her jaw tightly and took her seat again.

"Okay. So what is going on here?" Hazely asked. "I want

the truth. The whole truth. Then I'll decide whether or not to haul your ass to jail."

The Mayor nodded, seemingly un-phased by her threat. "In 1666," he began, "the priest who built the church here—"

"Vincent of Wales," Hazely interjected.

"That's right. You have done your research." He seemed slightly impressed.

"Well, Vincent of Wales went missing and, shortly after that, a large wolf of unimaginable power began to stalk through the town once a month—every full moon—and began to kill the townspeople. It would kill on those nights just for the pleasure of killing, never eating its victims, and it would only kill one or two at the most. There were many theories at the time as to why it only killed the amount it did. In truth, it could have killed the entire town on the first night. Some believed it killed only to satisfy its need to take life, others thought it was so it wouldn't deplete the population of the town and always have fresh meat. Still, others thought that it might be fighting its urges and, therefore, limited its kills. But who really knows."

"Why didn't the people just leave?"

"Many tried, but the creature woke the next night, even though it wasn't a full moon, and hunted them down. The town's people of L'accord were imprisoned in this place to wait for death.

"The explanations I received from my parents, and their parents before them and so forth, was that the town became a place of torment: a veritable purgatory. No one knew if they only had a month left to live. They couldn't leave as that meant immediate death, and to stay meant eventual death at the hands of the beast." The Mayor looked to the side as if trying to collect his thoughts.

"Did anyone try to kill the wolf?" Hazely asked, leaning forward in her chair.

The Mayor nodded. "But it was impossible."

Hazely looked at him skeptically. "Everything can be killed," she stated matter-of-factly.

"I wish that were true. But because it wasn't, our ancestors found a way to deal with it."

"What *way*?"

"Well, even though witchcraft was abandoned and the books burned, there was a woman named Celeste who knew what had happened. She found a book that wasn't burned—the 'Lupus Est Scriptor Noctem'—'The Wolf's Night.'"

Hazely sat back. She tried hard not to reveal her shock that she had found that book. She still didn't know what the Mayor's motives were and how much he was involved with Jeremy's killing.

"Celeste found the book in the church, and suspected that father Vincent became enamored with it and was consumed by it. He transformed into the beast, only to awake once a month in order to sate his need to kill." The Mayor paused again, as if deep in thought.

"And?" Hazely prodded. She wanted to hear more about this book and its connection to the ... werewolf? The thought of it almost sounded ridiculous, but what else could explain what she experienced the night before? If this priest did indeed turn into a wolf once a month, then the term werewolf would be fitting. She almost laughed but caught herself. If anything, she was more confused now than ever. No. Not confused, torn. Torn between reality and myth. She didn't know what to believe.

"She was able to form a covenant—a pact—with the

creature," he continued. "Every full moon the citizens of the town were to leave their barns open which would act as a draw to bring the wolf in, giving him the ability to fulfill his desire to kill. He would choose one house and slaughter all their livestock, but the people of the town would be spared."

"So what you're telling me is that Jeremy got killed by this creature during a full moon?" the woman asked.

Mayor Boucher nodded. "He was in the wrong place at the wrong time I'm afraid. He died at the doorstep of Tristan's house as he beat upon his door pleading, in Tristan's own words, to be let in."

"But Tristan didn't open the door," Hazely reasoned. "And that's why he believed that he killed Jeremy, and why he tried to kill me: he was afraid that I would find out the truth that he let this man die."

The Mayor nodded. "The pact is specific about people forfeiting their lives if they are out when the beast prowls."

Hazely didn't know what to think. This sounded like a ghost story to her—like a fantasy—but she kept coming back to that horrifying experience the previous night when she was under the bridge.

"You know now what happened to Jeremy, so now your missing persons case is solved."

"And what happens when the next poor soul wanders into your unassuming little town? Is it going to be another case of being in the wrong place at the wrong time?" she asked accusingly.

The Mayor looked as though he didn't know what to say, but then he steeled his expression and tightened his jaw.

"You do realize that, with the way the world is changing, you won't be able to keep this a secret forever. Eventually someone is going to have to come in here and exterminate your werewolf problem."

The Mayor laughed. "As I already said, no one can kill the creature," he stated confidently, almost as though he was defending it.

"How do you know? Have you ever tried? Technology has advanced quite a bit since the 1600's," she retorted.

"Others have tried and have paid the price for it. Every generation or so some get filled with a righteous indignation and try to kill the creature, but the result is always the same: a most painful death to those who are idiot enough to attempt it.

"No, we can't. This creature comes right out of the darkness of hell and will not be put back."

The fighter in Hazely reared up inside as she balled her fists. She wanted to throttle the man at that moment. She was infuriated that they were content to live under this slavery. She was angry that they did nothing to help Jeremy when he needed them. And she was incensed that the deception had almost gotten her killed twice!

Hazely narrowed her eyes dangerously at him. "With our modern weaponry I'm sure there's something we can do," she stated confidently.

The Mayor laughed, which made her even angrier. "And how are you going to call in this *modern weaponry*? No one is going to believe you."

That comment sent Hazely reeling inside. At that moment she was that little frightened girl again, trying to get others to believe that her Dad's abuse was real! No one believed her then, and Mayor Boucher was stating that no one would believe her now. She felt as though she was shot in the stomach and left on the ground to bleed out and die.

Hazely shook the nightmarish thoughts aside and rose from the chair, slamming her fists down on the desk. "I have my ways," she stated resolutely through gritted teeth, determined to overcome the wall of ignorance she constantly battled.

Mayor Boucher leaned back in his chair. His eyes narrowed and his expression became cold once more. "You're missing one thing about this tale Miss Silverston," he said smoothly.

"Oh ya? And what's that?"

"No one leaves L'accord."

That statement, and the way the Mayor said it, rocked her back. She heard a footfall on the wooden floor behind her and spun around. A fist smashed across her jaw which sent her sprawling to the side. Pain exploded through her face and her vision blurred. Hazely groped around, trying to rise. She felt herself being hoisted up by strong hands. She looked up and saw the man she had seen outside, Mathieu, grab her in his iron grip. He pulled her arms behind her back and the other man who was with Mathieu when she approached the crowd outside punched her in the stomach three times. Each thunderous blow blasted the wind from her. After the third punch, Mathieu let her go and she slumped to the ground holding her stomach and coughing.

"You know what to do with her," she heard the Mayor say. His voice sounded closer, like he was right over top of her.

Hazely turned her head up. Tears rimmed her eyes from the pain. She saw Mayor Boucher stoop down to within inches of her face. "You should not have come here Hazely," he stated coldly. "I told you there were consequences for you acquiring the knowledge you so desired."

He stood up and peered down at her with that cold expression. “You see, there is something I neglected to tell you about The Pact. The preservation of secrecy is of prime importance. If any outsider finds out then the contract is broken. There’s only one way to avoid that terrifying outcome. The outsider needs to die before the evening or the werewolf is free to murder anyone it wants and is not limited to the full moons.”

Hazely’s eyes went wide with the Mayor’s statement. He had just said that she had to die!

“You sealed your fate when you crossed that threshold into our little town and determined to know what was going on. If you just left the town then everything would be alright. You could have gone back to your American lifestyle, and our town would continue on as it had since the 1600’s. But no. You *had* to find out what was happening here.”

He smiled wickedly, as if some evil thought just came to mind. “The contract is broken and needs to be repaired before nightfall. This is all spelled out in The Pact.”

Hazely was horrified. She could feel the despair creep into her like the chill of a cold winter’s night. These people were going to murder her. They needed to murder her.

The Mayor sat on the edge of his desk and sighed. “Now, you’ll be buried with the others who have tried to leave,” Mayor Boucher continued. “And no one will ever find out what happened to you.”

Hazely coughed again, still winded from the blows she received. She saw the Mayor stand up and back away from her. She wanted to rise but couldn’t. She tried to reach around and grab her gun, but Mathieu kicked her in the stomach, while the other man grabbed it away from her holster.

"I should have taken care of you when you first arrived," the Mayor said, almost as though he was speaking to himself. He looked to Mathieu and the other man. "Make sure no one sees you dispose of her. We don't want any questions. Do you understand the importance of this Mathieu, Nicolas? The Pact is broken without her death."

Mathieu nodded then bent down and grabbed Hazely.

Nicolas looked at her gun for a moment then pressed the weapon against her head. Hazely closed her eyes tightly, knowing that her brains were about to be splattered all over the floor.

16

LIFE AND DEATH

JUNE 20TH, 1989

"Not here Nicolas!" Mayor Boucher shouted at him. "You'll make a mess of my office. Take her to the hole first and do it there."

Nicolas shrugged. He bent down to within an inch of her face and gently stroked the gun across her cheek. "I guess you'll just have to wait a little bit longer," he said to her with a smile, then slapped her lightly on the cheek before standing and putting the gun in the back of his pants.

Mathieu wrapped a gag around her mouth, tied it tightly, then easily hoisted Hazely up. She wanted to struggle but couldn't find the strength. The two men herded her to the back side of the town hall and through the rear exit.

"What about her car?" Nicolas asked.

Mathieu struck a pensive pose for a moment then said, "Let's deal with her first, then we'll go to the place she's been staying and get her car at night when no one is around. It will be easy. Everyone will just think she gave up her search and left in the middle of the night."

Hazely was shocked that these two *enforcers*—or whatever they were—were speaking in English. She had to wonder why they were doing that when they could just as easily have kept her in the dark.

Unless ...

She glanced over to see the cold—almost dead—look in Mathieu's eyes. *He's enjoying this,* she realized. *He's probably been doing this for so long that he's developed a taste for the killing. He likes it, and he wants me to know that.* Those thoughts sent a shudder down Hazely's back. *What the hell have I gotten myself into?*

She struggled to loosen Mathieu's grip, but he just tightened it up more while Nicolas punched her in the stomach again.

She grunted and coughed. Nicolas cupped his hand around her face and yanked her head up so she could look at him. His grip was like iron. "You're a fighter aren't you?" he mocked. "And a pretty one too."

Hazely tried to pull her face away, but he held her fast. Nicolas reached up and yanked back on her thick blonde hair. She grunted as tears welled up in her eyes. "Don't worry it will be over quickly," Nicolas stated. "It's a shame we won't have any play time with you."

"I wouldn't discount that just yet Nicolas," she heard Mathieu add. "The hole is a long way from here. We can have our way with her when we get there."

Nicolas smiled, then let go of her. He stood up and slipped around the building leaving her and Mathieu standing there in silence.

The town hall backed onto a small green space and, just beyond—about twenty feet from the exit of the building—was thick forest. Hazley looked around, hoping there was someone around who would be able to help her, but she didn't see anyone or any other buildings that were recessed this far back.

No. She realized she would have to be patient and hope that an opportunity would present itself.

A few moments later she heard what sounded like a car pull up to the side of the building. Mathieu dragged her around the corner to see an older car backed into the alley with its trunk open. Nicolas was standing beside it, stone-faced. His dead eyes bore into Hazely as Mathieu pushed her along toward the car.

Neither of the enforcers said anything as Mathieu grabbed Hazely by her thick blonde hair and yanked back on it hard. Nicolas put one hand on her waist and slid the other one up under her shirt and around her breast. Hazely tried to scream out but couldn't.

"Oh ya. This is going to be good," Nicolas said as he groped her and pressed the bulge in his pants against her leg.

She struggled with all her might. Mathieu released her hair and punched her in the side. She crumpled to the ground and he released her hands. Nicolas had retracted his hand, grabbed her, and spun her around. He slammed her against the bumper of the car and Mathieu smashed her across the jaw.

Pain erupted in Hazely's head. Her vision blurred and she fought to stay conscious.

"I think she's had enough for now," she heard Nicolas state. "Let's leave the rest of the fun for when we get there."

Hazely felt herself being hoisted easily into the air and with one powerful heave Mathieu tossed the slight woman into the trunk.

Hazely spun her head just in time to see the trunk slam shut, leaving her in utter darkness.

She pushed and banged on the lid, but it was no use. Hazely groped around in the darkness, trying to find a way out. Her hand moved along the seam where the back seats met the trunk, but there was nothing.

Suddenly the car began to move and she felt the bumps of the uneven road. Her heart ramped up and anxiety flooded into her. Her breathing came in quick short gasps. She knew she had to calm down, but images of her lying on the ground with her skull shattered assaulted her mind.

Hazely grabbed the gag and pulled it off. "Help! Help!" she yelled. She knew no one would hear her, but she screamed the words anyway as she pounded on the trunk's lid. "Let me out! Don't do this!" As she screamed, the word *shame* flooded through her. How many times had she been locked in a closet when she was younger, screaming for help, only to have no one answer that plea? But she wasn't that person anymore. *What the hell am I doing?* she asked herself. *This isn't you. You're tough. You're a fighter.*

"Get a hold of yourself," she said out loud.

Hazely took two deep breaths and allowed her heart rate to come down. Her senses came back to her and she reached into her pocket and pulled out her flashlight. She clicked it on and squinted at the sudden brightness. Once the shock of the light dissipated, she shined it around the trunk. She tilted her head up, looked to the side, and saw a tire iron. Quickly, she grabbed the iron and held it in close to her chest. It wasn't much, but it was better than nothing. At least now she knew she wouldn't be going down without a fight.

Hazely had no idea how far they had traveled—or for

how long. The car began to bump and bounce more fiercely and Hazely did everything she could to keep herself from smashing into the roof of the trunk. Eventually the car began to slow and grind to a stop.

She could hear the two talking, but couldn't make out what they were saying as their voices were muffled and they had reverted to speaking in French.

Hazely racked her mind trying to remember which side of the car Nicolas was on as he probably still had the gun. She was almost sure that it was the driver's side. Her heart began to pound more fiercely again. She knew that in a moment she was either going to get out of this or be dead.

The car doors opened and closed and she heard the men walking around back toward the trunk. She held onto the tire iron so tightly that her knuckles whitened. A few more frightening seconds—that felt like hours—drifted by until Hazely heard the click of the latch.

Everything seemed to slow down at that moment except for the beating of her heart. Light flooded into the trunk, but, as Hazely's eyes were already accustomed to the light. She sprung up and smashed the bar across Mathieu's face. He tumbled into Nicolas.

Bang!

Hazely felt the bullet whip just passed her head, but she didn't slow as she leaped from the trunk awkwardly. Unfortunately, she lost her grip on the tire iron and it fell to the ground. She knew she didn't have time to retrieve it so, as her legs hit the ground, she ran. She ran with all the strength she could. She ran for her life.

Bang! Bang!

A bullet ripped into a tree right beside her and another

soared over her head as she ducked around some bushes to the right.

Bang! Bang! Bang! Bang!

Hazely weaved and turned. She could hear at least one of her attackers crashing through the bushes after her.

Bang! Bang! Bang! Bang!

Bullets whizzed by her, blowing off nearby branches, and sinking into trunks.

As she glanced back, her foot snagged on something and she went down. She hit the ground hard and rolled down a small hill, coming to an abrupt stop with the side of her face slamming into a pile of dirt. She shook her head and wiped the dirt from her eyes. As she scrambled to get back to her feet she noticed that she was in a small clearing that had dipped down into a low spot that spread all the way to the tree-line on the other side of the clearing about twenty feet away. There were small mounds spread throughout the clearing. Most of them had thick grass growing on them except the one she had slammed into. It was mostly dirt with sparse amounts of grass beginning to show on its surface. Her heart sank as she knew what these were: shallow graves. There had to have been at least a dozen of them.

The sound of crashing trees brought her back to her senses. Hazely took off across the makeshift cemetery, zigzagging as she went.

Bang! Bang! Bang! Bang!

She flinched as the sound of the shots echoed through the air. Bullets bounced all around her as she ran—dipping, zagging, weaving, running for her life!

Somehow she made it to the trees on the other side and ducked to the left. Hazely ran for about fifteen feet then slid behind a large tree trunk. She looked around desperately for something, anything. Not more than ten feet from her she saw a large dead tree branch lying on the ground.

Hazely ran over and picked up the makeshift weapon then spun around, thinking to dart back behind the tree, when Nicolas appeared. He held the gun out at her and grinned wickedly.

"You gave us quite the chase," he said in his thick French accent. "It's too bad for you that there is nowhere else to run."

Hazely held the branch out in front of her defensively.

Nicolas tightened his grip on the gun and held it out straight.

Click!

Nicolas's eyes went wide as the gun didn't fire.

Hazely tightened her jaw and lunged at the man. She swung the branch and hit Nicolas' arm. The man grimaced and dropped the gun. Hazely swung again, but this time Nicolas grabbed the branch and yanked it away from her grasp.

She backed up a step. Nicolas leaped forward and swung the branch at her head, but Hazely was too quick for him. She ducked the branch then leaped forward and tackled the man into a large tree. Nicolas grunted as he slammed into the tree and dropped the branch. Hazely screamed and swung her fist into the man's face. She hit him three times before he managed to put up an arm to block. Blood flowed from his nose.

Nicolas grabbed her around the waist, buried his head into her neck, lifted her lithe form up easily, and drove her backward and to the ground.

Hazely knew she was in trouble. She looked around

desperately for something she could use against the man. The gun was within reach, but she knew it was empty. Hazely grabbed it anyway.

Nicolas reared himself up then swung down at her. Hazely managed to turn her head aside at the last moment and only received a glancing blow on her ear. The side of her head exploded with pain, however, and at that moment she knew she couldn't take a full-on punch from him, not in this position.

Nicolas pulled back for another swing, but Hazely was quicker, slamming him in the face with the butt of the gun. His head rocked to the side and he grunted as the hard metal slammed into the side of his head. Hazely hit him again, and Nicolas moved to the side which allowed her to squirm out from underneath him.

He reached for her, but she slammed him again on the side of the head. He went down, but tried to get up. Nicolas pushed to his hands and knees, his head hanging down. He blinked and swayed. His efforts to stand only resulted in him falling back to the ground.

For a moment, Hazely was tempted to just walk away. But this man wanted to kill her. She drew back her foot and kicked him in the face.

Nicolas fell to his back. He laid there and moaned, eyes rolled back whenever his eyelids fluttered open.

Hazely reached around and pulled another magazine from her holster. She released the empty one from her Glock and reloaded it. She cocked the action back and forth, placing a round in the chamber.

"I don't know why you're doing what you're doing, but you killed a lot of people haven't you?" she asked coldly as she approached the dazed man. "I could just tie you up and get the authorities to take care of you, but, as the Mayor says —" She aimed the gun at Nicolas' head. The man managed to glance up at her. Hazely saw fear in his eyes for the first time since she encountered this killer. "No one leaves L'accord."

Bang!

17

THE CHASE

JUNE 20TH, 1989

After Hazely took some pictures of the shallow graves she slipped through the woods and found her way back to the car. She crouched down behind a tree and scanned the area. The trunk of the car was still open, but there was no sign of Mathieu anywhere. Birds chirped and leaves rustled from the slight breeze that filtered through the forest.

Hazely glanced all around, half expecting Mathieu to come running out at her, but there was no one.

She pointed her gun in front of her and darted out from behind the tree. Coming to the car Hazely put a hand on the bumper and crouched down to where Mathieu should have been. There was blood on the ground which trailed off to the right.

"Shit!" she exclaimed.

Hazely searched around and saw the tire iron. She scooped it up and stood, cautiously glancing around as she slammed the trunk shut and moved to the driver's side of the car. Yanking the door open she threw the tire iron onto the passenger seat as she slipped into the car. The musty smell of old upholstery and cigarette smoke filtered through the air. Glancing over she saw that the glove box was open. She quickly peaked inside to see a pair of pliers, some wrenches, and a stray bullet. She slammed it shut, then fumbled around in her pocket for the keys she had pulled off Nicolas.

With shaky hands Hazely managed to get the keys into the ignition. The car fired to life.

Smash! The passenger window suddenly blew out.

Hazely yelped.

Bang! A bullet sunk into the dash just in front of her.

She glanced to the right and saw Mathieu about twenty feet away advancing, gun in hand.

Bang! Another bullet ripped into the passenger door.

Hazely threw the car into gear and slammed her foot down on the pedal. The back tires spun for a moment then the car lurched forward when it gained traction.

More shots rang out. Hazely ducked as the rear window shattered.

The car spun to the right. Hazely jerked the wheel back to the left, trying to stay on the gravel road. Another gun shot echoed through the air, then a loud bang rang out and she could feel herself losing control. Trees closed in as the car slid off the road.

Hazely screamed.

She slammed on the brake but that did little to arrest the momentum. The car sped down into a small gully and slammed into a tree. Her head smashed against the steering wheel and the gun slipped from her grasp as the vehicle came to a sudden stop.

Pain erupted through her head, but she shook it off.

Hazely knew that Mathieu would be on her in moments. She looked around for the gun but didn't see it. Panic set in. She saw Mathieu out of the corner of her eye at the top of the hill. He was running toward her, gun aimed in her direction.

Without thought, she grabbed the tire iron, opened the door, and slipped out of the car. She stayed low, hoping that Mathieu couldn't see where she was.

Hazely peaked her head over the hood and saw that he was coming around the back of the car toward the driver's side. She quietly slunk down and stepped around the car the other way. As quietly as she could manage, she slid around the car and peaked around the corner. She saw Mathieu reach the door and stick his head inside. She knew this was probably going to be her only chance. With as much speed as she could muster, Hazely sprang out from behind the car, tire iron held high.

Mathieu spun around, gun leading. Hazely swung. She struck him on the wrist, causing the gun to go flying from his grasp. Mathieu grimaced, but managed to reach up with his other hand and grab the front of Hazely's sweater. He moved close to her and threw her up against the car with frightening strength.

Hazely felt pain shoot through her back as she was slammed into the unforgiving metal. Mathieu brought his other hand up and tried to grab her arm that held the tire iron, but there wasn't much strength in his grip. She easily ripped her arm from his grasp and slammed the iron across his face. Mathieu spun away from her and landed on the ground, face first. He struggled to get to his hands and knees. She knew that last blow had dazed him.

Hazely tightened her jaw. She saw, represented in

Nicolas and Mathieu, all the men who had ever abused her. Rage began to course through her veins and consume her. Rationally, she knew she should restrain Mathieu and take him to the authorities, but she was way beyond being rational at this point. She wanted justice: justice for all the people these two had killed, justice for all the people who had been abused like her; justice for herself from all the abusers she had to endure over the years; and ... justice for their attempted murder of her.

Hazely growled and dropped the tire iron. She launched herself onto Mathieu, threw him onto his back, and began punching him as hard as she could, over and over and over and over again, until he stopped moving. His face was an unrecognizable bloodied pulp.

She wasn't sure how long she beat the man, but eventually exhaustion set in and, only then, did she notice that her fists throbbed. She stood up and looked down at him—at her work. Hazely glanced at her bloodied fists—most of the blood being from Mathieu. Tears welled in her eyes as realization sunk into what she had done. She put her arm across her mouth and nose as she began to sob and stumbled away to lean against the car for support.

Tears ran in rivers down her dirty cheeks.

Many minutes drifted by until Hazely was finally able to get control of herself. She wiped the tears from her face before going back into the car and finding her gun. She knew she had to get back to town and somehow call for help. This conspiracy ran deep, and she knew more people were going to end up dead if she didn't do something about it.

The car was wrecked. The only way for her to get back to town now was on foot and, with the sun continuing its slow march across the sky, she knew she had to hurry. Hazely knelt down beside Mathieu and quickly checked his neck for a pulse. Nothing. She stood and, with one more glance down at the broken and bloodied killer on the ground, Hazely turned, scrambled out of the gully, and jogged down the road.

She managed to find her way back to the town just after dark. The streetlights shed their dim glow throughout the town.

The hike back was harder than she expected. She didn't realize how far out Mathieu and Nicolas had driven in order to put her in the ground.

This was no case like she had ever dealt with. The secret the Mayor was keeping was something out of a fiction story. The rational part of her mind wanted to dismiss it as a campfire tale, but she knew that she saw something that wasn't ... rational, and that the Mayor's explanation—strange as it may have been—lined up with her experience under the bridge the previous night.

She stood on top of the hill looking down at the serene town. Everything was quiet. Hazely started down the road but then froze when she heard a deep howl echo throughout the valley. She knew immediately that it wasn't a normal wolf's howl. This one was full of rage, the rage of an animal that had been caged for centuries but was now free.

No. She knew this howl came from something not of this world.

The Mayor's words came firing back into her mind about The Pact being broken if she remained alive. Her presence here had unleashed the monster.

Now it was coming for her.

Mayor Boucher hugged his wife tight. Music filled the house from the small radio they had sitting on the stand beside the fireplace.

"What was that for?" the old woman asked with a smile.

"Do I need a reason to hug the woman I love?" he responded.

She looked into his gray eyes and must have seen that something wasn't right. "What is it dear?" she asked as she moved back to arm's length.

Jean didn't know what to say. He knew he had effectively dealt with Hazely, which would ensure the continuance of The Pact. Even though Mathieu and Nicolas hadn't checked in after they had finished their task, he knew everything was as it should be. Those two often never followed-up right away after taking care of some unpleasant business. So their lack of communication was of no concern to him.

"It's nothing dear," he responded. "I just had a difficult day at work."

He walked over to the window and drew back the curtains. The sun had disappeared over the mountains, blanketing the valley in darkness. The sight sent a chill down his spine, but he knew there was nothing to be worried about as the next full moon was now a month away.

"Are you sure you're alright?" his wife asked.

"Yes dear."

He walked over and turned up the volume on the old radio. He tilted his head slightly as he thought he heard something outside—like a howl—but shook the notion away.

"Not tonight," he whispered to himself.

They were fortunate to get a few signals through to this part of the mountains which made them feel as though they weren't totally detached from the world. The smooth sound of Edith Piaf singing her signature song from 1947, La Vie en rose, began to filter through the small house.

Agnès smiled then walked into the kitchen. She filled up the rustic-looking kettle with water then set it on the stove as she rocked slightly to the tune of the music and hummed softly.

Jean took a pack of cigarettes from the small table on the other side of the fireplace. He pulled one out, placed it in his mouth, and brought it to life with his lighter. His heart began to race a little with each successive puff and his body physically relaxed as his craving was satiated. Agnès smiled at her husband as she poured the fragrant liquid.

The two enjoyed their tea together as they sat by the roaring fire that poured forth its soothing heat.

Agnes glanced up and her eyes met Jean's. "What?" she asked with a small smile.

"I remember when I first saw you," he said.

"Oh, Jean, it's been fifty years!" she laughed.

"Seems like yesterday. To think, I never would have known the young woman you turned into if not for your father."

Agnes laughed again. "He thought he'd get a hard worker out of you—not a son-in-law! Oh, but he was furious when he found out we'd been sneaking out."

Jean grinned at her and took a long drag on his cigarette. "I'd do it again."

They were married a couple years later, and twenty years after that he became Mayor of L'accord. Life for them was good in L'accord as long as they followed the rules of the town. "Livestock can be replaced, but lives are precious," Jean used to tell Agnès and the rest of the towns' folk. "As long as we live by the rules which were laid out for us by our forbearers we will live peaceable and productive lives," was the mantra.

He would do anything to keep the pact they had inherited from their forefathers. Even murder, if he had to.

The fire burned low as the two enjoyed their tea and listened to the radio. Before long Jean leaned over and placed his hand on Agnès' arm. "I think it's time we retire for the night dear."

Agnès smiled and gathered up the tea cups while Jean made his way up the stairs. He readied for bed, put his hearing aids on the night stand, tucked himself in with a book, and waited for his wife to join him. After a few moments Agnès came into the room. She was about to climb into bed when she suddenly looked up quizzically.

"What is it dear?" Jean asked.

"Oh heavens," the old woman responded. "It's just that I forgot to let the cat in."

"Don't worry about Geoffrey. It's a nice night out. He'll be fine."

"I know he will, but you know him, he'll be meowing at the door for us to let him in at some ungodly hour of the morning."

Jean laughed and conceded the point. Geoffrey always loved sleeping curled up on his bed in the corner of their room. If he was close by he knew that Agnès would be able to coax him inside.

Agnès looked at him then turned and walked to the stairs again. "I'll be right back." She closed the bedroom door as she exited.

Jean watched her leave then returned to his book. A few minutes later the old man looked up and stared curiously at the bedroom door. *She's been gone a while*, he thought to himself. *It shouldn't take that long to get Geoffrey inside.* "Agnès! Are you okay?" Jean hollered.

No answer.

He thought he heard something downstairs, but wasn't sure. "Agnès!" He glanced over at his hearing aids on the table next to him.

Jean pulled himself out of bed, scooped up the hearing aides and placed them in his ears as he walked to the door. "Agnès!" he yelled again, but there was no answer.

He reached for the handle and, as he did, he noticed something seeping under the door and into the room. His mind was confused at the sight and didn't quite know how to process what he was seeing so he pulled open the door and there staring at him with her eyes wide open, gasping her last breaths—her lifeblood pouring onto the floor from a gaping gash in her neck—was Agnès! Her face was frozen in fear and pain—the light from her eyes disappeared as her lids closed for the last time.

Jean took a step back by instinct as he looked at the body of his wife—his love—going limp. Behind her he saw eyes of a different kind: large orbs that flickered yellow as they refracted the light from their lenses. He could also smell the stench of death as it rolled into the room and heard the low growl of the beast.

With a sudden fury the creature grabbed Agnès around the waist with its massive clawed-hands and tore her in two. Entrails spilled onto the floor with the lower half of her body. The werewolf then threw the top half of her body to the side of the room where it slammed against the dresser and crumpled to the ground. The beast then stepped fully into the room and glowered down at Jean who was now too shocked and stunned by what he saw to properly process what had happened to his dear wife and what was about to happen to him. He had never seen the creature before, only heard the tales and saw the depictions in the book. The sight caused him to blanch and his knees to shake so badly he feared he would fall over.

"How can this be?" he managed to ask aloud. "We took care of the girl!" he pleaded, speaking to the werewolf. "The Pact is intact. The Pact is intact I say! You can't do this! We have a deal!"

He backed away from the creature until he made it to the nightstand beside the bed. Without looking away from the werewolf he opened the drawer and reached inside. He pulled out a folded piece of paper and held it up. "Listen to me Vincent, the Pact is still good."

When Jean mentioned the name Vincent, the werewolf turned its head to the side slightly and seemed as if it had a moment of recognition.

"Yes. Yes. You are Vincent of Wales," Jean pleaded for the werewolf to recognize that.

Vincent—the werewolf—turned its head back to stare at him, then the look faded quickly as it stood overtop the man and snarled. Its lips curled back revealing large curving teeth the size of small daggers.

Jean said something indecipherable, his mind swirling. His heart pounded in his ears. He put his hands up to defend himself, but they were a feeble barrier to the raw power of the wolf's jaw, and those massive canine fangs. Pain exploded through his neck as those razor-like teeth cut into his tender flesh, severing arteries and tissue.

His life-blood pumped and sprayed from him. Gurgling —his own gurgling as he choked on the precious fluid exiting their vessels—echoed in his ears.

Jean landed on the hard floor when Vincent released him. He grabbed feebly at his neck; blood poured through his fingers pumping freely in bright lines.

Vincent stood over Jean staring at him with those terrifying, murderous, hateful eyes. Jean choked. His life drifted from him, and those eyes were the last thing he saw.

Hazely made sure the safety was off on her gun before continuing down the hill. All seemed still and quiet except for the sound of the river flowing through the valley. The old streetlight perched atop the pole near her flickered and swayed slightly in the breeze.

She wasn't exactly sure what she was doing. Hazely kept replaying the conversation she had with the Mayor who was absolutely resolute that the creature couldn't be killed.

She hoped he was wrong.

With renewed determination Hazely walked down the street. She kept her head on a swivel as she scanned around. As with most nights she had witnessed around L'accord, no one was out of their houses past dark.

An owl hooted in the distance and crickets chirped. There was a slight breeze drifting into the valley; the fresh scent of the forest accompanying it. If the woman's nerves weren't so taut, she might have actually enjoyed the evening.

Hazely peered carefully around every building she passed and scanned up each side of the roads she crossed. There was no sign of anything.

She continued up the main street. Nothing stuck out to her as abnormal. Suddenly the wind picked up, causing a slight chill to enter her body. She looked around some more then shook her head. This whole situation had her on edge.

Hazely jumped as the loud bang of a door caught her attention. She steadied herself and listened more intently. There it was again! It sounded like it was coming from the left, away from the town center.

With a sense of urgency Hazely slipped down the road and moments later, when she rounded a bend, noted the door of a small house swinging in the breeze. Slam! It hammered the door jam.

The house was dark except for a soft glow that faintly radiated through the blinds of one of the upper windows. The houses adjacent and across from it were also dark. Two old street lights flickered in the gloom, illuminating the street and houses under them in a dim glow.

A shudder went down the woman's spine. Something definitely wasn't right with this. She took a step toward the swinging door.

"Meow!"

Hazely jumped with a start and turned to the side. A large orange and black cat stared at her with big dark eyes.

"Meow!" it cried loudly.

"Holy shit," she said, trying to get her heart rate under control again. "What the hell!"

She took a step toward the cat. It hunched its back and hissed, then sped away between two of the houses.

The door banged again in the breeze.

Hazely looked over at the door. She took a deep breath then checked her gun again making double-sure the safety was off. Shaking her head she continued her approach. She made it to the stairs that led up into the house and tried to glance through the door as it swung. It opened about half way then closed again. She squinted into the gloom but didn't see anything.

Closed then open ... closed then open. She flicked her flashlight on then took a step up as she shined it at the door.

Closed then open ... another step. Closed then open ... closed then open ... another step. Closed then open ... closed then open ...

Hazely stuck her foot in the door.

She opened it up and stepped into the front room. The smell of cigarette smoke and tea lingered in the air. She crept up the stairs, heart pounding in her ears and making it almost impossible to hear anything else. She stopped at the top and gagged.

Light spilled from an open bedroom door to her right, revealing the bottom half of a woman's body laying in a pool of her own blood, just as half her insides were on the floor. The stench of death and rot filled the air.

Hazely swallowed hard and continued forward, to the bedroom door. She peered around the corner. The loud pounding of her heart stopped. Mayor Jean Boucher—his head at least—stared back at her. His headless body was off to the side, lying in a large pool of blood. In his hand was what appeared to be a piece of folded paper. It looked old. On the other side of the room was what had to be the other half of Mayor Boucher's wife, lying in her own blood.

She crept into the room, went to the Mayor's body, and pulled the paper from his grasp. She unfolded it. It had the same type of script she had seen in the book from the church. Hazely knew it had to mean something. She was about to fold it back up when the words on the parchment turned red and flared up. Hazely yelped and drop the paper to the ground where it burst into flames and became ash.

"What the—"

A low growl resonated from down the hall. Her heart leaped.

She stepped out of the room and saw a large dark form crawl out of the room at the end of the hall. The rotten smell of death hit her and she knew ... it was him!

Hazely ran down the stairs then turned around once she hit the bottom and trained her gun and flashlight. The werewolf stared at her from the top of the stairs. She saw the large snout, stained with blood. Her light danced off its dagger-like teeth, and its eyes refracted the light making them shine yellow.

Bang! Hazely shot, hitting it in the head.

The werewolf flinched from the blow, but then turned back toward her and growled.

Her heart sank. She fired again, and again, and again as she backed out of the house. Every shot seemed to hurt it. She just wasn't sure how much.

The creature roared and sped down the stairs.

Hazely fired again.

The door closed then opened and ... it was gone! The woman jumped off the stairs and scanned the front of the house. Smash! It came through the living room window with a growl.

Hazely stumbled back and fired again. Bang! Bang! Bang! She didn't know if she was having any effect on it as it landed on the pavement, tearing at the curtains and trying to get them off its body. If she did, the creature sure didn't show it!

Hazely trembled. Her heart raced and she knew she was

in trouble. Before the werewolf fully extricated itself from the curtains she turned and ran with all her might. She wound around the corner, pumping her legs furiously. A roar echoed through the air from behind her. She couldn't tell how far back it was, but didn't dare look; her focus was set ahead. She didn't even know where she could run to get away from the beast, she just knew she had to get away if she wanted to live.

Movement to the side caught her attention as a door opened slightly to reveal the face of a frighted man peering through the crack. He then slammed the door shut as she ran by. He must have heard the gunfire! Hazely could only hope that the townspeople heard, and were themselves doing what they could to survive from ... from whatever it was.

The bridge came into view a moment later as she spun around the corner and ran down the short hill that led to it. Her feet hit the creaking planks; the uneven surface caused her to slow up initially so she wouldn't lose her footing. Half way across the bridge she heard a crash from behind and glanced back to see the creature bounding towards her. The sight of the monster spurned her already fatigued legs to push harder despite the protest being issued by her lungs. She knew if she stopped or slowed she would be dead in a matter of seconds, and now that the werewolf was in full pursuit of her, she knew that hiding under the bridge wasn't going to be an option this time.

Somehow she managed to get across the bridge and pounded down the road towards her house. The beast roared. It was so close! She could see her house and, more importantly, her car sitting in front. Hazely turned slightly and saw that it was almost on top of her. It leaped! She spun and fired. Bang! Bang! Bang! Bang! Bang! Two bullets hit it: one in the chest and the other in the shoulder. Hazely fell to the ground as the massive creature soared overtop her. It crashed into the ground, slid across the pavement, and hit its canine head on a light pole which toppled over. The lens of the light struck the ground and shattered.

Hazely scrambled to her feet and ran to the car. She fumbled with the door, but it was locked. It was then that she remembered the keys were in her purse in the house! She ran around the car and saw that the werewolf was beginning to get up.

Bang! Bang! Bang! Bang! She fired as she ran.

With as much speed as she could muster she ran across the street and leaped up the stairs, crashing into the door. The old wood buckled under the force and the door flew open with a crack.

Hazely ran to her purse and grabbed it. Smash! The door shattered as the beast dove into the house. The woman jumped over the counter and landed hard on the kitchen floor. She scrambled back and somehow managed to stand. The creature narrowed its eyes at her and stalked in; thick saliva dripped from its massive mouth. Bang! The shot hit it on the side of its head but only seemed to anger the creature more. Click! "Damn!" Hazely screamed.

The creature crouched as though it was going to leap over the counter. That split second gave Hazely the time she needed to turn and lunge for the back door. A roar split the air as the woman turned the handle and pushed through.

Hazely felt the claws tear at her and a searing pain erupted across her back but she knew she had to keep moving. She ran around the house, every step causing waves of agony to course through her. The woman gritted through the agony and sprinted with all her might to the car. It sounded as though a wrecking crew was in the process of demolishing the house as the monster tore apart the door frame trying to get out.

Hazely grabbed the keys out, unlocked the door, and climbed into the car. Her hands trembled so badly she didn't know if she was even going to be able to put the keys into the ignition. The car rocked suddenly and she yelped. The creature was clawing at the metal frame with abandon. Tears streaked down her face.

The moments seemed like hours but Hazely somehow managed to get the key into the ignition.

Smash! The back window exploded under the ferocity of the creature.

The car came to life. Hazely slammed down on the gas pedal and the vehicle took off. Before she was able to get any speed though the massive beast ran up beside the car and shouldered into it. Hazely yelped. She tried to keep the car on the road but the sheer force of the creature pushed her down the embankment.

Hazely screamed as the car careened down the short hill toward the river. It hit a small lip on the edge which propelled it into the air.

Suddenly, everything felt as though it was moving in slow motion as she soared through the air. Then, the front end of the vehicle turned down and plummeted into the cold dark water.

18

HELP

JUNE 21ST, 1989

"What is it?" Captain Roux asked Lieutenant Matan as he approached the man. He could hear the nearby river lap gently on the shore from through the trees. Matan was staring down at the ground and shaking his head.

The sun was beginning its rise over the eastern sky again. The Alpine Hunters had slowed the pace significantly at which they were traveling so they could follow the trail of the creature who had killed their friends. Plus they had to take turns in carrying Toussaint's and Corbin's bodies.

They methodically moved through the forest with focus and intent. They searched throughout the night, and all the next day and night with barely a break. Now it was morning on the second day since the incident. Even the most hardened of the group was starting to show his extreme exhaustion and Captain Roux knew they needed to rest.

Cartier, the team's radio operator, continued to try and get a signal out, but the terrain prevented the communication from hitting any towers.

Lieutenant Matan glanced at the Captain and shook his head. "I'm not sure we still have the trail," he stated sombrely. "I was being careful. The depressions of the tracks were so deep and evident, yet ..." his voice trailed off as though he didn't know what exactly he should say.

"It's okay Lieutenant. You're exhausted. We all are," Captain Roux reassured him. "You haven't slept in well over forty eight hours. It's hard to expect—"

"I expect the best of me!" the Lieutenant snapped back. He must have realized immediately what he had done as his face calmed immediately. "I'm sorry Cap," he said apologetically, rubbing his hands over his face. "It's just that—"

"You want to find this creature and put it down for the sake of Toussaint and Corbin," the Captain finished for him.

Lieutenant Matan nodded. "And to make sure it doesn't kill anyone else."

"We'll find it," Captain Roux reassured. "But first we need to stop and make camp. We're no good to Toussaint, Corbin, or each other if we aren't at our best.

"We'll pick up the trail in a few hours."

The Lieutenant nodded again then walked away and began barking orders for the others to set camp. The men complied without complaint.

Captain Roux looked up to the western mountains where the sun's rays touched the peaks, spreading out in all directions in a glorious collision against the unmovable rock. He never got tired of seeing all this beauty before him. Unfortunately, the spectacle was spoiled by the gruesome discovery of his men. *What could have caused such destruction?* he wondered. *Any predator would have eaten the bodies, but Toussaint and Corbin were merely killed. No. They were slaughtered. It was almost as if they were killed for pleasure.* That last thought sent a shiver down the Captain's spine. *These men weren't just killed, they were murdered.*

He turned to leave when the sound of a moan caught his ear. He shook his head, thinking that the sleep deprivation was getting to him. Then he heard it again. It was coming from by the river. He moved some of the branches away with his hand and took a step into the brush. The sound of the river was close, but he still couldn't see it through the thick forest. He took another step, then another. Another moan. He knew he wasn't hearing things now. Someone was down there!

With urgency he began crashing though the bushes until he burst out onto a small bank. It was a little lighter out now as the sun was coming further up above the mountains, which allowed him to make no mistake at what he saw. Lying on the rocky beach face down was a woman with wild blonde hair stretched out across her back. She moaned loudly again and her arm moved as if she was trying to grasp onto more of the land.

The Captain stared, wide-eyed, for a moment, trying to process what he was seeing. Then he shook himself out of the initial shock and ran the last couple steps to her. He bent down and gently pulled some of her hair away from her face. Her skin was pale—really pale—but she was breathing.

He turned her over. She looked like hell! There was bruising around her neck as though she had been choked. Her face was red and purplish in many places, and a long cut ran the length of her forehead from the top of the left side to just above her right eye.

"Lieutenant!" the Captain yelled. "Lieutenant! I need you now! By the river!"

Captain Roux heard a commotion behind him as his men scrambled. Someone yelled something to him but he didn't register the words, being too consumed with the sight of the battered woman before him. Her body was still half submerged in the cold water so he repositioned himself and pulled her more fully onto the rocky beach. As he moved her some of her thick blonde—bloodied and tangled—hair fell to the side, revealing large claw-like marks that stretched from her left shoulder to her mid-back. Captain Roux lifted her torn sweater and saw four lines cut into her flesh. The sight of the garish wound was enough to cause the Captain's heart to skip a beat. He had seen similar wounds all over Toussaint and Corbin.

"Captain! Captain!" he heard the cries as his men crashed through the trees. Lieutenant Matan was the first on the scene.

"What the hell!" he cursed as he moved up beside the Captain. "Private Ricard!" he yelled, turning his head toward the trees. A few more of the men charged through before Private Ricard got there. The response of those men was similar to that of Lieutenant Matan, but they stayed back until Private Ricard made it there.

Private Ricard knelt at the other side of the woman and began assessing her condition. "She's breathing and has a pulse, albeit the breathing is shallow and the pulse faint," he relayed as he took her vitals. "Quickly! We need to get her warm. Someone grab a blanket, and get that fire going."

He turned and looked at the Captain. "We need to get these clothes off her before she dies of hypothermia. I also need to check her other injuries to see how severe they are."

The Captain nodded. "Is she safe to move?"

"I don't know, but we don't have a choice. Hopefully she wakes up and I can perform a better assessment. But for now, because we don't have any c-collars, we'll have to hope she doesn't have a spinal injury."

Captain Roux nodded. "Let's get her to camp quickly then."

With that, the Lieutenant, Captain, Ricard, and another Hunter picked her up and moved her to the camp as swiftly and carefully as possible. Once there, Ricard stripped her down and quickly assessed the rest of her body. The cuts on her back weren't as deep or severe as they first appeared, so Private Ricard bandaged them as thoroughly and quickly as he could.

"I think this bruising and cut on the forehead looks worse than it is, but we won't know until she wakes up and I can tell what her mental status is," Private Ricard reported to Captain Roux.

After the assessment, they placed her in a thick sleeping bag and Ricard stripped down to his underwear and climbed in beside the woman.

"What do you think, Cap? Do you think she's seen what got the others?" Private Voland asked. He ran a hand nervously over his bald head.

"I don't know for sure Private."

"But look at her! She's got similar wounds on her from what we saw on Toussaint and Corbin."

"I know she does, Private. But we won't know for sure until she wakes up. Now let's not make any assumptions until we have all the facts. Do you understand Private?"

Voland nodded and walked away.

Captain Roux glanced behind Voland and saw Kaplan

standing about fifteen feet away, staring at him and muttering something under his breath. He knew this could easily get out of control if he wasn't careful.

"Get yourselves something to eat and get a few hours of sleep," the Captain ordered. "You all know what watch you're to take. Make sure you don't miss it."

He turned and looked at Ricard in the sleeping bag with the woman. "Don't worry about taking a watch Ricard."

Ricard nodded, obviously trying to calm his chattering teeth. "She's so cold."

The Captain cracked a smile. "It's a small price to pay for sleeping with a beautiful woman." He turned to walk away but then stopped suddenly and looked back at the man. "When she wakes up maybe she'll be able to tell us what the hell it is we're hunting."

"Y y y y yes sir," Ricard replied through chattering teeth.

Hazely rocked slightly back and forth, whimpering. She was reliving her nightmare, reliving the night she should have died. Those reflective eyes, that smell, those claws! The water! The cold, cold, water. *I can't breathe! I'm dying!*

She struggled to stay above the water, then the image changed. She was back in the closet as a little girl. She was hiding. Her Dad was looking for her. She could hear his boots on the hard floor, coming closer—coming for her!

The door opened and she saw him there, staring over her. He reached down and put his strong hand around her throat. With frightening strength he lifted her up and pulled her out of the closet.

She struggled and clawed at his arm, but couldn't break his iron grip.

"No! Please!" she pleaded. "Kristine! Help!"

Hazley managed to turn her head slightly and saw her sister, Kristine, standing at the door, watching what Dad was doing to her. "Please!" she whimpered, extending a hand toward her.

Kristine—stone-faced—turned and walked out of the room. The door slammed!

She flinched violently and felt a pain erupt on the back of her head. The jolt rocked her back to consciousness. Her eyes fluttered open. It was dark, yet there was a small light. She was covered and warm. She moved her legs and felt ... felt someone else! The warm touch startled her and she turned her head to see a man beside her holding his nose. Her heart leaped and, out of instinct, she tried to move away but couldn't. The man reached for her, but she knocked his hand away and punched him hard in the face.

"Merde!" the man yelled. He grabbed his nose with both hands as blood flowed freely.

"What the hell!" Hazely screamed as she tried to climb out of the bag.

Instinctively, the man reached for her again. Hazely knocked his hand away again and punched him a second time. The force of her blow was minimized by his blocking hand but she could tell he was hurting. The man grimaced and tried to pull back from the fiery woman.

She squirmed out of the sleeping bag and looked around like some feral animal on the run. Hazely saw at least a dozen men scrambling out of their own sleeping bags. Her mind whirled as the scene in front of her didn't make any sense. It was as though her mind couldn't comprehend or reconcile the present events with her previous encounter with the creature.

Suddenly she was fully aware of the chill that touched her skin and looked down to see that she was only wearing her bra and panties.

A shorter man—two or three inches shorter than six feet —with a stocky muscular build and sharp intense hazel eyes approached with his hands outstretched unthreateningly and said something in French. He appeared to motion for the other men to back off.

Hazely looked at him wide-eyed, still in shock at the scene before her. He was wearing military camouflage. They all were.

He said something again.

"I don't speak French," Hazely replied, frustration rising in her voice. "Do you speak English?"

"Oui, madame. We do."

He helped Ricard out of the sleeping bag. "Can someone please get the lady a blanket."

"What are you doing with me? Where are my clothes?"

"We found you unconscious by the river. You were severely hypothermic. Private Ricard is our medic in charge of tending the injured."

Hazely looked at the man she had assaulted. "Sorry," she said as a pang of guilt struck her when she realized that he probably just saved her life by keeping her warm.

The man looked at her—still holding his bloodied nose —and just shook his head as he walked away to retrieve his clothes. Some of the other men chuckled as they saw him stumble away.

A moment later Hazely was covered with a thick gray wool blanket. "Thank you," she said. "Who are you guys? And where am I?"

"We are Alpine Hunters." He must have seen a sign of recognition on Hazely's face. "You've heard of us?"

She nodded. "I've heard you guys were doing maneuvers in the area."

"Really? From who?"

"Some jerk inspector I had dealings with a few days ago." She shook her head. "Don't worry about it. It's a long story."

The Captain looked as though he wanted to ask more questions, but restrained himself. Instead, he motioned for her to sit on a nearby fallen tree. "Men! Form up!" he yelled.

Hazely sat down as the men quickly lined up in front of the Captain and stood at attention. "I'm Captain Gabriel Roux, and this is my Lieutenant, Chase Matan, who is my second in command or 2IC for short," he said.

Matan nodded.

"Then you have Ricard—who you've already met—Cartier, Pelissier, Janvier, Voland, Kaplan, Farrow, Lamar, Faucheax, Fay, Chevrolet, and Page."

Hazely nodded. "I'm Hazely. Hazely Silverston."

The Captain dismissed them after the introductions. "I was hoping that you could tell us how you got here. We pulled you from the edge of the river. You were unconscious, hypothermic, and injured. You looked like you had been to hell and back again."

As soon as he mentioned the injury Hazely felt the dull pain in her back and remembered getting clawed as she fled from the house at L'accord. She reached around and felt a gauze pad taped from her shoulder down the length of her back.

Hazely nodded slightly. "Thank you for your help."

"You're welcome. Well, Hazely, please tell me what happened to you." He then motioned one of his men over. "Please make some coffee for our guest." The man nodded then slipped away.

Lieutenant Matan, who was quite a bit taller than Gabriel with short dark hair, then approached. The look in his gray eyes was no less intense than Gabriel's.

The lieutenant stood to the side with his arms folded across his chest.

"So what happened to you Hazely?" the Captain asked again.

Hazely swallowed and took a deep breath. She wasn't even sure, and she definitely wasn't sure she wanted to relive the experience by speaking about it, but she knew she had no choice. She knew that the rest of the townsfolk at L'accord were in grave danger and she needed help. It was difficult for her to admit that she was over her head, but she was. For the first time in her life she was faced with a situation she knew she couldn't handle alone. Whatever that thing was, it was beyond her.

The two men waited patiently for her to begin. After what seemed a long while Hazely told them her story. She detailed for them how she was hired to look for Jeremy Jackson thinking that it was going to be a mere case of getting lost in the woods. She explained about her investigation at L'accord, of how she knew that the Mayor was hiding something, and how she was almost murdered by Tristan. When she got to the part of her hiding under the bridge and of her description of the creature, she noticed that the two men glanced at each other with concern etched on their faces.

"What is it?" she asked.

Gabriel looked away for a moment as if he were collecting his thoughts. Then he looked back at Hazely, his intense eyes boring into her. "We were on an escape and evasion exercise, trying to hunt down two of our men who had a head start on us, when we came upon their bodies, torn and mutilated. At first, we thought it was some wild animal, but noticed that none of the bodies were eaten, or rather, no part of them was eaten. We were confused by this, but if what you're saying is true, then what happened to our men is starting to make sense. The timeframe you describe is pretty close to our own."

The three of them sat in silence for a long while.

"I got a better look at the thing when it did this to me," Hazely finally said as she motioned to her back. "It was huge. It had reflective eyes that shined brightly when I put my flashlight on it—" her voice cracked up as she choked back some tears. She silently berated herself. *What the hell are you doing? Crying like some schoolgirl!* "Sorry. I'm just exhausted and hungry."

She shook off the emotional response quickly and steeled her expression. "It killed your men, Jeremy Jackson, the Mayor of L'accord and his wife, and who knows who else. And I don't know if it can be killed. I hit it at least seven times, but that didn't even slow it down."

Gabriel looked to the Lieutenant then back to Hazely. "There's only one way to find out," he said sombrely.

Hazely nodded. She didn't want to admit it, but this thing scared her. She didn't even know if the bullets she put into it even hurt the creature at all. But she felt much better being with the Alpine Hunters. If anyone had the weapons to kill a creature like this these guys did. She told the Captain and the Lieutenant the rest of the story—even though it sounded crazy when she said it out loud—so that they would understand more fully what they were dealing with.

An hour later, the sun was starting to dip to the west and the camp was a buzz with men packing up and readying to leave. The Captain turned to Hazely. "We're going after this thing. If it's as dangerous as you say—and I'm inclined to believe you—we'll have to hit it hard."

"The problem is, Captain, we don't even know what it is, outside of what little information I was able to get from the Mayor and the research I did," Hazely commented. "We can assume, now that The Pact is broken, that it will be out again tonight."

"I'm counting on it," the Lieutenant stated grimly. "According to my map, we're not that far from L'accord which means we should have a little time to set up and prepare before it comes out."

Hazely looked at the determination on the man's face. She wished she felt that confident at that moment, but she didn't. These men were walking into a situation like nothing else they had ever experienced before. She just hoped they were up for the challenge.

"Get yourself ready," the Captain said to her. "We leave in ten minutes."

Hazely sipped the coffee she had in her hands and ate the rest of the rations they had given her. Her mind spun with images of the events that led her here. She didn't want to admit it, but the last place she wanted to go was back to L'accord. Unfortunately, she felt like she didn't have a choice. The soldiers weren't going to leave this valley until they killed the creature who had slaughtered their men. And she wasn't about to wander around in these mountains by herself without assurances that the werewolf had been taken care of.

19

CELESTE

JUNE 21ST, 1989

With the Lieutenant mapping out their course, and having the river to follow up-stream, the group made it to L'accord an hour before sunset. They rounded the bend of the river and saw the shape of the old bridge crossing the valley. Hazely stopped when she saw the image. Her heart pounded and she felt as though she might collapse. Her breathing came in quick short gasps. She feared what the werewolf had done to the town when it was unleashed the night before. She had barely escaped, but did anyone else? What about Isabella?

"Are you okay?" Lieutenant Matan asked. The man looked at her and extended his strong hand. "It's okay. We are with you. We're going to kill this bastard."

Hazely nodded and swallowed hard. She had never been so shaken before. It was not like her to lose her courage the way she felt she was. *Am I losing my mind?* She could almost see the creature in her head and smell its odor of death! She shook those thoughts away and continued toward the town.

As they got closer, Hazely knew something wasn't right.

It was quiet. Strangely so. She would have expected to see the last of the townsfolk putting their livestock away for the night but there was nothing; just the eerie sound of the steadily flowing river and birds chirping away. That sound wouldn't have been eerie if they were in the middle of the forest, but they weren't. There was a town in front of them. A town that was previously occupied and bustling with agrarian activity mere days before. But now it was a ghost town. She knew her worst fears were being realized.

They made their way onto one of the cobblestone roads at the edge of L'accord. Hazely stopped and looked around noting the conspicuous absence of smoke coming from the many small houses which dotted the hills on either side of the valley.

"Something's not right," she said.

Captain Roux stepped to the side and scanned the area. Then he turned back to his men. "Cartier, Farrow, there's a radio tower on that hill. I want you two to see if you can get a signal out from it."

Without saying a word the Lieutenant stepped forward and handed Cartier the map.

Cartier took it and nodded, then he and Farrow bounded off toward the bridge.

"This whole place is cursed," Kaplan stated, loud enough for everyone to hear.

The Captain spun on Kaplan angrily. "Maybe so Kaplan. But we're going to stop this curse in the ass!" he yelled.

That comment brought grim smiles and nods to the face of many of his men.

"Lieutenant, please set up the men in teams of two and sweep the town. Let's find out what the hell is going on here. I'll set up base camp and radio where that's going to be.

"Kaplan, Fay, you're with me. Grab the bodies of Corbin and Toussaint."

"Don't you think it would be better if we stayed together Cap?" Voland challenged. "I mean, if this thing is as dangerous as Hazely is saying it is, and as we saw demonstrated by the death of Corbin and Toussaint, I think we'll be better off in a large team."

"Point taken Voland, but we need to complete this search as quickly as possible with multiple teams."

"But—"

"Enough Hunter!" Captain Roux snapped. "Those are my orders. Now follow them."

Voland was silent for a moment then tightened his jaw and replied, "Yes sir!"

Lieutenant Matan steeled his expression, grabbed Voland by the shoulder and pulled him aside with the rest of the Hunters, and began barking orders at the troops.

"And make sure all your radio coms are in English so Miss Silverston here can understand what's being said," the Captain said, loud enough for everyone to hear.

With military precision and efficiency the platoon split and began spreading out amongst the town.

Hazely was thankful that they had found her, not just because they saved her life, but because she now had hope that they would be able to kill whatever this thing was.

She thought about the story the Mayor had told her, and how he was so committed to the secret that he would kill to keep her, or anyone else for that matter, silent. That, and her experience with the creature itself, solidified in her mind that there was some truth to the story. How much truth, she wasn't sure, but she wanted to find out.

Hazely nodded slowly to herself, staring at the church.

She knew there was something she had to do. She took off, determined to finish what she'd started.

"Miss Silverston, where are you going?" Captain Roux yelled after her.

Hazely paused and frowned at him. "To check out the church."

"It is abandoned. We need to—"

"Look, I have a hunch, okay? I'll meet up with you at the rendezvous!"

"Wait!"

Hazely grumbled and turned to face him again, only to find a handheld radio shoved into her face.

"Take this. You'll need it to find out where I set up the base camp. And if you need help, let us know."

Before she could leave he held out a flashlight, pulled a pistol from its holster, and handed them to her as well. "It's nearing dark. And if what you told me about this creature is true—that it comes out at night—you had better be quick about what you're looking for, miss Silverston."

Hazely took the items and nodded. She knew they should expect to see the werewolf shortly and that thought wrenched her stomach in ways she had never felt before.

She turned away and jogged through the streets making it to the back door of the church in no time. She walked by the bloodstained ground where Tristan squirmed in his last moments of life, and looked up at the shattered window. A shudder ran its course down her spine. All the horrible memories of Tristan, and of finding Jeremy's shoe, and ... and the experience of that room with the book—that horrible room!—assaulted her, and now Hazely knew she had to go back into that room and get that book. The answers they needed were in there, she was sure of it.

She walked up to the door and took a deep breath before pulling it open.

The inside was dim. Hazely brought the flashlight to life and moved quickly, but cautiously, to the stairs. She shined the light down the narrow corridor. The stairs were stained with Tristan's blood. She paused for only a moment but then pushed herself on down the stairs and around the corner.

Hazely was stopped immediately by the stench of decay that hit her when she came around the corner. She gagged but managed to keep the contents of her stomach down. She put a hand to her nose, attempting to block out the smell. It took a few moments, but eventually she managed to acclimate to the odor enough for her to walk the rest of the way down the hall.

As she neared the door she slowed up and glanced around. Her gaze fell over the door behind which lay Tristan's bloating, rotting, and rat-eaten corpse. Tristan's dead body flashed in her mind. She even took a step back as guilt —tremendous guilt—coursed through her. No. It wasn't her fault that Tristan was killed. She had to believe that. She grasped that thought and pushed the guilt away. If it wasn't him then it would be her! She shook her head and steeled herself then turned to the opposite door and twisted the handle. The door creaked open.

The room was exactly as Hazely remembered it. She shone her light, pushing away the darkness. There it was, sitting on the table just as she had left it.

Hazely glanced around nervously and waited, almost expecting something to lunge at her from the shadows.

Nothing.

She tentatively entered. Her heart raced, threatening to

pound out of her chest. She swept the light from side to side as she approached the table. There was nothing except dust and cobwebs. Hazely looked down at the book. She reached her hand for it.

Whispers echoed from the darkness.

Hazely spun around, gun raised. There was nothing.

She turned back to the book and grabbed it, pulling it from the table. The chill she had felt before radiated up her arms causing her to drop the book back onto the table. And the whispers came at her again, this time louder. She spun, trying to target the source, but couldn't.

"Who are you?" she shouted into the darkness.

"I ... am ... the pact maker," came the raspy reply.

"The pact maker? What the hell does that mean?" She was shocked that whoever it was spoke to her in English.

"I am the protector," it hissed.

"Protector?" Hazely moved around, aiming her light and pistol in every direction.

She flinched as a gust of wind brushed her cheek.

"You ... will not ... get out of here ... alive," the voice threatened. "I am ... Celeste ... and ... that book ... is staying with ... me."

Hazely panned her light around and suddenly stopped as a face began to materialize in the corner of the room. Her heart leaped and she began to shake.

The face was that of a woman with long flowing dark hair. Then the rest of her form materialized. She wore long blood-red robes that touched the ground. The robes were tied around Celeste's thin waist with a rope belt. Her eyes were black as midnight and pupilless.

Hazely stepped back. She glanced at the book, then the door.

Celeste smiled, revealing a row of sharpened teeth. Her form was no longer transparent. She seemed to have solidified. "You're not getting out of here with that book. I'll not let you harm Vincent," she declared.

"Vincent? You mean the werewolf. You made The Pact with Vincent didn't you?"

"Yes. And now it is broken because of you," Celeste said as she took a step closer to Hazely. Her finger nails began to grow into long sharp claws. "You saw it burn up in front of you."

Hazely took another step back. She remembered the paper she had taken from the hand of the Mayor and how it self-combusted in front of her and knew that must have been The Pact. "If The Pact is broken then why do you care if Vincent is killed?"

A shadow suddenly fell over Celeste's face. "Because I made Vincent! He is mine!"

"What do you mean?"

Celeste laughed. "The fool thought he could get rid of the old ways. I saw what he was doing to our way of life: converting all those unsuspecting idiots to the Roman Church. I knew something had to be done, so I made sure he would find the Lupus Est Scriptor Noctem: a book dedicated to the sin of wrath. I made sure it had the proper enchantments upon it so it would ... capture him."

As Hazely backed away she moved ever-so-slightly toward the door, hoping that Celeste wouldn't notice. "So you turned him into that ... that creature?"

Celeste shook her head. "No. His own greed and desires did that. The book promises eternal life, it just fails to tell the unwitting soul what form that takes."

Hazely still couldn't believe what was happening.

Celeste had been dead for hundreds of years and yet, here she was, speaking to her. Speaking to her in English! She didn't know how that was even possible, but then ... that was the least of the impossibilities right now.

"So you did this to stop Vincent and his crusade? So you could keep practicing your witchcraft." Hazely was trying to keep Celeste talking so she could make it to the door.

"Yes. The Pact was forged in order to keep the monster away from the people so I could bring them back to the old ways. I made sure enough people knew the extent of the agreement and instructed them as to how to keep it intact from generation to generation.

"The price I paid in all of this was being linked to Vincent. I exist still because he exists. Which is why I can't let you leave with this book. What happens to Vincent happens to me."

"Why didn't you just kill Vincent to bring the people back? Without him, there would be no conversions."

Celeste laughed. "The Church would have just sent more priests and eventually would have overrun us. Our way of life would have been lost. At least this way, if they did come, we could deal with them." She paused and smiled wickedly. "Vincent would deal with them."

"Hazely!" she heard faintly coming from upstairs.

Hazely lunged for the door.

With a flick of Celeste's hand it slammed shut. She ran at Hazely and swung for her face with her clawed fingers. Hazely ducked and rolled to the side of the room. Celeste's claws raked across the stone where Hazely was just a moment before.

Hazely turned around, trying to locate the spectre with her flashlight. A shadowy form dashed just outside the glow of the light. She tried to follow it, but there was nothing. Slowly, Hazely stood up and backed against the wall. She moved the light back and forth trying to locate Celeste.

Nothing.

Her hand shook so badly she feared she would lose her grip on the gun.

"Don't worry. It will all be over soon," Celeste's voice echoed in a raspy whisper.

Hazely heard movement to her right. She turned and saw the claws coming for her. With as much agility as she could muster, she dodged to the side. Pain erupted in her arm.

Hazely grunted then turned back and fired.

Bang! The room lit up for a second from the muzzle flash.

An agonized scream bounced off the walls of the small room.

Hazely panned her light over to where she had fired and saw Celeste standing there, holding her shoulder; black ichor oozed from beneath her hand.

"What magic is this?" Celeste screamed at Hazely. Her face was a mix of confusion and horror.

Hazely smiled wickedly at the witch. "Oh, that's right. You've missed a few things over the centuries Celeste." She held her gun up for the witch to see. "This is called modern technology bitch!" Hazely straightened her arm and aimed right at Celeste's head.

"Nooooo!" Celeste screamed. Her body began to transform again to become insubstantial.

Bang! The bullet ripped through Celeste's head, shattering her skull before she had time to ghost.

Celeste fell to the ground and her body immediately vaporized into dust.

Private Ricard and Corporal De La Rue stood in the church. They had come around a corner and seen Hazely enter the building from the rear. They walked around the front and pulled on the doors, thinking to meet her inside, but when they found them locked they decided to followed her in from the back. When they entered they called her but there was no response.

Ricard held the large Microbolometer up on his shoulder.

De La Rue had stepped in front of Ricard and scanned around with his light as he moved deeper into the church. "This place is a mess," he commented. He turned to Ricard. "Where do you think Hazely went?"

"I don't know," Ricard replied as he scanned back and forth with the night-vision camera.

"Hazely!" De La Rue shouted again.

"Do you think that's a good idea screaming like that?"

"Hey. Did you hear that, Ricard?" he asked a moment later.

"No. I didn't hear anything," Ricard replied as he continued to scan back and forth noting the dark images until his camera panned to the side. There was something on the back wall that emitted a heat signature. He took the camera from his shoulder and flicked his light on and shined it at the wall.

"I thought I heard a bang, or something like—"

"Would you look at this," a distracted Ricard interjected.

"What? What is it?" De La Rue moved up beside Ricard.

"There's heat coming from the crucifix."

De La Rue stopped. He fiddled with a necklace that was strung around his neck, then picked it up and kissed it. "Maybe that's what we need right now?"

"What?"

"A little faith." De La Rue bowed down before the crucifix, made the sign of the cross, and began to silently pray."

Ricard stood behind him quietly until he was finished. After a moment, De La Rue rose and tucked his own crucifix back into his shirt.

"Why do you think it's warm?" Ricard asked.

De La Rue merely shrugged.

The two soldiers approached, standing just feet from the hanging religious symbol. De La Rue went right up to the crucifix and examined it closely.

"What do you think?" Ricard asked. He wasn't exactly sure how these Microbolometers were supposed to work, and hoped that De La Rue had a better idea about it than he did.

De La Rue reached up and touched it. "I don't know. Maybe it's made out of a material that absorbs and maintains heat. It could be a residual signature."

"You're probably right. It is right in front of these windows which would allow significant light to enter the building and, with the heat of the days increasing as we start the Summer, then maybe it absorbs the heat."

De La Rue nodded, then he looked at the broken window to the left of the crucifix. "And with this window broken maybe there's also some direct sunlight hitting this thing as well," he stated.

Ricard slung the camera under his arm and walked to

the open window, looking out to the darkening sky beyond. It seemed like such a peaceful town. He watched as the sun shed its last rays of the day and dipped below the mountains, covering the valley in darkness.

"Sunray, this is Delta team, come in," they heard on the radio.

"Go ahead Delta team."

"There are a few empty houses, but we did come across one that was occupied. We found bodies in that house. They appear to have been torn apart in the same way that Toussaint and Corbin were."

The two men looked at each other. Ricard could see the concern in De La Rue's eyes, and he felt his palms suddenly get sweaty as his heart leaped in his chest. There was a long pause then the Captain answered, "Thanks for update Delta team. Please continue down the block and report in when you find something else."

"Copy that."

"We should go—" De La Rue began but stopped as he heard another bang; this one sounded like a muffled gun shot. He looked at Ricard. "Please tell me you heard that?" Ricard nodded and the two turned around and shined their lights toward the stairs. "Hazely!" he exclaimed.

They rushed toward the stairs when Ricard suddenly stopped. De La Rue looked back at him. "Come on!" Then his face twisted in confusion.

It was then that Ricard knew he could hear it as well: the crunching, popping, snapping.

20

THE CRUCIFIX

JUNE 21ST, 1989

Ricard and De La Rue slowly turned around. Ricard fell back immediately as he stared at the crucifix. The crossbeam warped and twisted. Out of the ends of it grew long sharp claws. The body of the crucifix seemed to inflate, and the bottom of the cross split in two; each side growing into large muscled legs. Bones popped into place as the crucifix continued to move and sway. Dark gray hair sprouted from the crucifix and eyes blinked from the top; large, dark eyes, not quite animalistic, intelligent somehow. Just below those eyes grew an elongated snout with glistening white fangs.

Ricard began to shake so badly that he dropped the thermal camera which smashed hard to the ground. He took another step back and noticed that De La Rue wasn't moving. The man appeared to be frozen in place.

More crunching, popping, and snapping resonated as the creature continued to take shape. Ricard backed again and fell over a piece of a broken pew. He scrambled to his feet. The creature was now fully formed. The smell of death that came from it almost knocked the man back again.

"De La Rue!" he managed to yell.

The wolf stared at the stunned man with a hateful look and issued a low growl. De La Rue must have come out of his shock as he raised his gun, but the creature leaped with frightening speed from the platform and swiped its massive claws across the man's chest and throat. De La Rue flew to the side, over the debris, and landed in one of the pews in a heap. Lines of bright red blood spurted from his neck. The man gurgled and twitched violently until his body rolled over and fell from the bench. His life's blood continued to pour from the wound causing rivers of crimson fluid to spread out from his lifeless body.

Ricard composed himself quickly and pulled his rifle around. The wolf shot its head in his direction and roared.

Bang! Bang! Bang! Bang!

Hazely heard the roar, then the shots. She spun around and looked to the closed door. Her heart leaped in her chest and she began breathing faster. She hurried to the book, slammed it shut, then grabbed it and ran to the door. She hesitated for a moment before opening it. She really didn't want to go out there, and even considered hiding, but she knew she needed the Alpine Hunters in order to translate the book.

The key to killing the werewolf was in this book, and she knew, for perhaps the first time in her life that she couldn't do it alone. Her whole life Hazely could only truly rely on one person: herself. But now, at this time in this circumstance, she knew she needed help.

She yanked the door open, ran down the short hall, and rounded the corner to the stairs. A scream pierced the air. More shots rang out. Hazely pulled out her gun and ran up the stairs but then stopped before she got to the top. She smelled it. The smell of death. Her hand began shaking so badly that she feared she would lose her grip on the gun. She took two deep breaths then walked slowly up the last couple stairs. It was now quiet.

"Can someone tell me what the hell is going on!" her radio blared.

She reached for the radio and quickly turned it down. Then she peeked around the corner. She saw the massive gray creature hunched over. It suddenly looked up and Hazely got a full look at Vincent—at the werewolf—who had almost killed her. It all seemed like a dream—a nightmare. It was more horrifying than she remembered from the night before. Blood ran down its snout and into its mouth to finally drip from its long deadly fangs.

"Come in! Where did those shots come from!"

The wolf cocked its head to the side when the Captain's voice sounded through the radios of the fallen men. It then nudged one of them with its snout.

"Come in! Does anyone copy?"

It flinched back and its ear twitched a little. The werewolf then slowly turned its head in her direction.

She ducked back around the corner, then lifted the radio to her mouth. "It's in the church," she said as loudly as she dared. "It's in the church." Then she turned it off, hoping that the Captain had heard her last transmission.

She heard the scraping of benches being moved across

the floor. "Oh god," she whispered to herself. She knew it was coming.

Hazely retreated a couple steps down the stairs and held her gun out in front of her. She knew she was about to die. Her hand began to shake again and tears started to roll down her cheeks.

She heard the heavy footfalls of the creature as the floorboards of the old church creaked and groaned under its weight; its claws tapped menacingly against the hard wood. It was close! So close!

Hazely descended another stair, then glanced back down into the darkness. She sighed as an idea—a horrifying idea—came to her. Before she had time to talk herself out of it she slipped back down the stairs and around the corner.

The stairs creaked behind her.

Hazely glanced back before opening the door of the room that housed Tristan's body. With as much stealth as she could muster, she opened the door and slipped inside. Vomit rose in her throat as the stench—which was far worse in the room than in the hall—hit her like a train, but she managed to somehow keep it down.

She hesitated for a moment, staring at the rotting corpse of Tristan laying where she had left it. Three rats looked up from their feast, then scurried away through holes in the wall. Hazely shuddered at the sight.

Tears welled in her eyes. She closed the door, sat on the floor, turned off her flashlight, and leaned against the wall beside the door, hoping that the stench of the rotting corpse would cloak her smell.

A low throaty growl rumbled from the hall. She knew it was just outside.

Not daring to breath, Hazely sat there in the dark, the

last image in her mind was that of Tristan's rotting half-eaten body.

The werewolf's claws tapped on the stone floor just outside the door. She could hear it sniffing into the air, and hoped its senses were similar to that of an ordinary animal.

The moments seemed like hours. What sounded like muffled gunfire and the sound of something being smashed broke the silence. The creature roared then bounded away.

Hazely sighed in relief, knowing that more Hunters had shown up—probably blowing through the front door. She flicked on her light, tentatively opened the door, and peered out into the hall.

Gunfire came in waves from upstairs and Hazely heard the wolf howl as if in pain. She heard more gunfire, an otherworldly roar, then screaming—so much screaming—the screaming of pain and defiance!

It was over quickly—quicker than she expected—then everything in the church went silent once more. She made it back to the stairs and waited for what seemed a long time before she could get the courage to move. When Hazely did move she bounded up the stairs quickly. She looked around the corner, shining her light. Nothing. It was gone. With urgency the woman moved over to the first two men who were laying amongst the pews. She almost threw up when she saw the amount of blood and gore that was strewn about.

The first man was mutilated beyond recognition. She went to the second one and turned him over, hoping he was still alive. She noticed immediately that it was Ricard, the young man who had tended to her when she was nearly frozen. His eyes were still open, but there was no light in them. His throat had been slashed. Tears welled up in her eyes. Hazely put a hand over his eyes and closed his lids. She spent a long moment looking at him. He appeared almost peaceful now, like he was sleeping. He was so young!

Anger welled up inside her! She clenched her fists and tightened her jaw. Hazely wiped her eyes with the sleeve of the jacket she had been given by the Hunters. She wanted this thing dead. She wanted it dead more than she had ever wanted anything in her entire life.

Hazely stood and looked toward the front door, which had been blown open—the light from the streetlights that were now on filtered into the entranceway—and saw two more Hunters laying there. She quickly moved over to them. They were both dead.

The woman grabbed her radio and turned it on. She walked to the front door and peered out into the night. There was no sign of the werewolf anywhere. "Captain, come in. Come in Captain," she whispered into the radio.

"Go ahead Hazely. What's going on?"

"The creature is out, and it's killed four of your men."

She cocked her head up and looked outside as she heard more gunshots echo into the night air.

"Hazely, meet me at the house just North of the cemetery. Can you do that?"

She looked up, then back at the broken window at the rear of the church. Hazely turned away and was about to depress the button on the radio when she snapped her head toward the wall. The crucifix! It was gone! Her mind whirled and spun. "The beast was the crucifix!" she mouthed to herself.

More shots went off in the distance and she knew she had to go. After grabbing a rifle and as much ammo as she could find on the bodies before her, Hazely darted out of the large doors and around the building. She sprinted to the cemetery with all her might. Her legs pumped furiously as she leaped over headstones and weaved around grave markers. More gunfire roared in the distance. She turned slightly and saw muzzle flashes coming from across the river. Her radio blared with indecipherable chatter.

She leaped the last of the headstones and broke free of the graveyard. Without slowing Hazely burst through the nearest door she saw of the house Captain Roux said he would be in.

The Captain spun around aiming his rifle at her, but immediately turned it away when he saw her. "What the hell is going on out there?" he asked. Two of his men had taken positions on opposite sides of the house; their guns trained out the windows waiting for any sign of the creature.

Hazely bent over trying to suck in the precious air she desperately needed after her all-out sprint. "It ... it ..." she gasped.

"It's what Hazely? What's happening to my men?" the Captain asked, his voice raising with concern.

"It transformed in the church," she managed to say.

"Transformed from what? A person?"

Hazely was shaking her head. "From the crucifix."

The Captain stepped back and his eyes went wide at the proclamation. "What are you talking about? None of that makes sense."

"I know it doesn't, but it's the truth." Hazely finally managed to stand up straight as her heart rate dropped and her breathing came easier.

"What's that?" the Captain asked as he pointed to the book that was cradled under her left arm.

She was about to answer when the radios blared again. “It went in the barn!” the soldier stated.

The Captain turned away and lifted the radio to his face. “Hunters, this is Sunray. Retreat to the North side of the river. Command is in the house North of the cemetery. Does anyone copy?”

There was a long silence. “Delta team copies,” came the response which caused the Captain to visibly relax.

“Bravo team copies. Redeploying to your position Sunray.”

“Sunray, this is Foxtrot. Come in.”

“Go ahead Foxtrot,” the Captain replied.

“Cap, we haven’t been able to get a signal yet from the base station radio. We request permission to keep going. If we can get to the tower then we’ll be able to call in support.”

The Captain held the radio in his hand and visibly sighed. Hazely could see the concern etched on his features. “Affirmative Foxtrot. Keep on your previous mission to establish communications. Sunray out.”

“Copy that.”

Hazely wanted to reassure the Captain at that time that everything would be okay, the problem was that she wasn’t sure of that. She had seen the power of the creature up close and wasn’t sure of anything anymore.

“Come on! You heard the Captain. We need to regroup,” Pelissier whispered harshly to his partner Voland.

Voland took his helmet off and wiped the sweat from this bald head. “But we just saw the thing slink into the barn,” he turned to Pelissier and whispered back.

"All the more reason to leave! You saw it. It had to have been seven feet tall, and it was hunched over!"

"Ya, but I think we hurt it. If we leave now then we may not be in as good a position later to kill it."

"But the Captain—"

"Will thank us when we kill it," Voland interjected.

Pelissier shook his head. "How did I get stuck with you?" he asked in resignation.

"I guess you're just lucky." Voland smirked then placed his helmet back on.

He knew Voland had a point, but he definitely didn't want to face the beast again without the support of the rest of his team. He had never been the most decisive person and so he often went along with the decisions of his immediate teammates. With a sigh he motioned for Voland to proceed to the barn.

Voland nodded grimly, then turned and began to stalk toward the barn door. It creaked on its old hinges as it swayed slightly in the cool breeze. When Voland made it to the opening he crouched down and held up his hand. Pelissier silently came up behind him. His stomach churned from the anticipation, and a significant amount of trepidation at facing the creature again. He heard a rattle—it could have been shuffling, he wasn't sure—from within the barn.

He grabbed Voland's shoulder. "Did you hear that?" he whispered.

Voland nodded. "We go on three," he whispered back as he held up his right hand, three fingers in the air—two—one. The man exploded into motion. He stormed the barn like he was possessed!

Pelissier was right at his back. He looked into the gloom and saw those yellow eyes reflect off their lights. Voland began firing. There was a deafening roar. Pelissier didn't know what was happening—everything seemed to be in slow-motion. The creature took one large stride which brought it right up to them. He knew Voland had hit it several times, but couldn't tell if it was being hurt or not. He wanted to fire, but was paralyzed with fear as he stared into those large yellow eyes. The creature was mere inches from him. It backhanded Voland who went flying into the wall. Pelissier turned to dive out of the way when he felt a searing pain course through his arm. Then—as suddenly as it came on—it was gone.

"Holy shit!" he heard Voland curse. The man was just getting up from the side. "What happened?"

"I ... I don't know," Pilessier stammered, holding his arm. "It was here, then it was gone. I think it jumped over us."

Voland was shaking his head. "Shit. Are you okay?"

Pelissier nodded. "I think so. Why didn't it kill us?" he asked dumb-founded.

"I don't know," Voland replied.

He reached down and grabbed Pelissier's rifle and slung it over his shoulder. "Come on, the Captain is expecting us."

Pelissier nodded and followed his friend quickly out of the barn and back across the river.

Cartier fiddled with the nobs of the large radio. He had unslung the base station radio from his back and knelt on the ground with it. It squelched and squealed. "Command, this is Charlie Alpha Tango 3. Do you read me command?" Nothing. "Command, come in. Command, I repeat, this is

Charlie Alpha Tango 3." The only sound that came back was static.

"Why won't this stupid thing work!" Cartier punched the side of the radio in frustration. "The tower is literally right over there!" He pointed his finger angrily at the Tower up on the mountain-side. Half of it was shrouded by dense forest, but the top half was definitely noticeable, even in the dim light of the clear night. Its form seemed like a shadow cast on the mountain background. Cartier estimated that it was maybe a kilometer up the hillside.

"Maybe we just need to be closer," Farrow commented, his eyes darting around nervously.

"Ya, maybe," Cartier conceded. He climbed up and slung the heavy piece of equipment onto his back again. "Worst case scenario, we physically tap into it from the control panel."

Cartier began the ascent again with Farrow closely behind.

"So, what do you make of the woman's story? Think our guys saw whatever it was she fought?" Farrow asked, concern edged his voice.

Cartier shrugged. "I don't know. But whatever it is, it killed more of our men." That thought, spoken aloud, sent a shiver down his spine, and urged him on up the hill with a greater sense of urgency. He knew he needed to get the radio working; he needed to get it working as soon as possible before things got worse.

The chill in the air further deepened with the encroaching darkness that descended on the valley. Cartier could feel it keenly. He had many years invested in the French special forces and had been on dozens of alpine exercises, but never in his life had he been so utterly shaken with the events that were unfolding around him. There was always risk inherent in the exercises, but he never felt that his life was in danger; that is, in *real* danger, like it was this time.

Cartier noticed that the trail grew less defined and steeper as they got closer to their target. He lost view of the tower many times, but then saw it again when they rounded a bend or came to a spot where the trees had thinned out. Farrow was always only two steps behind him, almost clinging to him. Before long the trail turned abruptly then climbed up at a steep incline. He stopped then looked at Farrow. "It looks like we need to climb this last hill in order to reach the tower. Why don't you spot me with the light then stay here while I see how close we are to the tower."

Farrow's eyes went wide. "I'm not staying down here!" he blurted. "Not by myself."

"Come on, Farrow. There's nothing up here but us. You heard all the fighting down at the town. That thing's either still down there or it's dead."

The look on Farrow's face told Cartier that he was less than convinced. "Fine. I'll radio in with the Captain and get a status update," he said.

"Sunray, this is Foxtrot. Come in Sunray." There was no response. "Sunray, please respond." Nothing.

Farrow looked like he wanted to say something but kept quiet.

"We're too far away now and this terrain must be blocking our signal," Cartier said, trying to reassure him.

Farrow didn't look convinced.

"Fine," Cartier said with a sigh. "You shine your light ahead of me so I can see what I'm doing then, when I get to the top, I'll do the same for you. We'll both go to the top."

Farrow seemed to gain courage from that idea as he nodded and shined his light on the steep hillside. Cartier began the climb. He slipped twice but managed to catch himself both times. Moments later he was sitting at the top of the hill. It took a moment, but he reoriented himself then spun around and shined his flashlight down the hillside. His heart leaped in his chest when he saw Farrow's flashlight by itself lying on the ground at the bottom of the hill spinning off to the side.

Farrow was gone.

21

THE TOWER

JUNE 22ND, 1989

Cartier fumbled to pull his rifle around. He clicked off the safety and pointed it down the hill towards Farrow's lone flashlight. He scanned the nearby forests but didn't see anything out of the ordinary. It was eerily quiet; the only thing he could hear was the sound of his own labored breathing as he tried to get it under control. But Cartier was a soldier, and he had dealt with life-threatening circumstances before. He was trained to handle the most adverse situations that could be thrown at him, especially being an Alpine Hunter.

With a calm that defied the situation, Cartier slowly picked up the radio with his right hand and slung it over his arm. He then backed away, never taking his eyes off the immediate area in front of him; he scanned with purpose and also managed two quick looks behind. After backing about twenty feet away from the edge of the cliff he spun and sprinted the last ten feet to the tower. He put the radio down and quickly went to the tower's control panel. He unlatched the small steel door and threw it open. Without even thinking about it he grabbed a small screwdriver from a pouch on the radio's webbing and unscrewed two wires on the panel. Then he detached the wires he needed from the back of the radio and quickly hooked them to the terminals on the tower.

Cartier then bent down and started working the dials. The radio squelched and hissed as he continued to tune.

"Command, this is Charlie Alpha Tango 3. Come in Command. Do you read me? I say again, this is Charlie Alpha Tango 3. Do you read me. Come in Command."

He waited for a moment and listened. He thought he heard something off to the right and quickly flashed his light in that direction and aimed his rifle. There was nothing.

"Command. Come in Command! I say again, this is Charlie Alpha Tango 3. Do you read me?"

"We read you Charlie Alpha Tango 3," a muffled voice full of static replied through the mic.

Cartier had never been so elated to hear another person's voice in all his life! He pulled the map out of a side pocket of the radio harness and glanced quickly at the coordinates Lieutenant Matan had scribbled down. Then he brought the mic to his mouth and was about to say something when he heard a low growl issuing from the darkness. He was suddenly frozen as a shiver went down the back of his neck. He knew he should be depressing the button and telling command about their need for extraction but he couldn't move. The growl deepened. The man knew it was getting closer, but he couldn't see it, or discern which direction it was coming from. Slowly he swiveled his head around, shining his light into the darkness. Eyes! He saw eyes to his right, coming up over the ridge and out of the trees.

Cartier swung his rifle around. Bang! Bang! The shots soared into the tree-line. The low growl was gone. He stood up and looked more intently into the trees with his light. The eyes were gone too.

"Come in Charlie Alpha Tango 3." The crackle of the radio snapped his mind back into focus.

We need help. Call for help! he screamed to himself.

"Command! We need immediate extraction! Our coordinates are ..." He glanced at the map again, "North, 45 degrees, 13.5 minutes, by East, 6 degrees, 28.5 minutes."

A roar shattered the darkness and froze the blood in Cartier's body! He turned to see the creature crash through the trees and lunge at him. Out of pure instinct Cartier dropped the receiver, placed both hands on his rifle, and rolled back. The creature soared overtop, swiping its hand across, barley inches from his face. Cartier flicked the rifle to full-auto and pulled the trigger. Bullets flew from the weapon digging into the chest and abdomen of the beast. Blood sprayed from the wolf, splattering all around as the monster flew over him mere inches from his face.

Cartier landed on his back and immediately rolled to his belly. The wolf laid very still only a few feet from him. He looked to the radio and noticed that it was smashed and laying a few feet away under the tower. He wasn't sure that his message had gotten through. All he could do was pray that it had.

With trembling hands he reached for his mobile radio, knowing that it probably wouldn't work, but he had to try. "Sunray, from Foxtrot. Come in Sunray."

Nothing.

"I say again, come in Sunray."

Silence.

Slowly, Cartier stood and trained his weapon on the beast. It was still—so still—and didn't seem to be breathing. He flicked the rifle back to semi-auto and pulled the trigger. Bang!

The bullet sunk into the back of the creature, right near where the spine should be. Blood sprayed but the monster didn't even flinch. He walked slowly toward the thing and, only then, did he notice the stench of death that surrounded the creature. He gagged once but managed to choke back the vomit.

Cartier kicked the leg of the wolf when he got to it and still there wasn't any movement. He made his way up to the body and marveled at the size of it! It had to have been at least seven or eight feet tall from foot to head when fully stretched out. He had never seen anything like this before and it unnerved him at the highest level of his being. His mind couldn't reconcile a creature like this with his knowledge of the known world.

He knelt down and looked at the thing's mass of scraggly wiry gray hair coming out from all over its body. He noted the spot on its back—near the spine—where his bullet penetrated; the fur being blown away. The wound—right before his eyes—sealed together.

That was when he heard the deep throaty growl.

Lieutenant Matan looked over at Corporal Janvier. The corporal's face was stern and his jaw clenched tightly as shots rang out in the air. The Lieutenant then turned and gazed up to the mountain side where he heard the shots echo from.

"Should we check it out?" Janvier asked.

The Lieutenant's mind spun. The Captain had ordered them back to base which is where they were headed when they heard the shots, but he knew that some of his men were up on that mountainside—Cartier and Farrow—fighting who-knew-what. Men had died—his men—just minutes before the order to regroup was given and now there were more shots. More men were going to die.

"Lieutenant?" Janvier said when Matan didn't answer immediately.

Lieutenant Matan looked again at the Corporal in all seriousness and shook his head. "No," he said.

"But—"

"No! I said," he cut him off before the argument was out of Janvier's mouth. "We can't risk it. Cartier and Farrow are on their own."

Janvier steeled his look and nodded.

"Now come on. We can't be caught in the open. This killer—what ever it is—has no preference who it murders." To accentuate the point he nodded his head down the street to where a body lay out on the stairs; it's dead form twisted and broken. This was the third body they had discovered. Then he nodded over across the street to where a cow was crumpled and bloated; beside that was what looked to be a goat at one time. "This place is hell, and we're walking through it without a clue as to who the caretaker is."

Lieutenant Matan then spun and sped away, Janvier tight on his heels. Another shot rang out as they ran. That concussive sound caused the Lieutenant to pause for a moment and look back. He then shook his head and ran on.

He wondered if he was doing the right thing leaving his men behind. These decisions were never easy, but he had to remind himself that they were dealing with something apparently more deadly than they had ever seen; something they didn't really understand. So he ran on, leading Janvier through the uneven streets of the small town.

It took them a little while after hearing the shots to wind through the town and make it back to the bridge which would lead to the other side of the river where their base of operations was set up.

The uneven cobblestone roads twisted and turned under their feet as they sped on. For a small town the distances were spread out far more than anyone would expect them to be, but eventually they came to the crest of the hill that led down to the old bridge that spanned the river.

Halfway across the structure Lieutenant Matan heard a roar pierce the darkness which caused him to cringe. He then felt the bridge shudder like something big had hit it. He managed a glance back and saw, to his horror, something bounding across the top of the trusses.

"Oh my god!" he heard Janvier scream. The man must have seen the shadowy form crossing the top of the bridge.

"Just keep running!" the Lieutenant screamed as he put his head down and tried to coax more speed from his already tiring legs. His muscles screamed in protest.

Bang! Bang! Bang! Bang! Shots pierced the night air. He glanced over his shoulder to see Janvier back-pedalling and firing his rifle up at the encroaching creature.

"Janvier! Run!" he yelled.

Janvier turned and started sprinting hard again, but Matan could see that he had lost significant ground. The end of the bridge was so near! It was only twenty feet or so away, but then a shadow passed over them and landed at the exit they so desperately needed to get to. Lieutenant Matan slowed up then stopped about ten feet away from the creature. Janvier was at his side a few heartbeats later.

The creature was crouched and had its back to them.

Bang! Bang! Bang! Bang! Bang! Bang!

It flinched with each shot but remained on its feet. The monster then rose and turned around. Its lips curled up revealing large fangs—fangs tainted red from the blood of those it had killed already. It snarled.

The Lieutenant had never seen anything like it before! His eyes went wide at the mere sight of it. The wolf—yes, the wolf, for that is what it looked like to Matan: a huge horrifying resemblance of a wolf that walked on two legs—began slowly stalking forward. The movement was enough to break Matan out of his shock. He lifted his rifle, but as soon as he made the movement the creature lunged faster than he had anticipated. Matan went left and Janvier broke right as the thing crashed into them. It slashed Janvier across the arm with its long, curved claws. Janvier yelped as he was thrown to the side and crashed hard into the thick timber of the bridge.

Matan rolled around into a kneeling position and fired. The bullet tore into the arm of the beast spraying blood into the air. The creature roared and turned its hateful eyes to Matan. He pulled the trigger again shooting it in the chest. The bullet made it flinch back, but seemed to anger it more than hurt it. The creature advanced with amazing speed considering how big it was. Matan fired again just as the thing swiped its clawed hand across, knocking the rifle from Matan's grasp and sending it fifteen feet from him. His eyes went wide when he saw the sheer force and power of the wolf.

It leered over him and snarled. He knew his life was about to end. How could he fight against the destructive power of something of this magnitude? It roared, ready to pounce as Matan scrambled away to the railing of the bridge.

Shots rang out, and a scream of defiance that sounded like music to the doomed Lieutenant, sang out in the air. The wolf twitched weirdly, arching its back and roaring as if in pain. Then it turned and pounced. Janvier's clip ran out of bullets as he was buried by the weight of the seven foot tall monster.

"No!" Matan screamed, seeing Janvier disappear under the weight of the creature.

Timbers cracked and creaked as the creature and Janvier slammed into them. Matan pulled out his side arm and was about to fire, but then he looked up at the beam that Janvier and the wolf had hit. The cracks widened and spread rapidly. He felt the bridge shift violently.

"Oh shit!" he screamed as he clambered to get up.

Snap! The beam went and Janvier and the creature toppled from the bridge into the cold water below. The bridge rocked, and more cracks appeared on different support structures.

Matan ran. He scooped up his rifle and lunged for the end of the bridge. He could feel his feet begin to sink and leaped. He hit the pavement hard on his stomach then turned to see half of the bridge collapse into the dark water below.

Lieutenant Matan crawled to his feet and looked into the river. The clear sky, the bright moon, and the dim street lights, helped him to see well enough, but he couldn't make out whether or not Janvier or the wolf were alive. His mind told him that Janvier was surely dead; he was probably killed when the creature slammed into him, but his heart hoped for a better reality.

He pulled his flashlight out and began to scan the surface of the water. Back and forth, back and forth, back and ... a glint in the water ... eyes ...

Matan jumped back when he saw the eyes staring at him, studying him. Then, long thick claws emerged from the river grabbing on to the bank and digging into the soft dirt. He knew he should be running but was frozen—wide-eyed—at the powerful creature.

Its head emerged slowly and Matan back-pedalled faster as he saw Janvier's severed arm in its maw. The sight made Lieutenant Matan blanch and was enough to release him from his stupor. His mind began to spin and he knew there were but two options before him: fight or run. With new energy propelled by the latest infusion of adrenaline now coursing through his system, Lieutenant Matan ran with every ounce of energy he could muster.

Behind him he heard a deafening roar echo through the valley that sent a fear through him that he never knew existed. And so he ran on. He ran for his very life, and for the lives of those he knew were still alive.

He got to the graveyard, leaped the small fence with ease, and began jumping and twisting around the scattered headstones. He could hear the sound of the wolf bounding after him; its heavy paws hitting the ground and pushing off powerfully. He dared to glance back and saw the shadowed form charging at him from through the darkness. It closed the gap fast with its powerful leaps.

The Lieutenant turned his head forward again and charged with all his strength but couldn't coax any more speed from his pumping legs; they screamed in defiance at him and he could feel the lactic acid build up in the tiring limbs. He dared to look back again.

A shadowy clawed-hand reached for him.

22

CRYPTIC WRITING

JUNE 22ND, 1989

Bang! Bang! Bang! Bang! Bang!

Lieutenant Matan saw the shadowy form flinch as the bullets streaked into it; the last one sunk into the side of its left shoulder which caused it to stumble and arrest its momentum. He thought the creature sounded pained as the stinging bullets penetrated its flesh. Those few precious seconds were enough for Matan to breach the gap between him and the house. The door flew open just before he got to the building and he barreled through like a man possessed.

He heard the door slam shut as more shots rang out. Lieutenant Matan hunched over the counter of the small kitchen sucking in the precious air his body desperately needed.

"It's moving off to the West!" Kaplan shouted from upstairs.

"I see it!" yelled Private Fay who was positioned at the large window in the main room of this small house. Bang! Bang! Bang! Bang! Bang! he fired.

"Oh shit!" he heard Kaplan yell. "More of our men are out there, coming in from the West and East."

Captain Roux lifted the radio to his mouth and ran to the window that Fay was shooting out. "All teams! Hostile is heading West of the command position!" he yelled.

"Damn! I lost sight of it!" Private Fay exclaimed. He moved his rifle left and right, trying to locate any movement in his scope. "It went behind that building. Third one West of the church."

Captain Roux pulled his binoculars up. "The team that is West of the church beware that the hostile is heading towards you," he said into the radio.

A moment later the radio blared: "Sunray, this is Delta team. We're West of the church. We will engage the target."

"Negative, Delta team! I repeat, negative! Do not engage the hostile. Continue to base camp. Do you read?" Captain Roux commanded.

Silence.

"Delta team. Do you read me?"

"We read you Command. Proceeding to ... what the hell is ..."

Bang! Bang! Shots could be heard in the distance.

"Delta team. Come in Delta team."

Lieutenant Matan shook his head, still trying to make sense of what was going on. He saw the concern etched on the Captain's face and knew that Delta team had just been killed by this murderer.

He felt a hand on his shoulder and looked over to see Hazely there. He stared her in the eyes for a moment, then his gaze dropped to the book she had put on the counter, a large dusty leather-bound ancient-looking book. "What is that?" he asked.

Hazely shook her head. “I don’t know exactly. I can’t even begin to explain to you what I had to go through to get it.” She paused for a moment as though she was collecting her thoughts. “It’s like a dream. I ... I don’t know what to believe anymore.

“It has something to do with that thing out there. I think this book created that ... that werewolf.”

The Lieutenant cocked his head to the side.

“Listen. This may sound crazy—“

Lieutenant Matan laughed. After all he’s been through tonight he’d believe anything he was told at this point!

“This book holds the key to killing that thing, but I can’t read it. It looks like it’s in Latin and French, but even the Captain had difficulty with it. He said it was in an old dialect. Do you think you can take a look at it?”

“What makes you think I can read it?”

“Captain Roux said you spent some time in Quebec, and that the French there evolved differently than it has in France. He said it’s considered by some to be Colonial French, whatever that means. Maybe that will be enough to help you decipher enough of it for us to understand it?”

Lieutenant Matan let his gaze drop from Hazely to the book. He reached over and grabbed it, pulling it open.

Hazely waited patiently as he scanned through it. Many awkward moments drifted by as the others were busying themselves with locating the werewolf. “Can you read it?” she finally asked.

“I think I can muddle my way through it to get the gist of what it’s saying, but I don’t see how this is going to help with our men dying out there.” He slammed it shut.

“Please,” Hazely pleaded. “I know you’ve had good men

die tonight, but unless we find out how to kill it we're all going to die."

He looked at her for a long moment. He could see the fear in her eyes, fear that was completely justified in the face of this monster. He then nodded and opened the book again.

Lieutenant Matan flipped through the delicate pages, skimming most of it, but slowed down on some parts that spoke about calling forth a beast. The language was hard but he managed to discern that the book claimed to be able to offer immortality to the soul who would bind himself to the night.

Hazely must have seen the confused look on his face. "What is?" she asked.

"It says here that someone can become immortal if they would bind themselves to the night, but it is really vague on the details as to what form this immortality would take."

"It doesn't say anything about becoming this murdering beast?"

The Lieutenant shook his head. "No. Not specifically. It just says that you would have to forsake the day and walk at night ... I think," he replied. "It doesn't even say that you would be confined to only once a month, but mentions that your power would be manifested during the full moon.

"The language is really vague."

"But does it say how to stop it?"

"I ... I don't know. I didn't read anything that talks about that. But there is one thing here ... it's a rhyme of sorts. I think I can give you the gist of it. This part is in old French."

"*The one who seeks tranquility*

Will not see immortality
It is he who offers up his soul
That will live forever full
The truth—the stalker of the night—
Is revealed in he when the moon shines most bright
But beware those who take on this guise
For a desire you will have that goes forth and cries
A thirst, a thirst that will not be quenched!
By blood, by blood only to be drenched
Live forever, this will not be undone
To walk at night, the daytime you must shun
Beware, beware the truth of this
And seal your life here now, of that you must not miss."

Lieutenant Matan looked up at Hazely when he was done and shrugged. "I don't know. What do you think?"

Hazely stared at him and shook her head disappointedly. "I ... I don't know either. Maybe this has a clue but I really don't know. The one thing I do know is that Celeste didn't want me to take this because she knew it had the answer as to how to stop the werewolf. It has to be in here somewhere!"

"Who's Celeste?"

Hazely shook her head. "It's a long story and we don't have time for that. All I know is I'm sure this will tell us how to handle the creature."

She flinched and turned toward the window as she heard more shots outside.

"Those shots were from Delta team!" Private Fay exclaimed. "They're still alive."

Lieutenant Matan could see that Hazely was frustrated and scared. "It's okay. We'll get out of this." The truth was, however, that he didn't feel as confident as he just sounded. The sheer destructive power that he witnessed of the wolf unnerved him to the core. He stood, checked the ammunition in his current magazine, and slipped it back into his FAMAS.

Hazely seemed to gain strength at that moment as she steeled her expression, pulled out her handgun, and cocked the action.

Lamar jumped to the side and slammed into the house just in time as the powerful clawed-hand came within inches of his face. He knew the creature would be on top of him in a moment if he didn't get his feet back under him. He managed to spin and get his rifle in front as the monster turned its head, opened its maw wide, and moved to snap at the soldier. Lamar fired. The bullet blew a large piece of the creature's jaw away. It yelped and spun its head.

Lamar scrambled along the wall, trying to put some distance between him and the murdering beast. Bang! He fired again hitting it in the shoulder. Blood sprayed from the beast as it roared and back-pedaled a step.

"Come on Page!" he screamed, looking to his fallen friend who was laying prone a few feet away. He was about to fire again when the creature snapped its head toward him. What he saw caused him to pause: the creature's jaw he had just blown apart was reforming before his eyes!

"How is that—" His voice trailed off as he reached Page and grabbed the man's shoulder. He felt moisture on Page's jacket. With a tug he pulled him over. His eyes went wide as he stared at the man's missing neck. Pieces of arteries, the windpipe, trachea, and veins were exposed and dangling out. The man's dead eyes were wide open; the lights having fled from them, and his face was ghostly pale.

Lamar was ripped from his horror by a low resonating snarl. He turned and saw the creature fifteen feet from him. It was hunched over. Despite the dim lighting provided by the sparse street lamps, Lamar could see the werewolf's eyes boring hatefully into him. It appeared to him as a harbinger of death. As it stalked in, it didn't advance straight at him, but rather, moved slightly to the side then changed direction. To Lamar it seemed as though it was toying with its prey before going in for the kill.

Lamar backed away, too afraid to even shoot the beast again. It closed on him and the snarl turned into a growl. Its lips curled up revealing those awful fangs that tore out the throat of Page.

The wolf stood over him. He could smell the rot, the decay. He held his gun up in shaky hands. The beast pulled back its right clawed-hand, and Lamar knew it was over.

Shots rang out behind him. Bang! Bang! Bang! Bang! Bang! Bang! Bang! Each bullet pushed the creature back that much more, and was enough to pull Lamar out of this shock.

"Come on!" he heard someone yell from behind.

He didn't waste any more time but leaped up, turned, and ran. He was grabbed by the shoulder and pulled along by Pelissier as another soldier he recognized as Voland, continued firing at the beast. Roars—shrieks—pierced the air as the creature took shot after shot.

Lamar glanced back and saw that Voland had now

turned and was running with all his might. The three men charged down the cobblestone road. They rounded a corner and Lamar could see the graveyard. Beyond that he noticed a house with the lights on. Someone was in the window facing toward them. He saw a flash and heard the concussive sound of the bullet. The round whipped passed Lamar and he heard another roar. More shots rang out from the house and Lamar knew that the creature was closing in on them. He dared to glance back and saw that a great hulking form in the darkness was almost on top of Voland, the man who had laid down the fire on the beast so he could escape.

"Look out!" he screamed, seeing the darkened form take a powerful leap that was impossibly high.

Voland jumped the small fence to the graveyard but the beast descended on him like an avalanche, burying him under hundreds of pounds of muscle, claws, and teeth. The man's screams were cut short as the creature ripped his head and part of his arm from his body. The wolf shook the man back and forth like a dog would tear at a bone. More shots streaked in, but they seemed not to harm the creature at all while it was in the midst of its frenzy.

Lamar's eyes widened when he witnessed the destruction of his fellow Hunter, but there was nothing he could do except run, and run he did. A moment later he and Pelissier burst through the door to the small house. Captain Roux was there in a flash, slamming shut the door and locking it tight.

"Look out!" Fay yelled, firing shot after shot out the window.

Lamar turned. He was about to say something when the door exploded off its hinges! It smashed into the Captain, knocking him to the ground and landing on top of him. The massive beast had one huge clawed-hand on the door, holding the Captain down. It roared, spraying spittle from its deadly maw.

Lamar stumbled back to the base of the stairs and everyone else scattered, screaming.

"Run!" he heard the Captain yell.

"Like hell!" yelled Kaplan, who sprinted down the stairs, shoving Lamar aside and advancing on the beast, shooting —muzzle-blasting Lamar in the process. The bullets hit the werewolf tearing flesh and bone from its monstrous body.

"I told you this damn place was cursed!" he screamed out.

Fay must have regained his sense as he too began to shoot at it from the side. Every shot from the two caused the creature to flinch back a little, slowly removing it from the door. Lamar knew he should help, but he was too disoriented to even get his rifle into a firing position. He looked to Pelissier who had stumbled toward the fire place when they burst through the door. The man was holding his arm which was dripping with blood; he knew Pelissier wouldn't be able to help.

The Lieutenant climbed out from behind the counter and started shooting. Fay's clip emptied and he scrambled to remove it and get a new one loaded. The creature howled and roared with each hit. The Lieutenant's magazine emptied as well, and Kaplan was now mere inches from the beast. Bang! Bang! Bang! Click!

There was a momentary pause after the resounding click of Kaplan's rifle that, to Lamar, felt like an hour. Everything seemed to be moving in slow motion. Lamar saw the sudden fear in Kaplan's eyes as the werewolf—its face and body dripping with blood—narrowed its eyes on the soldier and snarled. With lighting speed the creature shot its clawed-hand out and grabbed Kaplan by the throat. With impossible strength it pulled the man into the darkness. His screams echoed in the ears of Lamar.

Fay got his weapon reloaded and aimed it out the window. "I see nothing!" he screamed.

Captain Roux extricated himself from under the door. Lamar could see the look of fear in the Captain's eyes when he climbed to his feet. He knew the Captain well enough to realize that it wasn't so much fear for himself, but for the men who were being killed.

"Captain! Are you okay?" Lieutenant Matan asked, slipping the rest of the way around the counter to stand before him.

The Captain nodded. "We need to retreat to a more defensible position."

"Why didn't it kill me? Why didn't it kill me? Why didn't it kill me? It had the chance, but didn't kill me. Why ..." Pelissier mumbled to himself, rocking back and forth by the hearth, cradling his arm.

Everyone turned to look at the dazed man, then Lieutenant Matan stepped forward. "Pelissier?" he asked the mumbling man as he put a hand on his shoulder. Pelissier kept rocking and muttering the same words over and over, seeming not to notice the Captain. Lamar knew that the man was on the edge of his mental limits.

"When was that Pelissier?" the Lieutenant asked.

"We don't have time for that now," Captain Roux snapped. "We have to get to a better place."

"The foundry!" Hazely suddenly yelled which drew all their eyes to her—except Fay who was focused on looking for the creature.

"The foundry up on the hill," she reiterated as she pointed her finger in that direction. She picked up the book from the table. "The foundry's walls, doors, and windows are more heavily made than even these stone houses. Maybe we can defend ourselves from there until we find out how to kill this thing?"

It only took the Captain a second to contemplate the idea before nodding. "But how are we going to get there without being slaughtered? It's a ways up the hill."

"Why didn't it stay to kill the rest of us?" Fay suddenly interjected.

"What?" the Captain asked.

"If this thing is so invincible then why didn't it just stay and finish us off. Or why hasn't it come back yet?"

"Well, it did take quite a bit of damage with all of us firing at it. Maybe it needs time to heal?" Lieutenant Matan suggested.

"Good theory. So if we can do enough damage at one time then maybe it will die," the Captain added. "But right now, we need to get to that foundry so we have a chance of fortifying and hopefully doing the kind of damage we need to in order to put it down for good. And since we don't know when it will be back, any suggestions as to what we can do to make it there without being caught in the open would be appreciated."

There was a momentary silence, then Lieutenant Matan spoke up, "I'll lead it away. I'll light a flare and draw it off, then you can make a break for it."

The Captain was shaking his head before Matan even finished the sentence.

"Yes, Captain. It's the only way. We won't all make it if it's right on top of us. As we've already seen this thing heals way too fast."

Lamar looked from the Lieutenant to the Captain, then back again. "I'll go with the Lieutenant as well." He could barely register what he was saying. The last thing he wanted to do was to face that creature again, but he couldn't let the Lieutenant go alone. It wasn't the Hunter's way. "The thing does heal quickly, but the damage we do seems to slow it momentarily and can even back it off, so if we take all the grenades, and have enough ammo, we may be able to draw it away from you and then get away ourselves."

"But if you think that plan will work, then why don't we all just go and hit it hard as it chases us?" Hazely put in.

There was an awkward silence for a moment. "Because we don't know for sure if it will, and the Lieutenant and Private want to make certain we get to the foundry," Captain Roux answered for them.

Lieutenant Matan nodded. "Come on then, give us all the grenades you have. Be quick about it!" he said as he went to Pelissier and grabbed his explosives. Lamar also began gathering up ammo and grenades.

"I think it's coming back!" Fay yelled from the window. "We have to move." He threw his three grenades to Lamar then headed for the back door.

"Alright then. You lead it away and we'll make a break for the foundry," the Captain said as he gathered up the injured Pelissier and headed to the back door. "Don't spend more time out there than you need to," he said to the Lieutenant. "I expect to see you two at the foundry shortly after we get there. Do you understand?"

Lamar saw the Lieutenant nod, then he looked right at him. "You ready Lamar?"

"All teams, this is Sunray. We are retreating to the foundry. If you copy, meet us at the foundry," the Captain said into his radio. He then looked at the team. "I'm just hoping there is someone still alive who heard that."

Lieutenant Matan nodded as he walked to the door.

"Lead the way Lieutenant," Lamar said as he pulled the butt of his rifle into his shoulder.

Lieutenant Matan took out a flare from one of many pockets on his webbing, lit it up, then ran into the darkness. Lamar sprinted out into the cool night air right behind him. He heard a roar pierce the darkness to their left and knew the creature was hunting them down again. He and the Lieutenant ducked around a corner and kept sprinting parallel to where the foundry was on the hill to their right. Lamar hoped that the Captain and the others were quickly making their way up the hill.

The Lieutenant stopped at an intersection and knelt down as the flare dimmed and died out altogether. It took a second for Lamar's eyes to adjust to the low light of the sparse street lamps. There was an eerie silence that almost seemed to drift upon the air around them. Lamar's heart pounded furiously, and he wasn't sure if that was mainly due to the running or the adrenaline pumping through his veins, or from both.

"Did you see it follow us?" the Lieutenant asked.

Lamar shook his head. "No. But it sounded like it spotted the light and started to give chase."

"Well, let's get it's attention again." Lieutenant Matan took out another flare and sparked it to life.

Lamar squinted from the light and turned his head to the left. His eyes opened wide when he saw the yellow flash of the creature's eyes reflect off the flare's glow.

23

RELENTLESS

JUNE 22ND, 1989

Hazely heard the roar echo throughout the valley as soon as Lamar and the Lieutenant ran from the house with the glowing flare held high. She turned her head and saw a large shadow dart out from around the back of the house and down a street adjacent to the one Lamar and the Lieutenant sprinted down. Captain Roux grabbed her by the arm and pulled her out into the night air. Her nerves felt strung out as she began moving—slowly at first—but then gaining speed and running with a sense of urgency. No. Not a sense of urgency she realized, a sense of dread.

Since the attack on her the night before, she felt as though she had been slowly losing her nerve. She always prided herself in being tough and being able to handle any situation. But this creature had changed that. Now she felt like a frightened child trying to avoid the inevitable: death. She knew she had to get her focus and toughness back, but the power of the wolf seemed to steal everything from her.

Was this going to be the end? she thought to herself as she stumbled up the hill. *No! It can't be the end.* Her resolve strengthened as she picked up her pace and pushed in front of the three men. She clenched her jaw in sheer determination.

Pelissier was running under his own power now. His gait was a little awkward due to cradling his injured arm, but he was still able to, surprisingly, keep up. Hazely marveled at the toughness of these Alpine Hunters.

"Pelissier!" the Captain whispered to him as they slid through the dim streets.

"Yes sir."

"You said that the thing could have killed you and Voland, but that it didn't. When was that?"

Pelissier glanced over at the Captain for a second. "Voland and I were searching a house on the Northern side of the village when the radio went off with Foxtrot telling you they were going to carry on to the radio tower and call for help. That's when the thing came out and leaped over us. It got me in the arm, but then pounced away into the night."

The Captain looked deep in thought. He crouched at a corner of a house and quickly looked around the corner. "That means this thing must be intelligent. That's going to be an issue."

Hazely shuddered at the thought.

"Okay Hazely. Get us to that foundry," he said, turning to her.

Hazely slipped around the corner. She led them around a few of the buildings and onto the wide main road at the top of the hill. She ran across the road and into the wide parking lot.

Bang! A shot rang out.

She faltered at the sound and glanced in the direction.

An explosion rocked the town and a flash shot into the sky down the hill around some houses where Lieutenant Matan and Lamar had gone.

Lieutenant Matan dove to the side as the grenade went off causing pieces of shrapnel and chunks of concrete to spray everywhere. He felt a sharp pain in his left leg and his ears rang from the explosion. The grenade was close when it went off, too close.

He shook his head and looked around, trying to see Lamar in the midst of the confusion. A huge portion of the wall beside where the creature was standing when the explosion went off was blown away, and the small house looked as though it was going to topple at any moment.

The Lieutenant tried to stand up but grimaced from the pain in his leg. He managed to roll over and grabbed at the leg in order to examine it. His pants were soaked with blood and there was a small piece of metal shrapnel protruding from his thigh. He grabbed at the metal shard and tugged slightly. The pain intensified and he grunted, but he knew he had to get it out. With a yell the Lieutenant gave one sharp pull and the piece came free. He gritted his teeth with a groan, and placed a shaky hand on the wound.

Almost from out of nowhere Lamar swooped in. "Lieutenant!" he yelled, crouching down beside him. "Are you okay?" He quickly pulled a roll of gauze from one of his pouches on his webbing.

Lieutenant Matan nodded. "Ya. I'll be fine. What about the creature?"

Lamar shook his head as he began wrapping the Lieutenant's leg. "I don't know. I saw the grenade go off right beside it which launched it away, but I have my doubts as to whether or not it's dead."

He finished wrapping the bandage around the wound and tied it off tightly. "That thing has taken a lot of hits and it still keeps coming," he stated through heavy breaths. "The bullets rip through it but somehow the wounds seal up quickly." Lamar shook his head as though he was in complete disbelief.

Lieutenant Matan saw the fear in the man's eyes. This thing had shaken the entire platoon to its core. They had seen close friends torn apart by the unrelenting, merciless, savage creature. They had hit it, and hit it hard, but still it kept coming.

A sudden low growl echoing on the night air from somewhere he couldn't discern pulled the man from his thoughts. "It looks like you were right," he said in a pained voice as he shifted his injured leg and looked at Lamar. The man's face had paled. "Let's move private!" the Lieutenant yelled in order to shake the fear from the man.

Lamar nodded and helped to pull the Lieutenant up. Once standing, Lieutenant Matan could feel that his leg wasn't as injured as it first appeared, and that he could support his weight, and even walk on his own, albeit with a bit of a limp. Lamar tried to help, but Lieutenant Matan pushed him away. "I'm okay. Just head up that hill. The others must have made it to the foundry by now."

"Yes sir." Lamar moved in front of the Lieutenant and began to weave through the broken streets.

The growl had disappeared; the only sounds were those of crickets, and a couple owls hooting in the distance. The Lieutenant could see that they were only a couple of lower streets away from the main road that paralleled the foundry. Each corner the two came around, he thought would bring them face-to-face with the wolf, but there was nothing.

Lamar looked back at the Lieutenant. “Maybe we *did* kill it,” he stated more than asked.

“Do you really believe that?”

Lamar shook his head, almost in defeat.

The Lieutenant put a hand on the man’s shoulder. “But it doesn’t mean we can’t,” he said reassuringly, trying to bolster the man’s faith that they would get out of this alive. “We’ll find a way.”

Lamar seemed to solidify at that moment.

Lieutenant Matan looked around the corner then scanned the streets on either side and back at the one they had come down. “This thing is smart. There’s something about it, like there’s an intelligence behind the eyes. And, as you said earlier, our weapons only seem to slow it down.”

He paused, deep in thought, then looked directly at Lamar again. “No. It’s out there. Playing with us. Toying with us. It’s as though it savors the hunt and takes pleasure in the kill. It’s the perfect killing machine. It has the mind of a human, but the instincts and abilities of this ... wolf it becomes.”

“What do you mean?” Lamar asked. “This thing’s human?”

The Lieutenant nodded. “I was able to read some of the book the girl carries. It’s a man. He was cursed somehow, and now he walks the nights as this monstrosity.”

“Did the book say how to kill it?” Lamar asked expectantly, almost pleadingly.

The Lieutenant thought about all that he had read and skimmed through. He wasn’t sure. He didn’t have enough time with the book before the creature attacked. Finally, he shook his head. "I don't know." Seeing Lamar's face fall he added, "But I'm sure there is a way. Everything dies."

A roar shattered the silence! Lieutenant Matan looked around desperately, expecting the beast to descend upon him and Lamar at any moment. But then he realized that the roar came from ahead of them, up the hill toward the foundry. Another roar split the air. It was moving toward the foundry.

It was moving toward their friends.

Hazely could see the large front doors. They weren't more than a hundred feet away. She ran desperately for them when a deafening roar echoed through the air. It was close! She stopped with the others and looked back. A large shadow leaped through the air and landed on the road just outside the foundry parking lot. It hit the ground on its powerful legs and began to sprint toward them.

"Hurry!" she screamed before turning and running toward the door again.

Shots rang out and the creature howled. Hazely got to the door and saw again the large chains that were wrapped around the handles. She looked back. Captain Roux, Pelissier, and Fay were almost there. The creature had slowed its pursuit. Bang! Another bullet ripped into it from behind and it jerked its head around. There, standing on the edge of the parking lot were Lieutenant Matan and Lamar. They were hitting it hard and drawing its attention away from the others.

"Quick! This way!" Hazely screamed as she ran around

the corner to where the broken ground-floor window was. Hazely shined her light at the opening. "In here!"

Fay and Captain Roux helped Pelissier to climb through the window and, once he was safely inside, the Captain motioned for Hazely to go through. Without a thought, she climbed through the window and landed hard on the floor beside Pelissier. Fay came through next. Hazely leaped back to her feet and glanced out the window. Captain Roux was running back toward the corner of the building, toward death incarnate.

"Captain!" Fay screamed after him.

"You take care of those two!" he yelled back. "I have to help the Lieutenant and Lamar."

Fay placed his hand on the seal and was about to jump back through when Hazely reached out and grabbed him by the shoulder. "We can't do this without you," she said to the man. "The Captain knows what he's doing."

Fay looked at her for a moment then back out the window to where the Captain disappeared to around the corner. Shots rang out.

"Come on. We're sitting ducks without you. If that thing gets through then there's nothing stopping it from killing all of us."

"If that thing gets through then we're all dead for sure. We can't stop it," Fay replied grimly.

"Maybe. But I think there's an answer in this book," she replied, holding the tome up for Fay to get a good look at it. "And if we can find it then there's a chance ... for us."

"But what about them?" Fay asked indignantly.

"They're doing this for us," Hazely replied. "Don't cheapen their sacrifice."

Fay seemed to think about it for moment then nodded. "I'm with you."

Captain Roux charged around the corner like a man possessed. Bang! Bang! Bang! He let three quick shots go into the back of the creature. It flinched and spun its head his way. *Good! You bastard. Keep your attention on me.*

He saw the Lieutenant and Lamar running up to it on the other side, one slipping to the left and the other to the right. With military precision they hammered the beast with ripping rounds of bullets. The creature spun and flinched as the bullets tore through its flesh, but the barrage only seemed to anger it more as it roared and leaped for the Lieutenant. The Captain saw that Lieutenant Matan was about to get buried by the monstrosity when Lamar, almost out of nowhere, ran in and shoulder-checked him away.

With terrifying fury the creature landed on the man and began to tear into him. Even with the bullets that Captain Roux was putting into the creature he knew there was no way he was going to stop the slaughter. He kept firing as he ran to the Lieutenant who was pulling himself up from the pavement. The screams coming from Lamar as he battled the beast sounded like pleas for mercy. Captain Roux knew that Lamar was pleading for an end to the pain he was suffering under the fury of the creature. He grabbed the Lieutenant and noted the last three grenades he had taken hanging on his webbing. He slung his rifle and quickly grabbed two of them and pulled the pins. He knew that Lamar also had a few grenades still on him.

Could this finish the beast here and now? That thought,

however, wasn't what motivated the Captain at that moment. The only thing the Captain cared about was giving his soldier the dignity of a death he deserved.

Captain Roux turned and threw the grenades beside the creature. He pulled the Lieutenant away from the beast and Lamar, but only made it a few strides before the grenades went off. He felt the concussive blast—which was amplified multiple times over with the explosion of all the grenades—and was thrown through the air. The Lieutenant was hurled away from him as the Captain flew twenty feet and more before hitting the hard pavement and rolling uncontrollably into the wall of the foundry.

The captain smashed his head and heard a loud crack. Pain erupted throughout his body and his vision blurred. He tried to will himself to stay conscious, and even attempted to move, but his body wouldn't respond to his commands.

With all the energy he could muster Captain Roux glanced around, trying desperately to see the Lieutenant. He closed his eyes tight then opened them again hoping his vision would clear, but it didn't. He thought he saw the Lieutenant laying to his left, unmoving. He took another long blink and when he opened his eyes he turned his head slightly and saw, laying a few feet from him, a large torn arm that was from the werewolf. Its hand, with its long curved claws, was half curled and twitched as it lay there. Most of the hair had been blown from the limb which revealed charred pieces of sinew and exposed muscle tissue.

Captain Roux issued a long sigh of relief. They had done it. They had killed it. They had survived.

He tried again to rise, but his vision clouded over, the world spun, and darkness took him.

24

HIDING

JUNE 22ND, 1989

Hazely heard the explosion. It sounded like a bomb had been dropped just outside. She silently prayed that the Captain and his men were alright, but didn't dare go back into the other room and out the window to find out. Instead, she led Fay and Pelissier through the winding corridors. She figured her best chance of survival—if the creature was still alive—was in the maintenance room, with its lower ceiling and many places to hide. The tight quarters would take some of the advantage away from the werewolf. At least that's what she hoped would happen.

"We should go back to help them," Fay stated, and not for the first time.

Hazely shook her head. "We can't. The Captain ordered you to help us. Pelissier is in no condition to fight, and my weapon isn't going to do anything against that creature. We have to find a defensible position and plan out how we're going to kill it."

"Do you really think we can stop it?" Fay asked skeptically, stopping in the middle of the hallway and looking at Hazely with a steely expression.

Hazely didn't know, but she knew she had to have hope; if not for herself then for these two who were with her. She clenched her jaw and returned Fay's steely expression with one of her own. "I do."

Fay looked at her for a long awkward moment then nodded slightly and motioned for her to continue on down the hallway.

Hazely led them quickly to the maintenance room and, once inside, she and Fay looked around for something to bar the double doors. Fay found an old pry bar leaning up against the wall and jammed it between the handles.

"Come on. This way," Hazely said once the doors were secured.

She led them deeper into the room, around old boilers, motor control centers, and various machines. She moved carefully, as the only lights they had were from their flashlights which only illuminated a few feet before the outer edges of the light faded into darkness again. More than once she bumped into a piece of equipment or almost tripped over a broken tile on the floor. Each time, she shook off the pain and disorientation and pushed on. Eventually they made it to the maintenance crib: a fenced off area that housed the maintenance worker's tools and office equipment.

The door to the cage was locked. Hazely took out her handgun and pointed it at the lock.

"Wait! What are you doing?" Fay asked.

"What does it look like? I'm going to blow this lock open so we can get inside."

"But we won't be able to lock it up again afterwards," Fay argued.

Hazely looked at him and arched an eyebrow. "Do you honestly think the thing out there is going to be stopped by a little bit of chain-linked fence, especially if it gets through the door with the pry bar in it?"

Fay was silent.

She knew that he was processing everything he had seen about the creature and was coming to the same scary conclusion that she was: it was near unstoppable. After a long moment the soldier nodded.

Hazely aimed her gun again and squeezed the trigger. The lock blew out and she opened the door. The large room had various tools hung throughout—all had a large coating of dust on them. There were three desks and five chairs. It looked as though, when the foundry went under, the people operating it just up and left without any regard for the equipment it contained.

Hazely was exhausted: mentally and physically. All she wanted to do was to curl up in a ball and go to sleep, but she knew that wasn't going to happen. With a sigh she threw the book down on one of the desks and sat in a chair. Fay and Pelissier did the same.

After a moment of silent reprieve Fay got up and went over to Pelissier and started to help bandage his arm.

"Do you need help there?" Hazely asked.

"No. I think I have it."

Hazely nodded and slid her chair up to the desk where she opened the book. She began thumbing through its pages, mainly looking at the pictures again as she couldn't read the content. It was clear to her that this creature was connected to the full moon but, now that The Pact was broken, it was free from that restriction.

She flipped more pages and saw more depictions of the creature but nothing came clear to her. She looked over at Fay who appeared to be almost done with Pelissier.

The little poem that Lieutenant Matan read from the book kept coming to mind, but she couldn't remember the details of it. The one phrase she did remember was when it spoke about the werewolf being a walker of the night and something about daylight, but she couldn't recall the details.

She found the page that the Lieutenant referenced, but it just looked like gibberish to her.

Hazely sighed. *Maybe Fay would be able to muddle his way through it?*

She looked over at him and Pelissier. "When you're done over there, I could use some help reading this," she announced.

Fay looked up for a moment then went back to his work. When he finished wrapping Pelissier's arm with a field dressing he stood up and came over. "What is it?"

"Can you translate what this is saying?" she asked as she pointed at some of the text on the page. "Particularly near the end here. It said something about walking at night and shunning the daytime."

She pointed to a picture of the wolf on the next page standing with its arms outstretched and staring at the full moon.

Fay looked at the book and began skimming his finger across the text she had pointed to. "This is hard to read. It's in French, but it's so old that I'm not sure what it's saying exactly. It looks like some sort of warning but ..."

"But what?"

He shook his head. "But I can't be sure. Maybe it's just telling the one who turns into this thing that he has to sleep during the day? I ... I don't know."

"But why would it be worded as a warning?"

"That's just it, I'm not sure it is," Fay responded. "The language is really archaic."

Hazely sighed. "Well do you think you could look through more of it and see if you recognize anything that could help us?"

Fay looked into her eyes. He must have seen the desperation there and nodded. "I'll try."

He flipped through more of the pages and continued to scan, then stopped on a certain passage. Hazely looked at him expectantly. When he didn't say anything she asked, "What is it?"

"I think it says that it only stalks at night which confirms our assumption, but I can't be sure. But look here." He pointed to a picture that depicted the werewolf retreating into hiding at the rising of the sun. "It also says something about the full moon. I think it's only supposed to come out in the full moon. If that's the case then why is it out now?"

Hazely knew the answer to that. "It's because the Pact that it made with the town is broken and now it's free to come out every night." Celeste had told her that terrible truth, and she was sure that the actual document vaporized in her hand when she took it from the Mayor.

Fay looked at her. He seemed like he wasn't sure what to say at that, or if he should say anything at all.

"I found The Pact in the possession of the Mayor after the werewolf had killed him. Someone had told me that it had been broken and the paper burned up right in front of me."

"I don't understand."

"I mean, it's like any contract. If any party breaks the deal then it's null-and-void."

"And how was this one broken?" Fay asked.

Tears welled up in Hazely's eyes. She quickly turned away and wiped them with the sleeve of her jacket. "It's because I was here during the full moon and found out about their secret."

Fay looked at her curiously.

"After that, the only way for them to restore what was broken was for them to kill me before the next night, which they failed to do. I'm the reason this thing is now loose. I'm the reason it's killing everyone. The reason it killed Isabella and the rest of the town."

"Who's Isabella?"

"Never mind," she replied more sharply than she intended.

Hazely looked up at Fay, but his face was unreadable—cold. Hazely wasn't sure if he was on the verge of an explosion, or if he was passive about her part in this. At that moment she resigned herself to whatever judgement anyone would lay on her. She just didn't care anymore. She was weary—spent—and just wanted the nightmare to end, even if she had to die in order to bring it to a close.

Hazely sat in silence staring up at the soldier for a long while, trying to comprehend what she had done.

Fay's penetrating gaze and steely look bore into her. After a long awkward moment he turned away and walked over to Pelissier. "What's done is done," he replied coldly.

The words cut through her. Could she ever be forgiven for what she did: unleashing all the death in the valley? The entire town had been killed and most of the Alpine Hunters.

Anger suddenly welled up in her and she balled her hands into fists and slammed them down on the desk.

Fay and Pelissier shot their heads in her direction, startled by her outburst and probably a little concerned about the noise she was making.

"You're right," she said through gritted teeth. "What's done is done, and now we need to kill that bastard."

She glanced over at Fay. The man clenched his jaw and nodded slightly.

"And I'm sure this book has something to say about—" Her words faded off as a low growl drifted into the old room.

"Captain! Captain!" he heard as though someone was calling him from a distance. "Captain!" The call was closer now and his eyes fluttered open. He could feel someone shaking him. His body ached, and he wasn't even sure if what he was feeling was real. The last image in his mind was that of the creature's arm laying a few feet away. His eyes opened more and he could see a battered Lieutenant Matan staring down at him. His voice still seemed distant, but eventually his vision cleared and his ears responded fully to the call. He coughed a couple times and lifted his arm to the Lieutenant's shoulder.

Lieutenant Matan smiled. "Are you okay?"

"I'm ... I ... think so." In truth, he wasn't sure but he knew he would find out as soon as he tried to stand.

With help from the Lieutenant he was pulled to his feet. It didn't feel like anything was broken. He had a splitting headache. He put a hand to the back of his head. When he pulled it back around he noticed a little bit of blood there, but it wasn't significant. He felt lucky at that moment as he recalled the force involved when he smashed his head on the wall.

"We killed it," he said in a shaky voice and managed a weak smile.

The Lieutenant looked at him grimly and shook his head. "No, we didn't," he responded.

The smile disappeared from Captain Roux's face.

"When I came to, I caught a glimpse of the monster slip into the shadows behind the building."

Captain Roux was too stunned to say anything.

"I think it's going after the book."

"The book? What do you mean?"

Lieutenant Matan seemed to collect his thoughts at that moment, looking around, then back to the Captain. "After Lamar and I hit it with a grenade, we were stalking it and, when we stopped at an intersection, we talked about it as being smart, and that it was toying with us, and ..." he paused.

"And what?"

"And I mentioned to Lamar that I read a little bit about it in the book that Hazely has. That's when we heard the roar and it seemed to totally ignore us and come after you and the others; but I think it was really after Hazely."

The Captain's eyes opened wide. "It understood you and changed its tactics?"

"I think so."

"Pelissier told me that he thought the creature understood the radio communications too," Captain Roux responded. "I think he was right. It heard the radio comms and knew that it had to get to Foxtrot team before they could call for help."

"It appears so, but it seems ridiculous that a creature from a few hundred years ago would even understand what we meant by calling for help, doesn't it? Or even understand English? But that's the only conclusion I can come to. Somehow it understands us, and that fact unnerves me almost as much as not being able to kill it."

"Then getting to the book is the most important objective of the creature right now," Captain Roux concluded.

Lieutenant Matan nodded. "It probably figured you and I were dead, or at least out of the fight, and that it needed to get to Hazely before she discovers its secret in the book."

"Then we have to get to them quickly!" Captain Roux replied with urgency but, when he went to bend down to grab his rifle, he nearly fell over.

Lieutenant Matan grabbed a hold of him and pushed him firmly up against the wall. "Easy Cap. You're not going anywhere in that condition."

Captain Roux pushed the Lieutenant's hand away. "I'm okay. I just need a second to get my bearings."

The Lieutenant nodded and bent down and retrieved the Captain's rifle for him. Captain Roux grabbed a hold of the stock and held the weapon in close. He took a couple deep breaths then nodded to the Lieutenant to indicate that he was ready. With tremendous effort he pushed off from the wall. At first he felt as though he was going to fall again, but the feeling quickly went away and he was able to take another step, then another, then another.

Moments later he was at the ground-floor window with Lieutenant Matan looking through with his light. There was no sign of anyone, but the sill was coated with blood. He figured it was probably the creature's. He would have been hopeful if this was a regular wolf, but he knew that, even at this moment, the monster was reforming all its parts and healing the rest of its injuries. That thought—the thought of the futility of fighting such a thing—almost knocked him back down, but he shook it away with the knowledge that the creature was scared of Hazely having that book. There had to be a reason behind that.

The Captain climbed through the window and, shortly after he landed, Lieutenant Matan joined him.

"Where to now?" the Lieutenant asked.

As soon as the words were out of his mouth a roar echoed down the hall to their right and the Captain knew they had their answer.

25

HOPELESSNESS

JUNE 22ND, 1989

The roar bounced off the walls of the maintenance room. Hazely fumbled with her flashlight and managed to flick it off as she desperately scooted down behind the desk. Pelissier and Fay did the same. Hazely's heart began to race; it felt as though her chest would explode. *Calm*, she told herself. *You need to relax.* Her breathing came in short quick gasps and her hands trembled violently. She put them under her butt and started to try and control her breathing. A few moments later she could feel her heart rate come down and her hands stopped shaking. Slowly, she pulled them out from under her and reached to the top of the desk, blindly feeling around for the book.

A violent rattle in the distance caused her to flinch and pull back. She knew the werewolf had found them and was trying to get in the room. A tear streaked down her cheek. Suddenly a bright light shined in her face causing her to back away into the wall.

"Hey," Fay said as he crouched beside her. "I don't think hiding in the dark is going to do any good for us. This thing hunts at night right?"

Hazely nodded.

"Then I think one of us should go and find the switches to turn the power on, if there's even power still coming to this building. At least if we can see too we might have a better chance of escaping."

Hazely thought about his logic for a moment. It did seem plausible that this creature would have superior night vision which would put them at a severe disadvantage. It seemed like as good a plan as any. "Okay. What's the plan then?"

"The plan is that I'll sneak out before that thing gets through the door and find the main power switch. Once I turn it on, you two come out and we'll try and sneak around it when it gets in the room and find a better place to hide."

"That doesn't sound like much of a plan," Hazely remarked. "But it's better than just sitting here and waiting for the thing to get us."

Fay nodded then slipped out of the maintenance crib and into the mechanical room.

As soon as the man left Hazely flicked on her light again, grabbed the book off the table, then scrambled over to where Pelissier was. The throttling on the door got louder, then there was a distinctive cracking sound as the doors were being ripped from their hinges.

Pelissier was huddled in a corner when Hazely got to him. He flinched when he heard the doors break.

"It's okay," she said to him. "Fay is going to get the power on for us so we can at least see where we're going. Once he does, we need to make a break for it. You got that?"

Pelissier seemed to solidify at that moment and nodded. He grabbed the rifle that Fay had left for him in his off-hand.

"Okay. Let's get to the door of the crib and get ready," Hazely said. She turned from the man and led them to the gate. Once there, she turned off her light again and crouched down just behind the fence by the door. Pelissier slid in beside her. There, they waited.

Fay slipped between the equipment and headed for the motor control centers: tall steel boxes that housed the breakers for power distribution. He hoped the main power switch would be there that would bring in the electricity from outside to the rest of the building.

He made it to the electrical cabinets—the MCC's. The rattling at the door continued until he heard a loud crack as the doors must have broken. The fact that the creature had found them so quickly unnerved him.

Sweat dripped down his brow as he frantically panned his way up and down the gear. He heard more cracking and then heavy footfalls coming into the room. The werewolf seemed to be out of its element as it sounded as though it banged into tables and equipment as it tried to maneuver its large body through the shop. That didn't surprise Fay at all as the creature, by nature, was designed for the outside.

Frantically, he read the labels on the doors of the units until his eyes fell upon one that said "Main Breaker." He looked above the unit and saw that large thick cables came down from the roof and fed into the top of this electrical panel. He knew this was it. He reached for the handle of the breaker when suddenly a stench hit him: a stench of death itself!

He turned his flashlight to the side and flinched back. The beast narrowed its yellow eyes at him.

Fay reached for the switch. The werewolf roared and came in at him. He felt a sharp pain erupt in his side as the dagger-like claws tore into his flesh.

Hazely heard the roar coming from the other side of the room where Fay had disappeared to. She brought her light to life, looked to Pelissier, then ran from the crib. Pelissier raised his rifle and followed close behind. Another roar rang out and Hazely could see a form moving in the distance as her light jostled around when she weaved between machinery, tables, and shelves.

Within moments she saw the back of the werewolf. It lifted its arm, claws held high.

Bang! Bang! Bang!

Hazely saw the muzzle flashes come from the other side of the werewolf and knew that Fay must be fighting for his life.

The creature flinched back for a moment then looked like it was about to dive back in. Pelissier stepped in front of her, levelled his rifle, and began firing. Some bullets hit the creature and some ricocheted off the surrounding equipment. Hazely put her hands on her head and ducked down when she heard the ringing of the bullets bouncing off the equipment.

The monster spun on them and Hazely could see in its murderous eyes that they had gotten its attention. She backed up as Pelissier continued to fire. It flinched back with each hit, then jerked forward as Fay shot at it from behind.

It roared! Then its large eyes looked from Pelissier to her to ... the book. When it saw the book it took a step forward, its eyes not leaving Hazely. She stepped backward, seeing its intent.

Pelissier put his rifle on a nearby table and tried to reload, but with one good arm the process was slow as he stumbled to pull the magazine out from his webbing.

The thing stalked forward, accepting more shots at its back. Hazely didn't know what to do. She knew it had come for her. It wanted the book back, she could see that now; could see it in its hateful eyes. It was mere feet from them and stood up to its full seven foot height. Hazely had never felt so minuscule and unimportant than at that terrible moment. She knew she was dead, they all were.

It opened its maw wide and issued the most blood-curdling roar she had heard up to that point then ... the lights flickered then flared to life! The creature seemed stunned by the sudden brightness and even shrank back, blocking its eyes from the glow and appeared to be in distress for a moment as the bright lights beamed down on it.

Hazely saw a glimpse of Fay fall to the ground behind the werewolf and heard a moan come from the man.

Pelissier had finished loading his rifle and began emptying the clip into the side of the creature.

"We need to get out of here!" Hazely screamed to Pelissier, knowing that their bullets only slowed it down at best.

"Not without Fay!" Pelissier screamed back.

The beast growled, stepped forward, and backhanded Pelissier in the chest. The blow lifted the solider from his feet and sent him flying through the air. He spun awkwardly then smashed into a metal shelf before crumbling onto a drill press with a sickening crack. He slid onto the floor and laid there, unmoving.

Hazely wanted to run, but instead she pulled her gun and aimed at the monster. She knew it would do nothing but she had to try. She was about to pull the trigger as the wolf hunched over and appeared as though it was getting ready to pounce when it took a round in the side of the head; the impact causing it to snap to the side violently. She glanced over and saw the Captain and Lieutenant there, hollering for her to run. The distraction was all she needed to slip around the beast and behind the Captain and Lieutenant.

"Go!" Captain Roux yelled. "We'll be right behind you."

Hazely ran. She charged into the hallway and turned right, running with as much speed as she could muster. Shots echoed from the maintenance room and a horrifying roar, the sound of which eclipsed that of the machine-gun fire, bounced from the room and down the hall. She got to the stairs which led to the upper-floor offices and, without thinking, she bounded up them two at a time.

She burst through the first room she saw. There were large windows overlooking the plant floor and an old desk sat just off to her left, two couches lined the walls, and a few broken office chairs lay strewn about.

She heard more gun fire and another roar, but couldn't tell if it was closer than before. Hazely ran to the window and looked out onto the massive plant, noting the various train cars which were being assembled before the foundry shut down. She was about to turn away when suddenly she saw the wall explode down below, across from where the maintenance room was. A form flew through the air and landed hard on the concrete floor. Amazingly, whoever it was stood up on shaky feet. Then she saw the beast step through the wall and stand before the doomed man. The man didn't have his rifle anymore, and, as the dust settled, she saw him pull a large knife from a sheath that hung on his belt.

The creature stalked in and the man stared it down. She couldn't tell who it was, but she knew he was going to die. Hazely frantically looked around for something, anything. She knew she had to help, and she knew the creature was after *her*.

Hazely put the book down on the desk and grabbed one of the chairs. She lifted it into the air and ran at the window, swinging, and smashing it into the glass and through it. The chair flew the twenty feet down to the concrete floor and splintered apart on impact.

The beast and the man—who she now recognized as Fay—looked up at her. She grabbed the book and began waving it out the window. "Is this what you want you bastard!" she yelled at the creature. "Come and get it!"

The werewolf narrowed its large eyes and turned toward her. Fay took the opportunity and shoved his knife into the beast's neck. With frightening strength the monster back-handed him. Fay went flying away as though he was a mere puppet.

Shots fired from the hole in the wall and hit the creature. The wolf flinched and roared. But his attention was still fixed on Hazely. It began walking in her direction and she just knew that it was going to try and leap through the window at her.

She backed away and started to look around frantically. She knew she couldn't outrun it or fight it. Her only option was evasion. Hazely looked up at the ceiling and saw a large air duct opening. Without another thought she pushed the desk under it and leaped on top. She was just barely tall enough to pull the cover free, but did manage to get it popped open.

More gunfire and another roar, which sounded much closer now, resounded. Hazely leaped and threw the book up into the shaft. She then took another jump and grabbed the edge of the duct. Her fingers slipped and she fell back down on the desk. She jumped again and managed a better hold. She used every ounce of strength she had and was able to get her elbows up over the ledge, but her energy was spent and she couldn't get up over the lip.

The sound of crunching glass came to her ears and she lost her concentration and slipped back down into the room. She landed on the desk hard. Hazely looked over and saw the massive claws of the creature gripping the windowsill. It pulled its canine head over the lip and looked around. It spotted her and narrowed its hateful eyes. Its lips curled up into a snarl revealing those murderous fangs. It easily pulled its head up into the window.

Hazely froze. It was mere feet from her and she knew she couldn't escape. Her mouth went dry and her heart raced.

She knew that her life was about to end. She would never experience another sunrise. She would never have that relationship with a man that she so desired but that always evaded her. She would never feel anything again. All was hopelessness.

All was darkness.

All was at its end.

26

INTO THE DUCT

JUNE 22ND, 1989

Despair like she had never before felt sank down into Hazely's very soul. She was about to commit her fate to the rage of the creature when ... Bang! Bang! Bang! Bang! Click. The bullets hit the beast with such force they rocked its head back and it appeared to be losing its grip.

A man yelled and charged into the room right at the monster. It was Lieutenant Matan! He sprinted to the window and spartan kicked the beast across the jaw. He winced slightly with the impact but recovered quickly. It lost more of its grip, but still held on stubbornly. It tried to whip its head around and snap its maw at the Lieutenant but the man now held his rifle like a bat and levelled blow after blow across the jaw of the creature causing its head to rock back and forth. Lieutenant Matan yelled as he beat the beast, but the thing wouldn't let go. It snapped and grabbed the rifle in its massive maw. With one twitch of its powerful neck muscles it yanked the weapon from his hands and threw it to the floor of the foundry.

The wolf looked hatefully at the Lieutenant and growled. It seemed oblivious—or just didn't care—about the item Lieutenant Matan now held in his hand.

With a flick of his wrist he lobbed the grenade into the air just above the beast then ran back toward Hazely who was now up again.

The creature scrambled to get into the room but the wood of the sill tore apart under its weight. The grenade came down just under the outside of the window. The explosion rocked the room and the beast roared as the shrapnel tore into its flesh. The Lieutenant dove toward the desk and Hazely lost her balance and fell back down, sliding off the hard surface and onto the floor on the other side. The blast dislodged the creature from the windowsill and sent it careening back down the twenty feet to the concrete floor of the foundry.

Hazely laid there for a moment trying to get the breath back into her lungs. That moment seemed a lot longer than the mere seconds it actually took.

"Are you okay?" she heard the Lieutenant ask, then saw his face peering over the top of the desk at her.

"Ya. I think so.'

"Good. Then we have to go. That blast won't keep the creature down for long." The Lieutenant offered her his hand. "I hope you've discovered something that will help us kill this thing, because we've thrown everything at it and it still keeps coming."

Hazely took his hand and pulled herself up. "Nothing yet, but I did notice that, when Fay got the lights on, it seemed more than unnerved by them."

"What? Like it gets hurt by them, or just doesn't like them?"

"I don't know. I was going to hide in the ventilation system and hopefully figure something out," she said, pointing up to where the vent was open. "I figured that the creature was too big to get in there which would give me some time to think about it."

The Lieutenant nodded. "Good idea. It certainly seems bent on getting that book back." Suddenly, a panicked look came across his face. "Where is it?"

"Up there." Hazely pointed again into the shaft, then she jumped back up and grabbed the edge.

With help from the Lieutenant she scrambled up into the narrow steel shaft. A moment later, Lieutenant Matan was with her in the tight space. He reached back around and pulled the duct-opening closed and latched it again. "Which way?" he asked, looking back at Hazely who now had her flashlight back in her hand.

"I don't think it matters," she whispered back, then began crawling away as fast as she could go.

She made it about twenty feet or so when she suddenly stopped and turned back to the Lieutenant, her flashlight illuminating his face. "What did you say back there?" she asked.

The Lieutenant looked at her with a confused expression.

"You know, after you hit it with the grenade? You said that it won't keep it down for long."

"Yyyes ..." Lieutenant Matan replied, obviously unsure of where she was going with the thought.

"Maybe that's it. Maybe we just need to keep knocking it down—slowing it down—until sunrise?" She shifted around as much as she could in the tight space so she could face the Lieutenant more fully.

"The book is pretty specific that this werewolf can only come out at night right? There was that line you read which said *the daylight you must shun*. And the sudden exposure to bright light in the maintenance room unnerved it until it probably realized that it wasn't daylight.

"Think about it. This thing is from the seventeenth century and, even though it seems smart, must be still constrained intellectually by the man it was when it transformed back then. Meaning that it has no knowledge of modern technology except for the interactions it's been having with us." She thought of Celeste and her response to the gun.

"But how then could it have understood Lamar and I?" Lieutenant Matan asked. "It would only know a really old dialect of French."

Her thoughts again went back to her encounter with Celeste in the room under the church. She didn't have any answers, but knew that a creature who used to be a man from the seventeenth century understanding modern French or English wasn't the strangest thing she'd seen all day. "It just does," was the only answer she could give him.

"So what you're saying is that we just need to survive until sunrise?"

Hazely nodded.

"Okay then. Sounds simple."

The Lieutenant's sarcasm wasn't lost on her.

Lieutenant Matan looked at his watch. "Okay, it's 05:07. Sunrise is a little more than a half hour away."

"Great. So all we have to do is survive until then and, hopefully, the werewolf will be forced to retreat."

"That sounds easy enough," the Lieutenant responded dryly.

Hazely just shook her head then turned and led the way through the ducting, turning right, then left, then left again. She had no idea where they were, but that didn't matter to her. Her only thought was to get as far away from the creature as possible. She knew that it would probably be able to track them down with its heightened senses and that thought didn't sit well with her at all.

More than once they came to other vent panels which led into different rooms. When she approached these hatches she would creep up slowly, stop, and listen to see if anything was stirring below. Lieutenant Matan would wait patiently until she declared that it was clear.

After that, she would carefully climb over the panel and move on. They ran into a few of those rooms before the second left turn, then it seemed as though it was one dark tunnel.

After crawling for what seemed a long while she stopped and turned to look back at the Lieutenant who was right on her heels.

"What is it?" Lieutenant Matan asked.

"Do you think we lost it?"

The Lieutenant shook his head. "I don't know. But I really don't want to stop to find out."

Hazely offered him a forced smile before turning back and leading on. A few minutes later she came to another hatch. The light coming from this one was dimmer than all the previous ones. She slowed up as she approached. The panel itself was a lot larger than the other ones. She looked up and also saw light coming through vented slats from the end, about twenty feet away and knew that it was the vent that led to the outside. With the sunrise coming soon, she hoped she and Lieutenant Matan could make it outside and be protected by the sunlight if her theory was correct.

As she got near it she looked through the slats and saw that they were up high, really high. Her heart leaped in her chest as she realized that they were crawling across the factory floor, probably at least forty feet off the ground.

"What is it?" she heard the Lieutenant ask as her mind spun with the realization of where they were.

"Hazely?" she heard and realized that it probably wasn't the first time he had called her name.

"We're over top the plant floor," she replied. "It's pretty high and the panel is wide. Not to mention the fact that this foundry was probably closed about twenty years ago and that no one has serviced it since." She could feel the panic rising in herself, which definitely wasn't normal for her. She was fearless … wasn't she?

"It's okay," Lieutenant Matan reassured. "I know you can do this. I'm with you all the way."

Hazely swallowed hard. She didn't like heights at all, and the thought of getting across the grate, and the fact that they were sitting in a thirty-plus year old metal duct, didn't sit with her well. "What is wrong with you?" she whispered to herself.

"What was that?" the Lieutenant asked from behind.

"Nothing," she responded quickly.

After a couple deep breaths Hazely tossed the book across the grate. It hit the other side with a dull thud then slid about three more feet until coming to a stop. She reached out her hand over the slatted area and felt around, testing its strength. The grate seemed solid enough. Looking at the length of it she figured she only needed to be supported fully by the grate for a second or two if she hurried.

With one last breath she crawled as fast as she could across the hinged section. Just as she placed her hand on the solid part of the duct on the other side she heard a snapping sound and felt herself falling!

She let out a yelp as her legs and body swung through the opening. Her hands slipped from their hold. As she slid down the grate she managed to slip her fingers through the last rung which yanked her arms violently and caused the steel to bite into her fingers. She let out a terrified scream as she hung there, suspended over the concrete deathtrap.

Her arms and hands throbbed with pain, but she didn't dare let go. Her heart raced, threatening to pound through her chest at any moment.

"Hazely!" she heard the Lieutenant yell and looked up to see him staring at her from the duct.

She tried to pull herself up, but the energy seemed to be rapidly fleeing from her. Lieutenant Matan reached his hand out, but couldn't reach nearly close enough to grab onto her.

"You're going to have to climb Hazely," he called to her.

Hazely nodded weakly, but wasn't sure she would have the strength to pull herself up—not with how much her arms and hands ached. She could feel something warm running down her wrist and into her jacket sleeve and just knew that it was blood.

"Come on Hazely. You can do this!" she heard the Lieutenant yell.

Then she heard the all-too-familiar low resonating growl. Her heart leaped again, and she managed to turn her head to see the massive wolf standing in the broken window of the second floor room she and the Lieutenant barely escaped from just minutes before.

They had moved quite a distance through the ducting away from the room and were now well above and distanced from that second floor window, but somehow Hazely knew that it wouldn't stop the monster from getting her.

It leaped down to the main floor and slowly stalked toward where she was hanging, its intelligent eyes darted back and forth and she just knew that it was formulating a plan as to how to catch its prey.

"Oh god," she said aloud as she began to scramble to get the next hold.

"Come on!" the Lieutenant urged.

Somehow, Hazely found new strength and began to pull herself up, one slat at a time. The blood ran more freely and the pain intensified, but she knew she had to climb—she had to climb or be killed.

The beast jumped on top of the roof of one of the half-made railcars. It creaked and groaned under the werewolf's massive weight. That still put Hazely about thirty feet above the beast, and the car was about twenty feet away from being under the ducting, but somehow Hazely knew she wasn't safe—she wasn't safe at all.

She swung and grabbed onto the next slat. The metal dug into her already injured hands. She grunted with the effort. She went for the next slat and one of the hinges broke off causing her to swing awkwardly. Hazely looked up at the Lieutenant and she could see distress in his eyes. He tucked back into the duct. Was he leaving her? Of course he was leaving her. Just when she thought she could depend on the people around her, they left her. Just like her sister. Just like her Dad. Just like her Mother. Tears stung her eyes as she struggled to control her unbalanced swing. It was just her. Her gaze landed on the beast, backed up and hunched on all fours. Her and the monster. There would always be a monster

The werewolf snarled and looked like he was going to break into a great run with its powerful legs.

She swung and glanced up. The hope had all but fled from her. Either she was going to fall to her death, or the creature was going to leap up and tear her from her perch. Then she felt something on her hand. She looked up and saw a leather belt.

"Wrap your hand around this!" the Lieutenant yelled at her.

He had come back!

A roar shattered the air.

Hazely let go with her right hand and grabbed for the swinging belt. After the second attempt she caught hold of it and wrapped the belt one turn around her hand.

"Now let go!" Lieutenant Matan yelled.

Hazely let go of the grate and desperately grabbed at the belt with her other hand. She swung around as she struggled to hold on, being supported by the Lieutenant, and, as she turned, her eyes widened.

The creature was mere feet from her, having sprang from its previous perch. Its murderous gaze fixed upon her.

27

MISSILE STRIKE

JUNE 22ND, 1989

Hazely shrieked.

The creature roared as it soared through the air; its long, sharp, claws reaching for her. She felt herself being pulled up but knew she wasn't going to make it: the wolf's momentum was too much for her.

She stared it in the eyes as it got closer—those hateful, cruel, evil ... almost human eyes. There was a man in there she knew; a man that she could almost sense wanted out, wanted release. Was he trapped in a prison of his own making? Was he forced to kill month after month *ad infinitum*?

No. If there was a man, he died a long time ago. Now, there was only the creature. The relentless, murderous, beast.

As she stared down death she felt a new surge of adrenaline and pulled up on the belt as hard as she could. The claws came in at her. One caught her in the thigh, opening up four lines of blood, tearing easily through her jeans. Hazely screamed out when the dagger-like claws ripped into her tender flesh, but that made the Lieutenant pull even harder. He yanked her up and into the ducting in one final heave. The other clawed-hand raked the duct as the creature flew by. It shredded the metal like it was nothing more than paper mâché and tore the door off the vent.

Hazely landed hard on the Lieutenant. She laid there for a moment trying not to pass out from the pain she felt in her thigh.

"Are you hurt bad?" the Lieutenant asked, moving her aside and trying to inspect the cuts.

"I … I think I'm okay," Hazely managed to reply.

There was a loud creak, then the whole ducting shuddered. The Lieutenant braced himself and looked around as though he thought the whole shaft would plummet at any moment. Hazely looked back to the other side of the torn duct and saw the book sliding toward the opening, as that section was now slanting downward due to the damage the creature had inflicted on the whole structure. Before she thought about what she was doing she spun around, ignored the pain in her leg, and leaped for the other side.

"Hazely!" she heard the Lieutenant scream.

She landed with her elbows and upper body inside the duct while her legs dangled precariously out, then quickly shimmied herself into it. Hazely grabbed the book then looked back. She heard a deafening roar and saw the Lieutenant leap from the other side. Just as he pushed off the duct, it shifted down, stealing his momentum.

Hazely saw the man's eyes widen as he flailed around trying to grab onto anything he could. The werewolf slammed into the metal where the Lieutenant was a moment earlier. Its claws dug into it, shredding the structure. Welds snapped and popped as the metal gave way and the duct and creature plummeted to the hard ground below.

Hazely reached for the Lieutenant and grabbed his forearms. He had enough momentum to almost clear the opening and, with Hazely's help, he managed to climb in the rest of the way.

Hazely and the Lieutenant laid there trying to catch their breaths. She was about to say something when they heard a snap, and then felt the whole duct shift violently.

"Quickly! Move up as fast as you can!" the Lieutenant yelled, pushing her along.

They scrambled down the tunnel for about fifteen feet. She could see the light more clearly coming from the outside vent. They were almost there! Then the structure came loose; it swung down as the bolts and welds broke all along the line. Hazely and the Lieutenant screamed as they lost their footing and began sliding back toward the opening. She tried to brace herself, but there was nothing to hold onto, and the inside of the duct was too smooth to get a proper grip.

Hazely launched out the end after the Lieutenant. She let out a shriek as she flew through the air—legs and arms flailing widely—to land on the hard floor on top of the Lieutenant. They rolled as she slammed into the ground, trying to absorb some of the impact. She felt a sharp pain radiate up her legs from the shock. The two tumbled together in a mass of legs and arms. They came to a stop right beside a train car a short distance from where they exited the duct.

Her head pounded and her body ached all over, but Hazely knew they needed to get up; they needed to get up fast! She scrambled out from under the Lieutenant who was trying to reorient himself.

She looked around and saw the book a few feet from her. She was about to lunge out and grab it when she saw the werewolf land right behind it. Hazely flinched and scrambled back.

The beast hunched over the tome, looking at her with those penetrating eyes. Its lip curled up into a snarl as it bent over and picked up the book. Once in its grasp the werewolf pulled it in tight and cradled it to its chest, almost as though it were a close friend.

Hazely knew she should be retreating, trying to find a place of safety, but she was transfixed on the scene. At that moment she almost felt sorry for the pathetic creature—no, not creature—man, Vincent. He had been deceived all those centuries ago and now he lived this hellish life month after month after month.

The werewolf closed its eyes as it cradled the book, then suddenly opened them and cocked its head to the sky and issued a deep smooth howl.

The sound shook Hazely from her thoughts and caused her to scramble back. She felt a hand on her arm.

"Come on! We have to hide," Lieutenant Matan said, pulling her back.

She spun around and saw that he was tugging her toward a railcar which was mere feet from them. He slipped underneath, pulling her along.

Captain Roux heard a distant howl. His eyes fluttered open. He wasn't sure if the howl was a dream or not. His head throbbed and his left arm ached with pain as he came to realize that he was waking up after being knocked out … again.

He was laying behind a piece of equipment and crumpled against the corner of a shelving unit. He shook his head to try and clear the fog from his mind. As he became more conscious he remembered being backhanded by the creature and sent flying through the air. Hazely ran out of the room as he and his team were fighting the monster, but it overpowered them, or him, at least.

He rose on shaky feet and started to make his way toward the door. He stopped in his tracks when he heard the howl again. He had no idea if any of his men or Hazely were even still alive, but he had to find out. He had to do something, even if he died trying.

He took another step when the radio on his hip squelched. The speaker spoke in French! "Charlie Alpha Tango 3 come in. Charlie Alpha Tango 3 this is Zulu 5 8, please respond with your current location. We are here for evac."

The Captain's eyes went wide. "Cartier and Farrow," he mouthed, understanding that they must have made contact with the Base.

He grabbed the radio off his belt. "This is Captain Roux. It's good to hear you Zulu 5 8!"

"Where are you Captain?"

"We're in the foundry up on the hill. Hurry, the enemy is still in play and we need immediate evac."

"Understood. ETA is two minutes."

~

Hazely and Lieutenant Matan looked at each other as they heard the communication over their radios. His eyes lit up for a moment then he shrank back as the massive creature stopped howling and bent down to stare at them under the railcar.

The Lieutenant grabbed his radio. "This is Lieutenant Matan. Captain. Do you read me? We are under a railcar in the factory," he yelled in English.

"I read you," came the Captain's reply a moment later. "I'm coming. We're going home."

"Negative. The creature is still stalking us."

The werewolf growled.

"Hold tight. I'm coming."

"What? Who was that on the radio, and what did they say?" Hazely asked, trying to inch as far back under the car as possible. The creature crouched down, set the book on the ground, and slowly stepped toward them.

"It's our evac. Zulu 5 8 is two minutes out."

Hazely's eyes lit up for a moment then she saw a shadow cross the Lieutenant's face as they looked out from under the car. The stench of death that was so familiar with this creature floated under the car to hit her and drain the little hope Hazely had left.

"We might not last two minutes," the Lieutenant stated. "That is an eternity, and I'm not sure how much help the Captain can provide."

The werewolf was mere feet from the car now, and its growl turned into a bloodcurdling snarl.

Hazely knew he was right, but she didn't know what else to do. She glanced around from under the railcar and noticed something curious. She saw what looked like beams of sunlight coming down from the ceiling. The duct that was attached to the roof must have pulled some of the wall—and maybe a portion of the ceiling—in with it, making holes which allowed the sunlight to come rushing through. It was sunrise!

She watched the werewolf closely and noticed that the creature paused for a moment when it came across a beam of light and carefully backed away from it, then looked up to where the light had come from.

The monster looked back toward them, but seemed confused—almost torn. It looked like it would enjoy nothing more than to tear them apart, but it also portrayed something Hazely hadn't seen in it yet: fear.

It shook its head and advanced another step.

Hazely was about to inch back more under the car when she heard a shot ring out. The creature flinched to the side and turned to face its attacker.

Bang!

It took another round in the body. With a roar it stood up and stepped toward the attacker, but inadvertently stepped into one of the beams of light. It yelped and pulled its leg out of the beam.

Hazely could smell something burn. She looked at the Lieutenant who glanced back, wide-eyed.

Bang!

The creature avoided the beams and began moving with greater speed toward the Captain.

"It doesn't just shun the light," Hazely gasped. "Sunlight hurts it!"

"Come on!" Lieutenant Matan cried as he unholstered his handgun and climbed out from under the railcar with renewed vigor.

Hazely wasn't sure what they could do. If the thing

avoided direct contact with the light then it could still tear them apart. All the Lieutenant had left for a weapon was a sidearm and his knife. That wasn't going to help much against this thing.

She scurried out from under the railcar. Her eyes immediately fell on the book that now lay on the floor. Hazely then looked to the left and saw a battered and bleeding Captain Roux firing single shots into the creature as it continued to advance on him.

She glanced at the book again, then at the beams of light coming through the many cracks in the wall and ceiling. Without another thought Hazely ran over and grabbed the book. She then went to one of the larger beams of light and began waving it in the air. "Over here! Vincent! I have what you want! Come and get it!" she yelled.

The Lieutenant glanced at her as he aimed his pistol at the back of the werewolf. "What are you doing?" he yelled.

"Trying to get its attention. Get it to come over here."

"You don't even know if that's going to work," he retorted.

"Just do it!"

The Lieutenant sighed and started firing into the back of the creature.

It flinched and whipped its head around. Its eyes narrowed on Hazely, but then it took another two rounds from Captain Roux on the other side, and spun back to him.

"It's not working!" Lieutenant Matan yelled. "Do you have any other ideas?"

Hazely didn't know what to do. If they had any hope of surviving they had to get the wolf into the light, but it wasn't taking the bait. Then a crazy idea popped into her head. She grabbed the radio from her belt.

"Zulu 5 8, you need to blow the roof off the foundry!"

"Qui est la?"

Hazely saw the creature running faster for the Captain who was firing back more aggressively now. He was about to die. "You need to blow the roof off this building or we're all going to die!"

The Lieutenant stared at Hazely for a moment, then must have understood what she was thinking as he grabbed his own radio. "Zulu 5 8, ici Lieutenant Mathan. Faites comme prévu!" he yelled into the radio.

There was a moment of silence that felt like an eternity.

"Zulu 5 8, bien reçu, missiles largués."

"Captain! Take cover!" Lieutenant Matan yelled as he scrambled back under the railcar. Hazely saw the creature close in on the Captain, but she couldn't make out if he had heard the command or not.

Suddenly the building rocked as an explosion erupted from above. Hazely dropped the book and dove under the car. Lieutenant Matan grabbed her, and the two huddled as a second explosion rocked the place. Debris fell and dust shattered the air.

Hazely coughed, and she could hear pieces of the building shift and crumble. The rumbling and crashing seemed to last forever then, after one final shudder, it all stopped. Wisps of dust and smoke swirled through the air.

After a moment she pulled back from Lieutenant Matan and looked out from under the railcar. Surprisingly, as the dust settled, Hazely saw that there was an opening for her to climb out from under the car.

Hazely and Lieutenant Matan picked their way carefully out from under their steel shelter. Large beams laid strewn about, cracked timbers stood in awkward angles—some of them were smouldering from the heat of the missiles while others were splintered into thousands of pieces.

The solid stone and steel walls that made up the main structure of the foundry still stood, although all the windows were blown from their sills.

Hazely's ears rang. She thought she could hear the sound of a helicopter, but wasn't sure. Suddenly she felt the wash of the blades as it flew over top the building. She looked up and saw that the sun continued its rise, slowly dissipating the shadows within the blown up structure. Then she heard shifting debris in the direction the werewolf had ran when it attacked Captain Roux. Her heart leaped as she saw a large piece of timber thrown to the side followed by the all-too-familiar throaty growl of the wolf.

She fully turned to where the creature was emerging and was about to walk in that direction when the Lieutenant grabbed her arm.

"What are you doing?" he asked, concern edging his voice.

"I want to see it." Hazely couldn't believe she said the words. She had spent the last two days running from the murderous creature—running for her life—but now ... now she didn't know what to think. Her mind rocked, and she felt like she was in a daze.

More timbers were thrown aside with incredible strength and Hazely could now see the massive paws with the wickedly curved claws emerge from the pile. Then its head came forth with those terrifying eyes. It spotted her and narrowed those eyes. Its lips curled back into a snarl as it climbed out from under the debris, but then the look on its face went from fierce to confused to pained.

Smoke began to rise from its body and it yelped.

Suddenly one of its arms transformed into what looked like the arm of the cross she had seen hanging in the church, then it turned into that of a human arm, and back to a wolf's arm. Its other limbs began to do the same thing. It whined and whimpered, trying to crawl away from the sun and find the shade again, but it couldn't.

Hazely could hear the sound of bones crunching as it contorted back and forth from cross, to man, to wolf. It tried to crawl forward but lost its balance and fell down on top of the debris. It howled, then shrieked—a very human shriek —then gurgled, then growled, then whimpered, as it continued to smoke and change.

Hazely walked forward and this time the Lieutenant didn't try to stop her. She came to within ten feet of the creature. It looked at her hatefully with the wolf's eyes, then the head transformed into that of an old man with long scraggly gray hair. His eyes were wide and wild as the rest of his body continued to twist and snap, but she didn't sense hatred in those eyes: the eyes of the man behind the beast. No. She sensed relief and ... was it gratitude?

"Merci," Hazely heard him whisper before he turned his eyes away from her. His face was locked in an expression of torture and pain, then his features began to twist into the wolf again but, before it was able to complete the transformation he screamed with the voice of a man and growled with the voice of the wolf before dropping and becoming very still.

Hazely looked down at the pitiful sight. Its entire body was twisted and contorted with portions of it in the shape of a man, others in the shape of a wolf, and the rest in the shape of a wooden crucifix.

She had no idea what she had just been through. It

didn't even feel real. But at that moment, looking at the grotesque mass in front of her, she didn't care.

She had survived.

She looked back at the Lieutenant and offered him a weak smile. He limped over to her and she wrapped him in a hug. All she wanted to do at that moment was to cry—was to release all the fear, anxiety, pain, hatred, and anger, but she couldn't. She felt numb.

The sound of shifting rubble to the side broke the two from their embrace. Dust still hung thick in the air, but through that dust they saw a hand, then a face emerge out from under the rubble.

"A little help here," the Captain said with a cough.

Hazely and Lieutenant Matan ran over and helped to dig him out. He was battered and bruised but appeared to be, for the most part, okay.

After being extricated Captain Roux sat down on the edge of a large piece of broken timber. He looked over at the two and just shook his head. "The next time you want to call in a missile strike on our location, could you please give me a little more warning?"

28

IMMORTALITY

JUNE 30TH, 1989

Hazely stared at the couple sitting across the desk from her. They stared back and looked as though she had just slapped them in the face. She knew they would never have believed her if she hadn't shown them the pictures of the mangled creature, the town, the helicopter, and the carnage.

"It's all true," she reiterated, and not for the first time. "I'm sorry. I don't know what to say. Jeremy was killed by something that defies explanation. A lot of people were killed ..." Her voice trailed off as she tried to choke back the tears. The images of the men who helped save her were still fresh in her mind: the men who had died.

Hazely wiped a stray tear from her eye. "I know this is a lot to process. You lost your son and I know that's not easy to accept, but at least now you can have some closure—"

"Closure!" Maria yelled, cutting her off as she stood up, clearly infuriated. "You think we can have closure with the fact that our son died, presumably at the hands of a monster! A monster that should only exist in legends and fairytales. Where are the newspaper stories about this, or … or the news casts?

"I can't accept this." She began to sob and slumped back down in the chair.

Her husband, Jonah, was quick to put a hand around her. "You'll have to forgive her," he started to say, but Hazely held up her hand.

"There's nothing to forgive," she stated. "I'd be angry too if I were you. You weren't there so how could you process what actually happened?

"You never saw those hateful eyes glaring down at you, or smelled the rotting stench of death, or saw someone torn apart right in front of you by razor sharp claws that cut through flesh as though it were butter."

Hazely stood up and shook her head. "No. You will never understand what your son felt right before he died at the hands of this … this thing." She motioned to the pictures that were strewn across her desk. "But I do." Her voice barely a whisper. "I understand Jeremy's last moments more keenly than you can imagine."

She wiped another tear from her eye then moved around to the side of her desk. "Now if you don't mind I have a lot of work to do."

Jonah looked up at her and she almost detected pity coming from him; or was it sadness? Was it sadness for the loss of Jeremy or sadness for her? She couldn't tell, but neither did she care. She just wanted them out of her office.

Without another word Jonah stood and helped Maria to her feet who was still sobbing in his arms. "We'll leave our final payment, Miss Silverston, with your secretary," he said. "Thank you for helping us understand what happened to Jeremy. We wish you well."

Hazely nodded.

The couple shambled out of her office and, as soon as the door was closed, Hazely lurched forward, clutching the corners of her desk, and began to cry. She tried to stop but that just made the cry uglier as her face twisted up and her sides began to hurt. Tears flowed in great rivers as she released all the emotions she had stored up and pushed down over the years. She now felt like a frightened child. The persona of a strong confident woman who would take on the world fled from her.

The werewolf had broken her. She had never felt so afraid of anything in her life. And now she saw its eyes in her dreams and in her waking moments. The wolf still stalked her—not physically—but mentally and emotionally. She felt as though its claws were piercing through her very soul, and that there was nothing she could do about it. She heard the whispers of Celeste and her haunting laughter.

After a few minutes Hazely composed herself enough to stumble back to her chair. She reached in one of her desk drawers and pulled out a bottle of scotch. She twisted the cap off and moved it toward her lips. The smell of the aged liquor wafted from the bottle giving her a good sniff of the bitter alcohol. She was about to take a long pull of the liquid, hoping to numb the pain and fear she felt, when she stopped.

Her mind suddenly flashed with the image of Ricard holding his nose after she had punched him in the face. Blood dripped freely down his arm and he yelled something in French, most likely profanities. That brought a smile to her face, not because she had caused harm to Ricard, but because he so willingly gave of himself to save her from hypothermia. He was a younger man. His youthful face was handsome, and his eyes sparkled with life and energy.

Then she saw the other men gather around as she felt the chill on her almost naked body. She saw the face of each and every Hunter and remembered what they all looked like that day in the forest in great detail: Cartier, Pelissier, Janvier, Voland, Kaplan, Farrow, Lamar, Faucheax, Fay, Chevrolet, Page, Captain Roux, and Lieutenant Matan. Without these men she wouldn't be alive right now.

Tears rolled freely down her cheeks again.

Then Hazely saw something out of the corner of her eye. She put the bottle down and looked over at the pictures she had strewn about the desk. Hazely moved them around so she could properly see them all. Her eyes went to the one with her, Lieutenant Matan, and Captain Roux at the headquarters after they had been rescued. The three looked like hell, but at least they were alive. The rest of the men and all of the townsfolk died at L'accord, but these two and her had survived. They had survived because they had each other and an indomitable will to live.

Hazely looked at the bottle for a moment then placed the cap back on it. She pushed it away from her, leaned into the desk, and picked up the picture. She knew they had survived because they had each other. They had each other's backs and they did what they had to in order to make it.

The thought rattled around her mind for many moments until she picked up the phone and dialed the number.

After ringing five times she heard a woman pick up the other line. "Hello."

Hazely didn't know what to say. She didn't even know how to start.

"Hello," the woman said again, a little more forcefully.

Hazely knew she was about to hang up and she needed to say something quick. "I get it," she blurted, not knowing what else to say.

"Hazely? Oh my god! Hazely? Is that you?"

Hazely tried to choke back the tears but couldn't. "Yeah. It's ... it's me Kristine," she replied through sobs. "Can we talk?"

The town was still abuzz with activity. Soldiers scoured every building at least three or four times in order to make sure they found every one of the massacred town's people. They even found three of them in the woods not far from town. It looked as though they were running away—trying to flee—when they were torn to pieces.

With the information Hazely had given them they found the makeshift graveyard outside of town. The military excavated all the graves and the forensic scientists began their long work of cataloguing the bodies for their records.

There was a large command tent set up by the foundry and military vehicles lined its parking lot. It had been only eight days since the event had taken place and, since there were no grounds on which to hold an American citizen, and by the testimony of Captain Roux and Lieutenant Matan that Hazely had been drawn into the events that led up to the L'accord massacre and not a participant in them, the woman had been allowed to return to the US.

The French government knew that if they ever needed to

find her again for further questioning they could easily do so. They also knew that word of this event would spread and, instead of trying to put a lid on it as the circumstances were outside of their understanding at the present time, they decided to not impose a gag order on the people who had experienced the event and those who came to clean it up. They would allow the tabloids and mainstream media access if they so desired. It would drive a lot of interest for a while then, like anything, die out in time. The only thing the government wouldn't give them access to is the remains of the creature. Eventually this whole event would probably be chalked up to the attack of some wild animal and people for generations would speculate as to what exactly happened here at L'accord.

The biggest concern the military had was for the families of the fallen soldiers. To them they explained the deaths as being from a wild animal during a training exercise which was pretty close to the truth. The nation of France would mourn for their fallen soldiers, but, in time, the people would move on to other business and other news.

"Let me know immediately when the extraction of all the dead is confirmed, Major," said Colonel Dupont—a tall man with short gray hair—as he stood from behind his desk. "It's a damn shame that something like this even happened. These men were on a training exercise and most of them were slaughtered like pigs!" he roared. He could feel his anger flare.

"Yes it is sir," replied the Major. He brushed a hand through his dark hair. "These are strange events. The Captain described something that came out of a horror movie. And the ah ... the ah ..."

"The find?" the Colonel finished for him.

"Yes sir, the *find*. It's more than convincing that the Captain's story is true."

The Colonel cocked an eyebrow. "Of course the Captain's story is true!" he shouted. "I've known Gabriel ever since he was a junior officer and he is one of the finest soldiers I have under my command. Every aspect of this tale is absolutely as he said it is."

"Yes sir."

"Which makes this all the more disturbing," the Colonel continued. "A beast like this is supposed to be make-believe. What if there are more of these things out there?"

The Major appeared not to know how to answer the question.

After a few heartbeats of awkward silence Colonel Dupont waved his hand dismissively. "There's no need for us to ponder that now, however. We have to first clean up this mess and, the sooner we are out of here, the better I will feel about this whole place."

The Major nodded and turned to leave. Before he could take a step to the door Colonel Dupont put a hand on his shoulder and stopped him. "John. I hope you cherish every moment you have with your wife and kids. You never know when tragedy will strike and it would be a damn shame to regret how we managed our affairs before an untimely death."

The Major turned his head around to look at the Colonel.

Colonel Dupont chuckled and waved his hand in order to defuse the tension. "Don't mind me John. Those are just the ramblings of an old man."

The Major smiled slightly and nodded, then stepped from the tent. As he departed, a private raced through the door holding something in his hands that was wrapped in a small canvas tarp. The Colonel looked at the man curiously. "What's that you have there private?"

The private stopped right before the Colonel, snapped to attention, and saluted. He appeared to be out of breath, but held his composure well. "Lieutenant St. Martin told me to bring this to you as fast as I could," the Private replied.

"What is it?" the Colonel asked again as he took it from the man and placed it on his desk.

"It's a book sir. A book that matches the description of the testimony of the Captain, Lieutenant, and the American."

The Colonel turned his head to see the private still at attention. "At ease soldier," he said, before turning back to the book and unwrapping it.

Colonel Dupont loved old books and when he saw this one his eyes lit up. It was large, and bound with aged leather. He brushed his hands over the intricate carvings and marveled at the handiwork. He then opened it up and brushed the dust off the parchment. The intricate penmanship was amazing! And he found the drawings remarkable.

He flipped through a number of the pages then closed up the tome. Colonel Dupont grabbed the edges of the cloth tarp and was about to pull it over when he thought he heard something.

"What did you say Private?" he asked, not even bothering to turn and look at the man.

"Nothing sir."

He shook his head. "You're dismissed private."

"Sir!" The Private stood to attention, saluted, then wheeled from the room.

Colonel Dupont was about to pull the tarp over the book

again when he did hear something. A voice. But this voice wasn't audible, it was in his mind. He knew it had to be. It was rough and deep, almost throaty. He shook his head, but it spoke again, and when it did, the Colonel's eyes lit up at the question it asked.

"Do you want to live forever?"

Colonel Dupont stared down at the book and felt himself drawn to it. The anger—the helplessness—he felt at having so many of his men die grew within him. He felt powerless. But maybe there was something he could do about that. He flipped the book open and saw the ancient text transform on the page. It blurred and moved, forming words he could read in Metropolitan French!

His heart leaped in his chest. Fear gripped him. He moved to close the book, unsure if this was actually happening or not.

"I don't offer this to just anyone," the voice insisted before he could close the tome. *"Vincent failed to attain that which you can have, Colonel Dupont. You can have immortality and power to satisfy your wrath."*

Colonel Dupont stopped. He looked around, then pulled his chair up to the desk, sat down, and began to read.

ACKNOWLEDGMENTS

I would like to acknowledge my family first and foremost for their great patience with me as I sit in my office night after night creating these stories for all you who love horror, suspense, and thrills.

I would also like to acknowledge Carol May Vaughn, my editor. She tells me the hard things that need to be said in order to make my stories better than they are. Her feedback is invaluable!

Finally, I would like to thank all of my readers and fans. Without you, The Pact would not exist. Thank you for having a love for adventure, horror, suspense, and action. I enjoy writing and making these stories, but beyond that I really love hearing how much you, my readers, have loved these narratives of fictional characters as they battle for their very lives!

There will be more to come. I promise you that.

ABOUT THE AUTHOR

Chad Stewart is the author of the YA action-adventure series, Dillon Hunt. He has also published four inspirational books, and one self-improvement. Chad loves to vacation, exercise, hike, bike, read, and of course write. He lives in Airdrie, Alberta, Canada with his wife Summer, and their children.

facebook.com/chadstewartauthor
instagram.com/chadstewartauthor

ADDITIONAL FICTION BY CHAD STEWART

Enter Orion: Heart of the Diablo

Dillon Hunt And The Desert Oasis Resort

Dillon Hunt And The Mask Of Time